"The first purpose of a garden is to give happiness and repose of mind."

Gertrude Jekyll

IT STARTED ON A GARDEN TOUR

A Novel

by

Georgia Brock

IT STARTED ON A GARDEN TOUR

Copyright © 1998 by Georgia Brock

Turtle Press
Georgia Brock
15290 Old Simcoe Road
Port Perry
Ontario L9L 1L1

ISBN 0-9683516-0-3

This is a work of fiction. Any resemblance of the characters to actual persons, living or dead, is purely coincidental.

All rights reserved.

Printed by:

Port Perry Printing Limited
201 North St,
Port Perry,
Ontario

Printed in Canada

for Sophia

ITINERARY

		Page
DAY 1:	Depart Toronto 6 pm	9
DAY 2:	Arrive London, Gatwick 6 am Half day tour Greenwich Boat ride up Thames to hotel	27
DAY 3:	London. East Anglia Full day at Beth Chatto Garden and Bressingham	39
DAY 4:	London. Portobello Road. Kew Gardens	59
DAY 5:	Depart London. Afternoon at Sissinghurst Castle Dover overnight	81
DAY 6:	Dover to Calais ferry Drive to Paris Evening tour of Paris lights	111
DAY 7:	Free day in Paris	125
DAY 8:	Monet's garden at Giverny	149
DAY 9:	Drive from Paris to Lucern	157
DAY 10:	Free day in Lucern	165
DAY 11:	Drive to Tuscany	177
DAY 12:	Free day in Florence	187
DAY 13:	Tour Tuscany gardens	205
DAY 14:	Full day in Pisa, Venice, or Siena	225
DAY 15:	Depart Milan for Toronto	235

DAY 1: DEPART TORONTO 6 PM

Syd looked up from the itinerary for A Garden Tour of Europe on his loaded clipboard to the clothes neatly hung and piled on shelves in his bedroom's wall-to-wall closet. He slid the list of fellow travellers between some tattered paint-smeared sheets and pages of calculations.

All of this was new to him. It had been a long journey to this point and he knew deep inside the changes he had made were for his survival. It had occurred to him many times over the past thirty years when he felt he had begun to come to his senses that the physical struggle for survival was over and the psychological struggle was on. It was still the survival of the fittest.

Sixty-two years old, he laughed to himself, and I'm back to square one, albeit with more moves up my sleeve than before. I've learned a few things that have lasted, and unpacked a lot of emotional baggage. That had taken some doing, because real men don't have emotions. Oh yeah? Says who? Emotions over Marjorie's death that he had examined, packed up, and laid to rest along with her. So that's the end of emotions.

He heard the back door open and close.

"Dad?" It was Hughie, Syd's older son.

"Upstairs," Syd called back.

Syd heard the back door open again, and he moved to the newly installed floor-to-ceiling windows.

"Boys!" Hughie's voice rang out. "Play in the garden or the lane, but don't go as far as the street." Three preadolescent boys waved in acknowledgement. They saw their Grandad and waved.

A narrow old-fashioned lane ran between the backs of the houses in some of the blocks in this neighbourhood. A throwback to the horse-drawn services for genteel households. Syd watched the boys creeping carefully and hiding about the paths of the garden overspilling with velvety-grey leaves of lamb's ears, small coral bells swaying over dark green foliage, creeping red flowering sedum: its leaves of deep red as well. All backed by a mass planting of showy Sweet William, variegated and mixed in pink, and red, and white, and wine, interspersed with stately spikes of mauve and true blue delphinium. Feathery cosmos was just beginning to bloom.

"I really like the different shades of yellow and natural stuff you've used throughout the house," Hughie commented as he walked over to Syd and gave him a friendly elbow in the ribs.

"I just finished the painting yesterday," Syd said as he gave Hughie a mock body-check that Hughie faked into a tumble onto the king-size bed into the down duvet and pile of pillows, kicking off his Birkenstocks as he sprawled, and in the same motion grabbing the big suitcase at the foot of the bed before it landed on the floor.

"All this yellow to neutral ... is ... is ..."

"Monochromatic," said Syd.

"Is that the old housepainter I knew, talking, or the new unknown watercolourist?" There was a note of teasing in Hughie's voice. Then, "Holy wick! Look at the size of that closet!" Hughie whistled in approval. "And what's in it. Jeans, denim shirts, and khakis. Eddie Bauer. You've got Birkenstocks, too! Taking your old blue blazer, I see. Very formal!"

"The closet was the last of the renovations, all the changes, included me." Syd's voice drifted afar.

"Stevie's timing was perfect." Hughie's voice brought Syd back to reality. "And he's really happy he took that job at the TV station in Barrie."

Syd nodded in agreement.

"We were both pretty worried about you, cooped up in that apartment, and we didn't know whether we should suggest you move, or if you could move and disturb your belongings as you had them with Mom. Sort of really leaving your life with Mom." Hughie was sounding a bit hesitant.

Syd reached past the suitcase and grabbed Hughie's foot and wiggled it back and forth. "I knew I had to do it. Leave my life with your Mother. We had talked about it. She was very brave and insisted I make a life for myself and she even said to marry again. Can't imagine even considering it. But I did appreciate your help ... your blessing ... you and Steve and your girls, women, wives, I mean."

"And you've no regrets dispensing with all the household stuff?"

"No," Syd said reassuringly. "I had to do it. It's part of moving on. I admit I have a box of special things, but I've put it in the attic. It's there if I need it."

"The house looks empty," commented Hugh.

"I want it that way ... minimalism. Funny, in my day we would have said Spartan." Syd made a little grunting sound as he remembered. "Now Japanese influence. Modern. Less is more."

"But not in your garden."

"Not in my garden," Syd readily agreed. "There I'm definitely old-fashioned. Victorian. Would you believe, fussy. I feel as if I've become a Jekyll and Hyde persona. But that's partly what this trip is about."

Syd picked three denim coloured chambray shirts from a pile in the closet and set them beside the suitcase.

"Victoria Sackville-West. Vita. She and her husband Harold Nicolson had enormous influence on gardening in England. I've read everything I can get my hands on about what they did. Their lifestyle too. I'm going to see their place. Called Sissinghurst Castle. And to look at the structure of some others. Then Monet's garden in France. Gardening and painting. That's what I do. My avocations!"

"What?"

"A word from what you call my old-fashioned vocabulary. From my high-school Guidance teacher! Right out of the ark!"

"God, this bed is comfortable." Hughie wiggled like the small boy he used to be. "Not like the one you and Mom used to have." He gave Syd a sly glance, "Ever think of having someone share it?"

"That's part of my life which is not an open topic of conversation." Syd sounded firm.

"That's true about you and Mom, but you're in a new league." Then teasingly, "As sons, we're old enough and with it, to be giving Dad advice. Like you did when we were growing up and new at it. An interesting switch!" And he winked at his dad.

"Well, you and Stevie persuaded me to take this trip. That advice I'll take. But I don't think anybody will be sharing this bed." Syd shook his head sceptically. "Steve talk to you?"

"No! About what?"

"Nothing."

"'Nothing' the man says in the most defensive tone I've heard since I cross-examined Two-bit Charlie, the thief, at the Old City Hall Court."

"Forget about it." Syd tried to sound indifferent. He didn't pull it off.

"Yo! I'm not dropping this one," Hugh teased. "I'll be sure to ask Stevie on the way to the airport."

A car stopped in the back lane.

"That's Stevie now," said Hugh. "Christine and Samantha are dropping him off and picking up my boys. The three of us will go to the airport in my wagon. I'll carry your case down. Your easel bag's in the hall? I'll take it, too."

"I'll close up," said Syd, "and be there in a jiffy, or is that an old-fashioned word I should eradicate from my vocabulary?"

"Just trying to help you be with it," said Hugh, heading for the stairs.

Steve was waiting at the garden gate that led into the alley to Hugh's car.

"You've bought a knapsack! Cool," said Steve admiringly. "Hey, Hughie, I always said the old boy would look better in jeans than we do." He gave Syd a light punch at the beltline. "No pot? Where'd it go?"

"Cowboy's breakfast. Baked beans, instead of bacon and eggs. Pizza and pasta are fast foods when you're labouring at home and have to cook for yourself. I've learned something of the new ways from your girls. Excuse me. Wives. Heather and Christine."

"Not to mention all the exercise in the Robinson Crusoe act he did here at the house," Hugh said to Steve, as he put the bags in the back of the wagon. "I don't think we realized how much physical work Dad's done here over the past year."

"I do," Steve said. "Totally immersed himself in renovating this place."

"Well, I did go down to the Canada Employment and hire a plumber, or an electrician or some plain labourers when I needed them."

"What did they think of this old character with a straggly beard and long hair pulled back with an elastic, plus the dress pants cut off at the knees and held up with a bit of rope?" Steve asked, when they were settled into the car seats.

"Nobody said anything. They got paid. That was all there was to it," Syd said as he ran his hand over the neatly cropped grey stubble on his face.

"Never thought you'd keep the long hair," Steve said from the back seat, scrutinizing Syd's straight hair just short of the collar, "although your Italian barber does a better job than you did. Can't decide if I like the beard or not."

"Neither can I, so it comes and goes."

Syd took one last look as Hugh pulled away. "Garden'll keep until I get back."

"But will that lady?" Steve asked with glee.

"What lady?" Hugh was navigating his way onto Avenue Road, and waited for an opening to make the left turn to take them north to Highway 401.

"I said forget it," stated Syd.

"That's the proverbial red flag in front of the bull," Hugh commented. "I'm not letting up on this one. Come on Stevie, spill the beans on the old man here."

Syd slunk down beside the door as Steve leaned on his elbows over Hugh's shoulder.

"You know my answering machine is still here at the house. I had to give up my Toronto number; Dad transferred his number from the apartment to the house here; and I've given Dad's number out so I

13

can keep in touch with my city friends. Dad either passes along the messages, or if I'm in town, I let myself in the house and check the machine.

"Well, last week," Steve's voice was full of high spirits, "there was this message for Dad. Maybe I shouldn't have said lady, because," Steve watched Syd slide lower in the corner, "because in the most breathy, sultry voice, she made the most unbelievable ... fabulous suggestions ..."

"Lascivious?" Hugh prompted.

"Yo, and she was wanton and lustful, too," Steve added with a whoop of laughter.

This was an old game of gotcha the boys had played with the encouragement of their mother. If someone came up with a big word, the other added a supposedly agreeable comment that was really the same meaning. The first time, it had happened by accident. Hughie had learned the word "miscegenation", and used it in reference to attitudes in the United States, at which point, in all innocence, Stevie had replied, "Ya, and they don't like black boys marrying white girls."

"Something to do with that big bed of Dad's!" Hughie hooted. "He was packing and I suggested he find someone to share it!"

"That's it. A woman. Shirley. Don't we know a Shirley somebody from the church ... Wallace?" Steve was reaching for memories.

"Her husband died just before Mom did?" Hugh was trying to put a face to a name.

"Now stop it. Both of you." This was Dad speaking.

With broad grins both boys looked expectantly at Syd as he drew himself upright into a posture of authority.

"I can't say there is nothing to this. How shall I put it? There is nothing to me having anything to do with this woman, but ... well, you know I haven't been to church for a while."

"Which was because Mom wasn't there any more, we thought." Hughie, the elder spoke for both of them still, on occasion.

"No. That's not the case. You know I'm no Bible-thumping Christian but it has a place in my life. I like singing and Thursday night choir practice for an hour and a half and the Sunday morning service for an hour is not a big tax on a person's time, even for me, the former high-powered executive that I was!" Syd said it with a self-depreciating tone. "Anyway, it was always a social outing with a broad swath of people. I was grateful to have it after your Mom died.

"However it came to my attention that I was being categorized as 'out of mourning'. Much to my surprise, and horror, I was being pursued by some of the widows in the congregation. All of these ladies had been friends or acquaintances of your mother's, and I discovered there had developed a pecking order as to who had the first shot at me." Syd's face coloured in disgust and mortification.

"Can you believe it? Attractive well-to-do matrons, rushing me like a college football hero. I felt worse than I had as a shy teenager. When I got home there were always two or three messages on the answering machine ... even before I moved out of the apartment ... some simply asked me over to dinner and to talk, or go to a concert. Others plainly making a pass ... and frankly, I didn't even expect Shirley Wallace to know about what she suggested let alone propose doing it." Syd shivered. "I have absented myself from church."

"It's that serious," Hugh said.

"It's that serious," Syd repeated emphatically.

"Why don't you look for some young woman?" Steve suggested. "Surely you met some single ones before you retired. There are tons around. One of your buddies still at the office should be able to introduce you to somebody."

"Huh." The sound from Syd was not a laugh, not a grunt, but definitely negative in connotation. "First and most importantly, I'm not interested. I'm what you might call a reconfirmed bachelor."

"You shouldn't close your mind completely," encouraged Hugh. "Get out and see what's around."

"Well, I did." Syd shook his head. "Remember I told you, years ago when you were beginning to date, how I met your Mother? Old Kenny at the tea dances after Saturday afternoon football game at University? He'd pick out a girl, dance with her and chat her up. If he didn't fancy her, he'd dance her over to me, make the introductions and go find another? Well, one of my colleagues from the office asked me out on a foursome for dinner. He said he had a blind date for me.

It turned out the guy did not bring his wife, but two younger women. He gave them the Old Kenny routine: picked the one he wanted, and 'fixed me up with the other'! It was one of the tackiest situations I've ever been in."

"We never heard this one," Hughie said.

"No. There was no point."

"So what did you do?"

"I spoke to the waiter with cash and asked him to move dinner along at a comfortable pace, and not to offer after-dinner drinks. Then I offered to escort 'my date' home, and included the other young lady as well. Both accepted, gratefully. My buddy was furious. It's ended our association. He's talked to a few other guys. Says I'm over the hill."

Syd didn't tell them the comment the colleague made as he escorted the girls away. Hard to tell if it was envy or just what, but he said, "There's Syd, never the star but always the winner."

The car approached the Airport Terminal.

"Good thing we persuaded him to take this trip," Hughie jerked his thumb back at Steve, "he needs something, anything, new in his life."

"Don't worry about me," Syd reassured them both. "I can take care of myself."

Arielle looked at the piles of clothes about the bedroom of her studio apartment and on the living room floor.

She was sorting them with the itinerary for A Garden Tour of Europe taped to the door between the two rooms, when she heard the scratching at the screen door up the three steps from her kitchen.

As she set the list of fellow travellers on the piano, she rested her fingertips for balance, and did a few first position plies, tendus and degages. As she made her way into the kitchen she paused step by step pressing her heel down for a runner's stretch. Long-limbed lithe body. Lean.

It was hot. Even at 8 o'clock in the morning.

She swept her long curly hair off the nape of her neck, and held it back with an elastic she picked off the counter.

"Well, Mr. Dog, you're finally up," she said, opening the door for the little grey poodle who was waiting patiently outside.

"Where's your girlfriend, Mrs. Cat?" she asked as she scooped the little dog up for a hug. She did a few releves, giving the little dog a cuddly bounce.

The pets belonged to her mother who lived upstairs, in the ground floor apartment.

Arielle continued a sequence of ronde de jambe, grande battement and battement cloche.

Technically, Arielle lived downstairs, in the semi-basement apartment. Lived here. Again. Sort of. No. Permanently now.

Years ago, it had started as her studio to teach piano and violin to her increasing number of pupils. She had used it to live in off and on since she had moved out of her parents' home, upstairs.

It had its own entrance from the common vestibule.

The vestibule, coming in off the side street on the south as the land sloped downhill serviced all four apartments. There were two more rented out on the top floor.

Arielle's English immigrant parents had escaped the European unrest in the late 1930s. Working class, they had nothing to lose, but everything to gain by coming. Working very hard for the well-to-do in Toronto; they saved every penny they earned and were at the right place at the right time to buy the converted duplex on Avenue Road just below Eglinton Avenue where Arielle was born.

Her name Arielle, was from the Shakespearean play The Tempest. Her mother loved Shakespeare; loved the English language; and was sorry she never had the opportunity for a higher education.

So Arielle was sent to Havergal College, the private girls' school, north of Eglinton. As well, she had been trained as a dancer and had been part of the City Ballet Company.

It had been her parents' ambition to give her something more than a simple, common state education, so they fostered her innate ability in music and her strong supple body with lessons in piano and dance. Her parents were immigrants to the new world, but strangely enough they sought to develop old world attitudes, skills and manners in her.

So any attempt at growing up a new world child was denied her.

It was the only way of life she knew; she was comfortable in it. By the age of twelve Arielle was different. She always knew she was different.

The discipline and structure in her world was satisfying. There was challenge in the build-up of knowledge and in the problem-solving of movement.

And then there was the feeling. Oh, the feeling.

Very soon, her piano teacher had asked her to make the sonatina blacker, to make the jig lighter, to stretch and compress time in the prelude.

She knew she could do it, too, with her body at the dance studio when she was asked to demonstrate the steps "with expression".

A life of music opened before her. Could she possibly take up the violin; her father was most anxious. He thought it was the aristocrat of the music world. Would it be possible for a young girl to play it?

Whatever Toronto teenagers did with their time on any given day in 1954, Arielle had no idea. She did hear phrases like "missing out on so many things" and "old for her age", but they simply didn't register.

She spent every Saturday at the dance studio in lands of make believe: fairies, nymphs, wilis. She read stories of Swan Queens, and Sleeping Beauties.

She thought some composers led pretty interesting lives and speculated on the love Chopin felt.

If anyone had pressed her about "missing out on so many things", she would have denied it, assuming that everyone else was as involved in their own rich world as she was in hers.

There were lots of young people in her dance class. Lots of kids took piano lessons. There were lots of kids at the Conservatory where she took violin lessons. There were young people at the ballet company when she was in the corps.

That had been a long time ago.

Her father had lived to see her dancing career on the stage give way to her accomplishment as a violinist in the City Symphony and ultimately be known in music circles.

She never gave up the body discipline of the dance; it was as important to her music as scales. She continued to teach dance every Saturday morning at the studio in Scarborough. She lived by her music: playing and teaching.

The little dog struggled to be put down.

"Good," Arielle said to him. "Ten No-chair Sits to do. Karen Kain can do thirty. But she's younger than I am. Then we'll get at it."

Arielle took a wide step sideways, bent each knee over its foot, back straight. She raised up on tip toes, both heels well off the floor. Heels down. Heels up. Ten times. Enough.

"Now," Arielle seriously addressed the quizzical looking dog, "You can help me sort out these clothes. They are from my past three lives, which you know all about."

No reply.

"I tell you all my secrets, but you never tell me any of yours. Fortunately, you don't tell anyone my secrets. You are the only man I can trust. So you can stay."

The dog settled on the floor, front paws crossed, head up, ready to give full attention to the task at hand.

"Those beside the suitcases are for the trip today. Great travelling wardrobe. Wear the brown crinkly Madras skirt, brown T-shirt, and tawny cowled sweater if it's cool on the plane. Black knit draw-string pants and a big black sweatshirt. Beige knit wedge dress. Long black denim dress. Covering the bod to avoid attention. Okay, my knees do show in the wedgie. But it might be really hot in some places.

"Throw this Indian shawl with the nice gold threads, in the carry-on. One pair of all purpose walking sandals, and my jogging shoes. Where is my camera?

"I'm going today. Did anybody tell you?

"And these clothes spread out all over are waiting to be kept, dismissed, put aside. Just like memories, which is what they are. Existential stuff from my first man ..." she laughed and corrected herself, "boy. Well, he did get older. He was twenty-six when we called it quits. After my boyish body developed, he realized he liked boyish bodies. The real thing! Maybe that had something to do with the beginning of my favourite colour: black. Right in style if I was still my skinny teenaged self. Imagine, these clothes in a box way back in the storage room.

"All of it into the garbage bag. Pow."

The little dog gave a jump and moved back ready for round two.

"Mini-skirts. I loved them. Still do. That college kid who painted houses along the street that summer. Before your time. You weren't even thought of yet. Now it's perfectly all right for a twenty-eight-year-old woman to be intimate with a twenty-year-old kid, young man. You're not shocked? Actually for us it was pretty all right too. And the fun we had, going to those dances. Jungle music. Drums. Speed ... no, not drugs ... foot and body speed. Terrific. Well, these are passe, but I think I'll put this black mini-skirt in the cedar chest. One for good memories."

The little dog barked.

"Oh, she's there, is she?"

Arielle went to her kitchen door again. The steps gave onto the lawn to the west of the house, and immediately to the right turned to go up some flagstone steps to the french doors leading into her mother's sitting room.

The ginger cat was sitting at the turning point to be seen from either household.

At the first sound of a door, the cat was in like a flash.

She walked haughtily around the muss on the floor, to the bay window facing onto the west lawn, sprang up onto the ground-level sill, turned two circles beside the huge hoya plant and settled down to make her toilette.

"I don't think she is interested in my present life," Arielle confided to the little dog, "let alone my past. Shall we finish this?"

"The psychedelic items go in there."

Once again the clothes were shoved into the garbage bag.

"As for these two piles ... old jogging shoes. Out. Dance leotards, where have these rags been hiding? Out. Black blouse and white blouse," she looked at the dog, "white, my second favourite colour ...

all right, don't be picky, I know they're not colours ... split at the back sleeve seams. Only so much a shirt can take, symphony after symphony; and these other work clothes, long skirts, dress pants have had it as well. Out."

"Room look better?" Arielle queried the dog.

"You bet," she answered herself.

The flat was still predominantly her studio for teaching piano, violin and other strings, and theory. She worked here, even when she had been living with B-Man.

How long since she had given up calling him by his name? She had switched to B-Man, short for Business-Man, even to his face. He had taken no notice, or let on he had noticed. She didn't know which.

She had left their downtown apartment each morning to come here to practice her own performance work, and to prepare for and to teach her pupils. She virtually lived here during the day, and had gradually transformed it into a home.

She had come to feel that B-Man really lived at his office. So fair's fair, she thought.

The studio walls were 1920's wood panelling, the floors, parquet. She had found an elegant baby grand piano at an auction house, a music cupboard, and a muted oriental rug, of the same era. From then on she sparingly added pieces of muted tones. It was not a room for the eye but for the ear.

Now it had a look of Armani, those colours of shadow. She was even about to branch out into those shades for her own personal wardrobe, like the brown crinkle skirt for the trip. Very daring, she said to herself. A new beginning.

It was two full years since she and B-Man had split. They had nearly married, but now she was so relieved that they hadn't. It wasn't what he wanted at all.

She counted out her life by the men she had been with, which might have been considered bohemian at the early part of her adult life, but which now was normal. Nobody talked of anything nowadays except lifestyle. Not the so-called traditional life for her. Slightly ahead of the times, she thought to herself sardonically.

Now she had her own life and very glad of it.

The taxi turned left onto Avenue Road. Arielle and Molly settled back into their seats.

"We're on our way," Molly stated.

Arielle smiled and nodded in reply.

"I'll say once more," Molly patted Arielle's hand. "It is wonderfully good of you to come with me. I did so want to make this trip. Gardens and gardeners are so special to me but the single supplement would have been prohibitive and at my age there are not many well enough to make this kind of a trip. Your mother didn't really pressure you, I know."

"Of course she did," laughed Arielle, "although it might be considered salesmanship. She can be very good."

Arielle could see Molly nodding her head in agreement.

"Mum's big points were," Arielle started to tick them off on her fingers, "I needed a big change to get out of myself, was the way she put it; you needed someone to go with you; while this might be a garden tour, my interest in cooking is vegetable oriented and surely there have to be vegetable and herb gardens; after England, I would appreciate the restaurants and cooking in France and Italy; I play, and am involved in, an awful lot of English and European music, and it's been a long time since I was there, and, I'll meet some new and interesting people.

"I could go on because she kept listing truths, like, she isn't well enough to go but would like an illustrated blow by blow account of the trip. She's already read more about the places than I have. I'm glad to be coming. Enough said."

The taxi wove its way onto Highway 401 west, heading toward Pearson International Airport Terminal 1.

Terminal 1 was still a zoo at 6 pm when they arrived at the departure desk. A charter company, adequate and suitable for their flight. The rest of the trip was first class.

Efficient Molly had a slightly larger than average suitcase with wheels which she could handle herself, and a many compartmented hand-bag.

Arielle lowered her big canvas tote-bag from her shoulder and swung the thin hand-bag inside it into her hands.

"Are we really supposed to put these name tags on?" Arielle asked Molly.

"I'm guessing the tour people want them for general identification purposes; for a head count more than specifically our names. But then again I suppose people have looked over the list and are curious as to how others stack up by their names." Molly made a few observations. "See the couple in his-and-hers track suits. They've got their name tags on. And those two women over there. One with the designer jockey-style hat over perfect hair with dressed-by-Tilley. And that man over there."

"The one who looks like Aaron Copland music," stated Arielle.

"That's interesting. Like?"

"Certain calm, clear ruggedness, about him. Still waters often run deep," said Arielle.

"You're attracted?" asked Molly.

"No. I'm past men," said Arielle with no trace of rancour. "About the travellers' list, did you look it over?" Arielle asked.

"Briefly," responded Molly.

"I was annoyed they put me as Ms A. Edwards. I usually arrange to be just A. Edwards. A for Anonymous. Avoids all kinds of bother."

"Avoid the inevitable gender count," said Molly. "Definitely more women. Ah, what does it matter? All of us over fifty, I bet."

"I'm beginning to believe that it takes age and wisdom for most people to become gardeners," commented Arielle.

"And by that time your knees and back won't take it," Molly added. "Check out Mr. and Mrs. His-and-Hers Track Suits. Can you see them in a garden?"

"Cross-filing with my stereotypes, not really," said Arielle. "Our turn here. Can I lift your bag onto the scales?" Arielle set it up before Molly replied.

Boarding passes safely tucked into passports and into handbags,

Molly and Arielle drifted toward the notice card held aloft that read: A Garden Tour of Europe. Mr. & Mrs. Martin and Isobel Bennett, Tour Directors.

"Now let me see," said the stylish jockey-hatted matron consulting her group list. She glanced at Molly, and then looked Arielle up and down very precisely. "You must be ..." she looked at Molly again, "Mrs.... Mrs.... Mrs...."

"Molly Barr," said Molly.

"Oh yes, I can tick you off."

You've already ticked me off, thought Arielle to herself.

"And your name?" Molly inquired.

"Grace," the woman stated, impatiently consulting her list.

"And you," said Grace with a hostile tone, "must be the Ms. My how I hate that. Never caught a man, and been to bed with too many is my interpretation of Ms." She looked knowingly around to see with whom she had scored.

Arielle stepped away from Grace and turned to look at the others in the group. Her eyes fastened on the tall lean sandy-grey-haired man, talking to two younger men. Enough resemblance to make them his sons, she thought. They don't look like Aaron Copland music though!

Grace walked around in front of Arielle. "Ms A. Edwards. What does the A stand for? Alice? Alva? Audrey? Annie? ..."

Molly could see Arielle bristling. She moved beside Grace and quietly said, "Her name is Arielle," and tried to steer Grace away.

"Arielle? Arielle? What kind of a name is that?" Grace's voice was louder than necessary.

Ever the conciliator, Molly said, "Perhaps, Grace, you could introduce me to some of the other ladies you have identified, I mean met."

Arielle could see Molly put a little pressure on Grace's elbow and steer her aside.

"Hello, everybody!" A cheery voice called out.

Arielle turned to see the large placard waving at the end of the stick.

"Welcome everybody, to A Garden Tour of Europe ... I'd ask you to make yourself known to me or my wife here. We'd like to start to get to know you all since we're going to be travelling together for the next two weeks ...."

A smiling wife poked the Tour Director and whispered something to him.

"Oh yes, my name is Martin Bennett and this is my wife Isobel. Call us Martin and Isobel. Now the most important thing to tell you at this point is that immediately clearing immigration and customs at Gatwick, we'll watch for a sign similar to this. That'll be our guide who'll take us to our coach, which will be our transportation for the next two weeks."

No one was particularly paying attention now, but Martin called out once again, "Make yourselves known to us ..."

"Or me," a voice called out. It was Grace. She looked at Martin. "I've already got fifteen of us identified. Hold up your hands, the ones I talked to."

"There they are: my friend Jean, Ross and Barbara, Mr. and Mrs. Phillips, and the Bobbsey Twins in their track suits." She consulted her list and rattled off women's names: "Lorraine. Marilyn, Helen, Peggy, Patti, Kath, Molly and Ar... Ara... Arielle," she smiled stiffly in Arielle's direction. "By the way, I'm Grace," and she beamed a big smile at the group.

"Thanks for the help, that will get the introductions underway. Please approach us, Grace, too, to make yourself known. Otherwise, see you all in London!"

Mr. Track Suit was standing beside Arielle and Molly. "The wife says there's always one bossy woman on every trip. Guess we know who it is on this one." Then addressing Arielle, he said, "What's a good-lookin' girl like you travellin' with her mother?"

Arielle stepped back and turned her body sideways toward Molly, hopefully ignoring the question and putting enough space between herself and the man to avoid answering.

Right in her direct line of vision was Aaron Copland and his two sons. Grace was with them, flooding a smile at all three. "And there you are!" Arielle heard Grace say to the father.

Arielle notice one young man nudge the other and wink. The other gave a thumbs up toward the older man, who gave a serious negative shake of his head.

DAY 2: HALF DAY TOUR GREENWICH. BOAT UP THAMES TO LONDON

"Where's my purse. Oh, my god, somebody's stolen my purse. Marl, Kath ..." The big woman was turning in circles amongst the baggage on the pavement in the coach bay.

"I have it," said Kath, a neat, tidy woman, "you handed it to me."

"So I did," said Julie sheepishly. "Losing a night's sleep on these trans-Atlantic flights mixes me all up."

"It's so damp and cold waiting for the bus. And they say it rains all the time in England." The woman was standing with all body parts pulled tight together, making her appear a taut skinny obelisk. "And I need my sleep." There was a near-whine in her voice.

Syd noticed the two ladies who seemed too wide a spread in age to be friends, yet appeared not to be mother and daughter, standing at the edge of the group. The younger one was saying, "I must admit I'm ready to get out from under this cavernous parking lot for some fresh morning air and the light of day."

Syd looked around him. Early on an English summer morning. A concrete carpark. Dull, dank, damp, dirty. Definitely a downer, if you were so inclined.

"And, I'm ready," the older woman commented, "for direct touch with England and it's history. To get our trip under way."

My sentiments exactly, thought Syd.

"The tour organizers must have had a real start in mind when they set up today," said the pleasant looking woman, standing next to Syd. "Coach ride to Greenwich, and then boat ride up the Thames to London. I was just saying to my husband ..."

"I wish we could just go directly to our hotel," the skinny obelisk whined at Molly.

Syd saw Isobel whisper to her husband. Martin listened intently, cleared his throat, and stepped toward the group.

"In planning our trip, we had to accommodate the hotel practice of not having rooms available for incoming guests until after noon. And we took into consideration that it's a grind through the suburbs of south London, so we were able to arrange the stop at Greenwich. You may wonder why ..."

"I sure wondered why." The obelisk didn't let up. She was obviously miserable.

Martin made a little simpering smile in her direction. "Well, we've found that many of our travellers have been to London and seen the regular things like Buckingham Palace, the Crown Jewels, St. Paul's, to mention a few ..."

"But we can duck out of some of the garden stuff to take those in." The interruption from Julie was a statement, not a question.

With a cursory nod of agreement toward Julie, Martin went on, "But visitors to Britain do like a touch of royalty, so we felt that Greenwich, with The Royal Naval College, designed by Christopher Wren, and Queen's House, designed by Inigo Jones in 1616 for Henrietta Maria, wife of Charles I, with the Royal Park which was 200 years old when Charles II commissioned the French landscape artist Le Notre to redesign it in what was, in the 1660s, the latest French fashion ...." He was speaking quickly to authenticate their reason for choosing Greenwich.

Martin continued, "The Flower Garden, on the southeast side of the park, and the deer enclosure nearby are both attractive. Also Cutty Sark and Gypsy Moth IV. And the Old Royal Conservatory. And besides, it's on our way."

"What I want to know," piped up the woman with two totebags, lined up on the same arm as her huge purse, "is, is there any shopping?"

"That a girl, Peg," said the woman with a similar line-up of bags on her arm.

Martin looked desperately toward Isobel. Isobel whispered into his ear.

"Of course ... certainly ... all the established tourist places have a shop." And switching back to the topic of the tour, "We'll have lunch at The Dolphin Coffee Shop on the royal grounds, or at pubs on the street that takes us to the dock. If you're unfamiliar with ordering your own food at pubs, stay with Isobel and me and we'll see you get a lunch ... we'll leave on the 1 pm boat for London."

"Where we'll get some proper shopping," concluded Peggy, which drew a small laugh from most of the group. "Make you happy, Patti?" she said to her companion.

"Makes you wonder why some people come on a specialized tour like this one, if shopping is their big thing," the pleasant woman next to Syd commented to her husband.

A coach pulled up to the curb. Most noticeable were huge windows and seats very high. It was theirs. A few 'hurrays' were heard from the group.

The luggage was stowed underneath and the passengers filed on, not without a bit of aggressive jockeying to be first and have the pick of the seats.

Martin was assisting people onto the bus, with a hearty voice reassuring everyone that "We'll rotate seats so everyone gets a chance for all views."

It actually was a grind through south London to Greenwich. However, teasing sleep fought the shifting of the gears, for most of the passengers, as a lull spread over the bus.

Syd was barely awake as they came upon the stately calm of Greenwich.

The coach pulled up in front of the gilded royal gates on King William Walk. Martin was on his feet with the microphone.

"Welcome to Greenwich. I'm going to give you a fast briefing, so you have plenty of time to enjoy this place. Straight out through the door is Romney Road, and it takes you directly into the grounds. The pubs are along this road. The docks are the other way. Be prepared for 1 pm departure. Have a nice morning."

All took their time gathering themselves together for the second start to the day.

Setting out on Romney Road, Syd worked at the stiffness and cramp in his arms and neck as he swung his knapsack over his shoulder. He felt the stiffness in his legs too, from sitting during the flight, and the drive. He stretched his step to pull out the kinks. Certainly a pleasant place, he thought, as he looked at the fresh dew-washed grass covering the hill of Greenwich Park up to the unassuming dome of the Old Royal Observatory. He hardly needed his guide book to tell him it was a Wren design as well.

Syd continued across to Park Row and then worked his way toward the river. The walk was a tonic. The sight, a refreshment.

He spent the better part of an hour, in and out of the buildings of the Royal Naval College. He had no idea that something as exquisite as the Painted Hall and the Chapel opposite it were here as well. He had only known of the Wren buildings as referred to the elegant and dignified facades.

And there, in bold contrast, was the Queen's House. Designed by Inigo Jones, Syd laughed to himself, remembering his school days when he thought it was Indigo Jones, a great name for a jazz musician!

He looked at the Queen's House again. White. Classical. Rectangular. Bold. Beautiful. "All those qualities I've forsaken to get on with my new life. Maybe I've made a mistake, giving up straight lines," he muttered under his breath. "Certain security in straight lines."

He walked to the steps of the Queen's House, sat down and opened his knapsack for a drawing pad and pencils.

The plain sweep of walk and lawn to the Thames was in direct contrast to the elegant lines and shapes of the Royal Naval Hospital. He established his point of view and started to sketch, capturing a figure walking which gave a comparable dimension on the human scale.

There were some footsteps behind him and he felt someone peering over his shoulder.

"Looks like her all right. Just gives the impression."

Syd looked up. It was the man in the track suit.

"That's her, all right," the man repeated, pointing first to the figure in Syd's picture and then to the figure on the landscape.

"Who?" asked Syd absently.

"She's on our trip," the man said.

"Is she?" asked Syd.

"Y' mean y' haven't noticed?" the man asked. "Are y' blind?"

"Bit coltish," said Syd absorbed in his drawing.

"For over 50, a bit coltish's not bad." The man whistled through his teeth.

"Come on, Jack, we gotta see the sights," said a woman's voice.

"The name's Jack," the man introduced himself to Syd, "and this here's the wife."

"I'm Syd."

"The wife says I gotta go, I gotta go. Bit coltish. Would y' believe it," Jack mumbled as they left, shaking his head incredulously.

Syd opened the small pocket on his knapsack and took out his wrist watch. It was coming up eleven o'clock. Time to finish if I'm going to have a quick look in the Maritime Museum, he thought. He put the watch back and packed away his drawing materials.

In the Museum Syd saw the man he had stood beside at the airport bus stop.

"I was in the Royal Canadian Navy during the war," Ross said directly to Syd. "Name's Wilson. Ross Wilson." He thrust out his hand.

"Syd MacKenzie." Syd gripped the hand. "Much here to bring back memories?"

"Not really, I just got in the war at the end," said the older man. "I've become a history buff ... I guess I should really say more than a buff. A student, really." Ross hesitated. "In truth, since I retired from business, as a corporate C.A. five years ago, I've completed an Arts degree from University of Toronto. A part-time mature student. Woodsworth College."

"I know the place. I've been taking some courses at The School of Continuing Studies situated, well, its headquarters is across the road on St. George Street."

"You. Retired?"

Basically a reticent man, thought Syd appreciatively. And a flash went through his mind: and a man of few words, too, as one of his boys would throw in!

"Yes," said Syd. Then equally concise, "Engineer. Civil. Construction. Roads. Bridges."

"What interested you in Continuing Studies? They offer a lot."

"Drawing and painting."

"Would have thought you'd had enough of that on the job."

"Complete switch. Botanical drawing and watercolours. Not a straight line, and the light touch."

"So you weren't drawing any of these magnificent buildings when I saw you with that sketch pad out there."

"I can't ignore them. Just try to give an impression of them. It's the landscape or some details of trees or plants I'm interested in now."

"We should get a move on," said Ross as he consulted his watch. "I'm to meet Barbara, my wife, at the shop. She's literary. Graduated from Vic. All those years ago. Likes to pick up postcards of places. Says they do a better job of photography than she could. Come with us for lunch? Barbara has a group of the ladies with her."

"Like to try the pub?"

They were on the Thames in pleasant sunshine. Looking back, Syd could see the broad green lawns rise from the blue water's edge and sweep up to the calm symmetry of the grey Wren buildings. The black pencil thin lines of rigging on the masts of the Cutty Sark cut dramatically across the scene.

The boat pulled into the centre of the Thames. Syd was sitting starboard, as he had said to Ross, to get a good look at Canary Wharf. "Officially it's called One Canada Square, but all the news refers to it as Canary Wharf. It certainly has the Reichmann's singing!"

There it was. Modern and crisp. Side buildings a kind of polyester blue.

"I've followed the rise and fall of the Reichmann's with horrible fascination. In the newspapers," said Molly.

"Horrible, is the best word to describe this complex," said Lorraine. "It really is too big. You'd expect a tower like it in North America, but not on the Thames with Wren downstream and upstream at St. Paul's."

"I think," stated Barbara, "that people are upset because of memories of paintings by whom? Constable? Maybe Turner? Or that Italian? Anyway, one of those painters of yore, who showed people working the river on boats or unloading cargo."

"And there is no evidence of the once proud trading nation that

Britain used to be," said Ross.

Syd settled back onto the bench. A coolish breeze was blowing, but in the sunshine, the cruising was pleasant. The Thames looked surprisingly clean. Even sparkling. He had heard it had been terribly polluted but environmental measures had been enacted to clean it up. He didn't honestly expect it to be so good.

The tour seemed to him to be divided into two groups. He could see Jack and the wife: surely those were not matching track suits they were wearing. Yes, they were. Light and dark grey parachute silk and light baseball hats. Which team or which sport, for that matter, he couldn't see. Jack Track and The Wife, Syd laughed to himself.

Jack seemed to be chatting up that woman with the long curly hair, the one he, Syd, had thought was with Molly. Molly was sitting with Barbara. So much for social structures, he thought.

"The tall office block," Ross said as he pointed, "has the Reichmann corners."

"What does that mean," asked Barbara.

"A special feature of their buildings, whether in Toronto or at the World Trade Centre in New York. They design double corners to double the number of corner offices, which are the most prestigious, and command the highest rents."

The boat plowed its way upstream.

"This has to be Tower Bridge," said Lorraine. "Coming up should be the Tower itself."

"Maybe not," said Barbara. "I think it's practically hidden by commercial buildings, even a hotel."

"Sounds as if you've read Prince Charles' book too!" Lorraine said to her.

"You've caught me out," said Barbara with a laugh.

"I have too," put in Molly.

They came upon the sights as described in the book: a glimpse of Wren's St Magnus Martyr hidden behind Adelaide House, that Egyptian-style office building; the grand Roman Doric Column of the Monument to the Great Fire of London beside the boxy National Westminster Bank Tower.

33

"Is that St Paul's?" It was Grace speaking. "Can I join this cozy little group?" She sat herself beside Barbara.

No one made any comment about any grouping.

"The river buildings around St. Paul's aren't in keeping or complimentary in any way, just as Charles says," Lorraine commented. "None of the little spires of the baby churches can be seen, either."

"It must have been wonderful to have seen it before all this new ugly development," said Molly wistfully.

"Look! There's the building Charles says looks like a word processor," Lorraine sounded pleased with herself at picking out the sights.

"Maybe more like a hovercraft or square space ship!" Ross was chuckling. "But remember this area was practically destroyed by the bombing in the war."

"And what did Charles say about that building on the south bank? It's the National Theatre." Lorraine was looking impish. "A nuclear power station! If it was one, everybody would have objected. But build one and call it a theatre, and nary a complaint!"

"There's a lovely building beside it," Grace said.

"County Hall, a kind of civic palace," said Lorraine. "And the Houses of Parliament. They're both a palace and offices. Classical. Gothic. Stunning."

"Now, Lorraine," Barbara said in a friendly voice, "a short quiz about that bridge where we are pulling into, excuse me, into which we are pulling!"

"Wordsworth," said Lorraine in the same friendly tone, picking up the challenge. "But from the wrong vantage point."

"I don't know what you are talking about," Grace said. "Why would you even ask?"

Syd was listening intently. Lorraine and Barbara were engaged in the kind of conversation Marjorie used to get involved in.

"The view would be from Westminster Bridge, not toward it. However I can see from here 'A sight so touching in its majesty'."

"I am impressed," said Barbara with a smile.

Their coach was waiting on the Embankment, and took them to the Regent Palace Hotel in Piccadilly.

Martin picked up the microphone. "We hope to see everyone by

7:30, pm that is, at the pub. Just around the corner. Details on your brochure. They're expecting travellers who have had more than a full day. We can use this opportunity to get to know each other a little better and to set-up our gardening for the next few days that we're in England. Don't sleep too much. You'll never get day and night sorted out. But I don't need to tell you that."

Deep red flock paper made the walls of the pub warm and inviting, out of the cool of the English evening. The brighter lights at the bar on the wall farthest from the entrance made it seem deep and intimate.

Syd went with Ross and Barbara to the bar end of the wall banquette, to one of the three round pub tables in front. The couples gravitated toward them as well. Group divided as usual, thought Syd.

Syd could see Molly and Lorraine and that woman with them. The one with the halo of curly hair.

"Quite a looker, eh?" said Jack Track, very wisely.

Who is this guy, thought Syd, and what's he up to?

"Didn't get much of a chance to talk to you this morning. How did your picture turn out?"

Syd made some pleasantries and let the jostle of the other men moving to the bar interrupt the conversation.

He did note that the women were already engrossed in introductions and chat, led by Molly who seemed a most gracious and sincere person.

Arielle and Molly were settled at the other end of the banquette with the women.

Grace arrived with Tilley-clad Jean in tow, and indicated a seat for her friend.

Grace was an attractive widow and she knew it. She had been kept in the style to which she had always wanted to become accustomed. She paid attention to her figure, which was full and mature but controlled; she paid attention to her make-up, which was smart but evident; she paid attention to her hair, which was elegantly cut, coloured and freshly coifed that very afternoon; she paid attention to her clothes, where she was borderline costumed rather than dressed.

This evening, she was wearing a fashion deer-stalker. Summer weight, of course.

"I'm Grace," she paused, and gave a little giggle, "amazing Grace, really. This is my friend Jean, and," she pointed to Syd, "I have my eye on him. I've been watching him ever since this trip started and he's mine, girls. So hands off."

"Grace always gets her way," Jean said.

"Look," said Grace, "they're short one woman to make it even couples. Here's my chance. One of the men will buy me a drink."

Confidentially, Grace leaned toward Arielle, Molly and Jean. "My man's not wearing a tie, but I'll fix that pretty soon. And get that hair cut. The beard'll be gone tomorrow. Come to think of it the blazer's the only decent thing he's wearing."

She stood up, patted her hair, smoothed her hips, set her smile, and sailed off to join the group.

"One woman short, I believe," said Grace, giving Syd a dazzling smile. "I don't have a drink," she announced and waited.

"Of course, my dear," said a courtly gentleman wearing a cravat tucked in his elegant shirt, "that would make for a proper introduction. My name is Leslie Phillips and you just talk to my wife Marcia while I get you ... what? ... gin and tonic? ... of course."

As Grace took her drink, she turned to Syd.

"I know you," she said charmingly. "At least I know of you."

Syd waited politely knowing he had never seen Grace before this trip.

"Yes," said Grace, "we have a mutual acquaintance. A dear, dear friend of mine, who goes to your church. Shirley Wallace. Told me all about you."

Syd nearly bit his tongue and at the same time felt the thunk of a blow to his beltline, or some damned place inside, he thought.

All? For God's sake I hope not all.

Grace was glowing.

No. No. I will not be sucked into anything here on this trip. But not too many places to hide or disappear when we are all thrown together like this.

Syd was silent.

He eased his weight onto the foot farthest from Grace, with the hope she would pick up some conversation with one of the wives.

Luck was with him. Marcia, took it upon herself to make a round of introductions.

"I think we all know Grace from our get-together last night at the airport. Grace I'm sure you have met Ross and Barbara, and this is Dr. and Mrs. Lewis, and Mr. and Mrs. Blachford, and I'm sure Mr. Victor has you filmed already and Mrs. Victor has full notes an you, and you already know Syd."

"And my name's Jack, and this here's the wife."

Syd shifted behind The Wife toward the bar to give his order for dinner.

Just as the group seemed ready to go back to the hotel, Martin called everyone's attention.

"I just want to say once more how happy I am to have such a pleasant group of people on my garden tour. Already many of us have made friends, and with our proper gardening getting underway tomorrow, we'll find, no doubt, we've much more in common. Areminder that if you're not going to East Anglia with us tomorrow to Beth Chatto's and Adrian Bloom's, I'd appreciate knowing so we won't hold the bus in the traffic, and prolong our departure. Tomorrow's a full day. Have a good sleep."

DAY 3: LONDON. EAST ANGLIA

Knowing it was going to be a day on the bus in spite of touring about the gardens, Arielle set off for an early morning run through London's traffic, avoiding attention in loose jogging pants and a big sweater. Her hair was tucked up into a peaked cap that pulled low over her eyes.

Out of the hotel, turn right onto Glasshouse Street to Regent Street. She had been here before and knew the streets. Now she just let herself feel the grandeur.

Across Regent Street, heading for Burlington Gardens. A quick look to her right down Saville Row but straight ahead to Bond Street. Turn right on Bond and left onto Bruton Street, left around Berkeley Square to the top, and out Mount Street.

This was Mayfair, in all its richness.

Turn right in front of the Connaught Hotel to Grosvenor Square. Head left toward the U.S. Embassy, a quick look at Franklin Roosevelt standing in the square. Complete it, and straight ahead on Brook Street past Claridges.

Keep going along the bottom of Hanover Square, keep going to Regent Street.

Get across Oxford Circus, in Great Marlborough Street to Carnaby.

Arielle jostled her way through crowds there already, turn right at the bottom, immediate left onto John and back to the front entrance of the Regent Palace Hotel, where she was surprised to see a familiar face. One of her fellow tourists. Out this early.

It was the still-bearded Aaron Copland. With a file folder under his arm? Business in London? So early in the morning?

He seemed to recognize her: a moment of knowing.

After all, she thought, we've been on the same trip for the better part of two days.

Keep going, she said to herself, still a shower and breakfast before the 8:30 am departure for the two gardens in East Anglia.

Arielle met Molly outside the hotel ten minutes before the coach arrived.

"Good run?" Molly greeted her.

"M-m-m-m," commented Arielle with a satisfied tone.

"We've a big but interesting day ahead of us," Molly said. "Beth Chatto's garden and then Adrian Bloom's establishment at Bressingham."

"You'll have to fill me in on what's special," Arielle said. "I'll like them, but I just don't know about plants and gardening like you do."

"Don't be impressed with me," Molly gave a little laugh, "I've spent my life in my garden and around plants and the longer I do it, the less I know."

"Yesterday afternoon, after we checked into the hotel ... our stop, on the South Bank, at the ... what was it? ... just beside Lambeth Palace ...?"

"You mean the Museum of Garden History, in that church, St. Mary's-at-Lambeth, I believe it was. Do you know that church was to be demolished for urban renewal, when some English lady, an ardent gardener, found out that the family tomb of the Tradescants was there. The upshot was that The Tradescant Trust was formed in 1977 to preserve the memory of those earliest plant collectors. Surely you have heard of the houseplant Wandering Jew?"

"Yes. That's the place. That's what I mean. Well, I focused on herbs. Some of them are very old, I'm discovering. And on some of my walks in Toronto ..."

"Hikes, you mean, or route marches," corrected Molly.

Arielle smiled, "Well maybe ... but anyway, around the ethnic parts of Toronto ... you know Kensington Market, or the Danforth with all the Greek population ... I'm seeing fabulous vegetables that I'm beginning to learn about cooking. I thought I knew something about them."

"Got an eye-opener," said Molly.

"I couldn't help overhearing your conversation," Ross said to Molly.

"Did you know that Captain Bligh of the Bounty is also buried there. Kind of ties in with our stop in Greenwich, yesterday."

"That must be coincidence, but then he was a plant collector, too" Molly said to him.

"He had breadfruit aboard, didn't he?" asked Arielle.

"Yes," answered Molly. Then, "Arielle, I don't think you've met any of these people. Ross and Barbara, I don't know your last name. Oh what does it matter? We all had lunch at the pub yesterday, and also Syd, and Lorraine was there too. This is Arielle. We're together. And over there taking our picture, with their camcorder are Mr. and Mrs. Victor. I met them at breakfast. We'll get everybody's name pretty soon. Formalities have to be over."

The coach pulled up. Those present boarded, stowing bags, cameras and general travelling gear in the bins above the seats.

Arielle and Molly were among the first half dozen on board and chose a seat mid-ship.

That man, Aaron Copland, thought Arielle. No, Syd is his name. What's that long zippered bag he's carrying? It bumped the seats. Bit wide at bottom, like a cello case. Surely not golf clubs. After the file folder this morning. This is a gardener?

"Look at Mr. and Mrs. Track Suit, as I call them," said Molly quietly, gesturing toward the couple, as they worked their way toward the back, "another matching set, with a pair of Blue Jays baseball hats." She could hardly contain a laugh.

They all settled and sat patiently as Martin checked his list. He did a head count again.

"We seem to be missing ... the ones who are going shopping!" He gave a nod to the anxious looking driver who closed the door of the bus, and cranked the wheel to pull out into the traffic.

"I have a microphone here," Martin was speaking into it, "and I thought we could make use of it this morning to get our gardening under way.

"First of all, I'm going to say that there isn't a gardening expert here on the end of this speaker, and I'm hoping we can all take part in sharing our expertise and our interests.

"The next thing I want to say is that as we're winding our way through North-east London, heading for the A12 to take us to Colchester, be aware that the British are great gardeners, and as we go through even humble areas, you'll see lovely bits of front gardens, window boxes, what have you.

"I'm going to sound like the ex-school teacher that I am, and say that, as we clear the busy inner city, I want you to think about these two gardens we are going to visit today: White Barn House of Beth Chatto, and Bressingham, the Dell, and Foggy Bottom of Adrian Bloom."

Everyone started to laugh.

Mr. Track Suit called out, "I didn't know Adrian's bloomin' bottom was foggy."

"Not a foggy notion about it!" an unidentified voice called out.

"This isn't the kind of thinking I had in mind," Martin said, sounding pleased with the participation, "but it is thinking. Anyway after we get out of so much traffic, I'm going to ask you to contribute things that you know about those places, so we can get to know each other a bit better and have some common ground to talk to each other in the garden itself.

"I've found that often we've a lot tucked in our heads from reading about these places, and a few of us carry our notes and clippings on a trip like this for reference."

Martin sat down.

The bus was in the Borough of Islington, heading out the Seven Sisters Road to the A127 which would give onto the A12.

"This is going to be a complete learning situation for me," Arielle spoke hesitantly.

"Not to worry, dear," said Molly, reaching into one of the outside pockets of her large handbag and pulling out a dog-eared notebook. "Gardens are wonderfully enjoyable places to be. In some ways I think you can appreciate the beauty of them better if you don't know. Just look. Then again I get curious about them."

"Actually I've been thinking about gardening. I've never had a place to grow anything outside, nor had the time ... well maybe taken the time."

"Your mother loves her garden."

"Yes. I guess I've just taken for granted that it's hers and she does it, and it makes the view from my studio window nice. I have that big hoya plant, and I grow and use herbs in the kitchen, and those vegetables I see around Toronto. It has occurred to me that they all grow somewhere! And I've done quite a bit of reading on how you cook them. Cultural and health info."

"I think you'll find out that you know a lot more than you think you do."

There was some oo-ing and ah-ing, as they passed a pretty English cottage garden in the front of a suburban villa. Colour at all heights and spilling over the whole area.

Just past it, a wall of beige-orange brick covered with cotoneaster caught everyone's attention.

With the fuss breaking the snooziness of the group, Martin took the microphone in hand. "We seem to be settling onto some fairly straight road ..."

"Corners every 200 feet instead of every 100," put in Mr. Track Suit, which drew a laugh.

"... so perhaps we could bring up some of the points we want to share about the gardens. Let's start with Beth Chatto's at White Barn House. By the way, has anybody attended Beth's talks at the Toronto Garden Club when she was there?" He looked around.

"Grace? Right here beside me. Yes? You did? Perhaps you could start. The microphone is handy for you. And a word about yourself." Grace and Jean were sitting directly behind the driver.

Grace half stood in the aisle as she took the microphone. She smiled graciously at everyone. "I've been a member of the Toronto Garden Club for years and took my turn as President, which is a great honour. We meet so many lovely people at the club, and Beth Chatto spoke to us at one of our meetings ... I can't remember just when it was. Very charming, and my gracious, she knew such a lot about plants. I do flower arranging, mostly. But she and her husband have done an incredible lot of work in developing their place. I'm really looking forward to it." She handed back the microphone to Martin.

"Thanks, Grace. Now anyone else?"

Quiet except for the noises of the road.

"Yes, I will," said a small voice from well down the aisle. It was Lorraine.

"Do come up to my seat," Martin said. "I can sit down in the courier's seat, which by the way is available for anyone. And," he spoke to Lorraine who was taking the mike from him, "something about yourself, remember."

"My name's Lorraine," she said confidently into the microphone. "I'm a librarian, and a gardener. I've taken some courses with the University of Guelph to become a Master Gardener. That's not as impressive as it sounds. It just means that any of us who completes this course is available in your community as a resource. Information about plants, conditions they like, pest control and if we don't know, we know where to direct you.

"About White Barn House. The garden there is quite new, like thirty years old. That's new! Somewhere around 1960 Beth Chatto and her husband bought the house with about four acres of land. Here in East Anglia, unlike the rest of Britain it can be quite dry.

"So they developed a garden with three contrasting areas, to suit the house and site. Where it was sunny on the gravel slopes they made a Mediterranean or scree garden. Aromatic plants like rosemary. Many herbs are aromatic shrubs from Mediterranean hill-sides, like cistus, evergreen sunroses, which should be in flower. Santolina. Grey cotton lavender, a sub-shrub, which acts as a ground cover. Artemesia, the family of sagebrush and absinthe. They endure droughts. Interestingly, grey-leaved plants are generally adapted to drought and heat.

"Enough about the scree garden.

"Then on the cooler slopes, they planted trees and shrubs for a shaded woodland, with foliage plants like hostas.

"And their famous water-garden. It was a spring-fed ditch and they've made it into a series of five large pools separated by mown grass-covered dams, surrounded by tall grass plants and a collection of moisture-loving trees, shrubs and other plants. Always water in spite of drought.

"Four acres. As Beth says, 'three aspects, three soils, three gardens'.

"Just let me add that part of the problem with a new garden, is that there's not the cheap labour available as in the late 1800s, when the wonderful gardens around the vast estates were developed, so this garden is pretty amazing.

"One other thing, about 1970, she started a small nursery, which has grown as she developed her expertise. She has a good Garden Nursery Catalogue.

"That's all I have to say. I hope I didn't bore you ... or lecture ..."

Applause broke out.

Molly said to Arielle, "Very informative. She knows what she's talking about. I want to get to know her a little better. Nice to talk to someone who really knows and is interested."

"Very nice, Lorraine," said Martin, taking back the microphone, "exactly what we wanted to know. Now for Bressingham. Volunteers?"

Martin surveyed the group hopefully. "Maybe just to jog everyone's memory, I have to say we are not going to see Foggy Bottom."

"O-o-o-o, not see a foggy bottom," Mr. Track Suit said luridly.

"Oh, Jack," admonished Mrs. Track Suit.

"It's only open one Sunday each month ... so we're not able to take it in."

"Showing yer bottom on Sunday!" Mr. Track Suit was getting on a roll.

"Cut it out, Jack."

"The wife says cut it out, I gotta cut it out."

With relief, Martin surveyed the group again with eyebrows raised. "Heathers. Evergreens." He was prompting.

"Well, maybe." It was Jean, tucked into the corner beside the window, behind the driver. She took off her Tilley hat as Martin handed her the microphone. Then she twisted around on her knees to face the others.

"I'm interested in Bonsai, as well as my little garden at my house. I visit the Japanese Cultural Centre, just off the Don Valley Parkway, around Eglinton ... but you don't want to hear about that ... Bressingham ... this Foggy Bottom is made up of heathers that have bright foliage and some flower in the winter. English winter. With these are conifers; tall, short and dwarf. Interesting shapes, like skyrockets, really narrow columns, some like pyramids, some round. Like that. Maybe hundreds or more. The best all in one place you'll ever see. These evergreens are not just green ... that's all I have to say."

"If I may add," Martin said, taking the microphone from Jean, "These evergreens are of all colours. A red heather. A golden juniper. Then a blue spruce. You'll see in his garden centre if not in the Dell, that's the garden up top of Foggy Bottom."

"Theya saya," said a woman with an accent, "ya, theya saya, big catalogue from nursery with heathers and conifers."

"It was the son Adrian who developed this," said a voice from the back of the coach.

Ross lifted his hand, to acknowledge this contribution. "It was the father Alan, who started it all along with his collection of steam-engines. Strange mix. Father specialized in herbaceous perennials and alpines, then son Adrian continued but specialized in heathers and dwarf conifers."

"And the gardens on the premises, is ... are called the Dell," Lorraine said. "This enormous plant collection is displayed in Island Beds. He developed the idea of amorphous flowerbeds. They are the shapeless drifts Beth Chatto used in her woodland garden."

Arielle saw Isobel give Martin's jacket a tug.

"Well, I think we've got a good handle on our two stops today."

Isobel tugged again, and Martin bent over to hear her. He straightened up to the microphone. "Some logistics. At Beth Chatto's, there are washroom facilities ..."

"Don't say nothing, Jack," came a warning.

"... and we have arranged some light refreshments, tea, coffee, donuts, scones, what have you as we will be here until, what is it now, just coming up to 10:20, let's say 12:45, with departure from the parking lot at 1 pm. We have arranged lunch at a pub on the road to Bressingham, and hope to get there by 2:30 at the latest."

About six miles along the A133 from Colchester was the sign for the village of Elmstead Market. Shortly the bus pulled off the road, along a drive marked by a tall hedge. White Barn House. The driver pulled forward to the path. The scree garden was in front of them.

Martin took the mike once more, "Two and a half hours from London. That's pretty good. Perhaps the people on the drivers side would like to get off first. We'll take turns. It cuts down the confusion."

Arielle lifted her big bag from the floor onto her lap as the large zippered bag brushed past her. Really, she said to herself, it can't be golf clubs, and definitely not a cello! But what? She was curious. Not a usual kind of travel bag.

Arielle and Molly took their time in the Mediterranean garden on the slope facing south-west. Even at mid-morning it was hot and dry.

"Look at that." Molly was surveying the plants. "As well as what Lorraine said, there are some old friends here. Lovely deep green spurges, with their yellow flowers. Bushes and pillows."

"Mixed in with those grey herbs," said Arielle, "and those spikes, I've seen those in Toronto, but not with those tall white flowers."

"Yuccas. Whole mix is subtle and stunning. Can those two ideas be put together? Well Beth Chatto did it."

"That fragrance." Arielle stopped and breathed deeply as a stir of breeze passed by. "Pineapple? It can't be. Yes, it is. Sweet and heavy." She had inhaled a second time.

"Just maybe," said Molly as she moved toward a twiggy looking shrub. "Yes. Broom. That's the name of these, and the label says pineapple. Lovely."

The crowd moved on ahead of them, and they made their way to the refreshment area beside the shed which seemed to be a shop and tourist center at the end of the Nursery area.

Clay pots, ceramic pots, any kind of container, any kind of shape or pattern were filled with strong thick succulent plants and cacti, to make a divider.

Coffee tasted good, and they agreed to progress to the regular garden by adding water, as Molly said, and keep adding water until the bog.

"Shall we head for the path through that stand of, I think, oak trees?" Arielle asked.

"Yes," said Molly. She was silent as they passed the line of trees. "Already the look of the soil has changed. Can you tell the difference?"

"Very obvious," said Arielle. "Darker. Moist. Like garden soil should look."

"Sheltered by the trees. Humus-rich loam. The plants should be wonderful."

"Just look at these trees," Arielle said as they came down the path around one of the island beds Beth Chatto also favoured. "The textures of the bark. They are all different. Molly, that one is gray-green and as rough as coral ... and look at that one, winey-red and smooth as leather ... but irregular circular rough rings ... how do you describe ?... you don't of course. You look and enjoy it ... and I do have a camera ... and it's completely different from what we saw back there where we got off the bus ..."

"Grabs you, doesn't it?" Molly said sympathetically.

"Fabulous." Arielle was overcome. "Wherever I look ... up, down, back where we came from, what might be around the corner." She fell silent.

"And a human has planned this, and done it, is doing it."

"A work of art."

"The best ones are. But so are the simplest and humblest." Molly had her camera and notebook in hand. She made a few notes and took one or two pictures. "I suggest we do once around and then return to places that specially interest you."

"How could you ever focus on a few things?"

"You'll be surprised. After we've done our survey, there will be one or two things that you remember, that you're curious about, want to check, see again. I have faith ...."

"Lorraine implied the woodland had a few plants, what did she say? Hostas?"

"Certainly an understatement."

"Do you know the names of all of these?"

"Not all, but quite a few."

"Name them as we go. I'd like to hear their names."

"Many are finished blooming now. Dog-toothed violets. The primulas ..."

"Primroses? Like they force at home in the springtime? Those sharp shades of purple, rosey-red, orange, creamy-white?"

"Yes. They grow naturally here in spring. Trilliums are cultivated in gardens," Molly said, loving to talk about plants. "By the way don't be surprised if you see a plant growing in one type of condition and then come across its close relative growing in a completely different environment."

"What's this low covering with these shiny green leaves and little purple flowers. It's in Mum's garden," said Arielle.

"Myrtle, or vinca. You also know delphiniums and salvias. Also campanula," said Molly.

"I can see common varieties like hollyhocks, and Sweet William. Maybe I'll just try to get a bead on them myself. Oh those have to be carnations."

"They belong to a big genus called Dianthus. Includes pinks. Sweet William belongs, too. Some are annuals. Some biennial."

They took their time, enjoying every inch of the way, through paths, past drifts of colour that moved from one shade to another.

They seemed to have the whole garden to themselves. Everybody else seemed to have gone the other route.

All of a sudden the woodland garden was full of people. Arielle and Molly were meeting the bulk of the tour group coming up the slope.

And just as suddenly they were in the water-garden.

"But where to look?" Arielle's voice was almost inaudible.

Yes, there were ponds in this shallow valley. But it was a garden. It was a painting.

Arielle could see plants with leaves like rhubarb, but twice the size; feathery ferns; huge clumps of strap leaves with a lily type flower sticking straight up. Iris. Here? Maybe that's what Molly meant when she said some family members could grow in completely different conditions.

Feathery flowers with hugely indented leaves. And grasses. Surely those must be grasses. Tall, thick, long striped blades of variegated shades of green. Massive clumps perfectly poised at the edge of the water. Lily pads. Yes, Arielle could hear a frog. And the water was moving, ever so slightly.

Arielle moved to the left from the path out of the woodland garden and stood with her back to the sun. It was stunning. The contrast of the flat water ... no, no the contrast first, of the water broken into patches by the grass paths, and then the flatness broken by these plants. The composition; the textures; the contrasts. It was a visual experience she had never had before.

She tended to live in an auditory world. She was caught in the middle of the visual.

For a trip of two dozen people, Arielle could hardly believe she had this garden to herself. But they had passed the others going the opposite way. That was a kind of magic in itself.

Molly was bent over some foliage as a coolie in a tea plantation. Arielle crouched down, to become an integral part of the scene.

A figure emerged from the path down from the house, kitty-corner to Arielle's position. It was Syd. He was carrying that strange canvas bag.

She watched.

He found a relatively flat place beside the first pond which was edged with blue hosta. He unzipped the bag. From it he took a number of sturdy wood slats, of various lengths, a thick rectangular form of shorter wood, and a small folded aluminium and canvas seat.

He briskly set about, with unhesitating skill, to form a tripod. Then he opened the rectangular form on hinges to double its size, secured it to the tripod to produce an easel. He tested the stability on the ground, made some minor adjustments and sat down. From the bag he took out a large drawing pad which he placed on the ledge of the easel, and then drew out a box of watercolours and some water containers.

Arielle looked at her watch. He had an hour and a bit to paint.

I can't sit here for the rest of the morning, Arielle thought to herself, but she was reluctant to move. She didn't think he had seen her; hadn't noticed.

Arielle just sat, basking in the warm sun, and being a part of the landscape. I have no idea what any of these plants are, she thought, but I have to believe they were all planted by design, in spite of it not looking designed. It is so perfect. It is a work of art.

She sat. Still. Looking and listening. A gentle movement of air ruffled the calm surface of her thoughts. Gradually a few phrases of music took shape in her mind's ear. A solo flute sliding and gliding. Debussy. Prelude a l'apres-midi d'un faune. So familiar. Languid wait for her violin entry.

The music faded from her mind.

Arielle decided to move on. Molly was right. There were two things she wanted to take another look at: the trees in the woodland for colour and texture on the bark; and back to the Mediterranean garden for the contrasts within it, and to contrast with plants she was seeing here.

As she reached the path to the woodland, Arielle heard a loud voice from the other end of the pond.

"Ah-ha," said Mr. Track Suit.

Arielle gave a quick look. Mr. Track Suit was bending over Syd's shoulder. "There," said Mr. Track Suit, pointing at the picture. He looked diagonally across the pond, then at Syd. "Gone. Ah-ha," he said knowingly.

Whatever that means, thought Arielle.

The group met as scheduled; were transported to a pleasant pub where lunchtime became a social event of gardening exchanges.

Arielle simply listened to all that was going on around her, until her prawn door-stopper sandwich was delivered to her. She took it outside to a table in the small garden beside a stream. Outside is always best, she thought to herself.

Then they embarked for Bressingham, fifteen minutes down the road.

The coach parked in a tree lined lane. Martin gave them their bearings: straight ahead to the railroad centre; left through the Dell with the island beds; and continue into the garden centre.

Arielle and Molly were together. Arielle knew Molly was a little tired after a full morning.

"I may just find a pleasant aspect and sit in the beauty of the flowers," Molly said.

"That sounds nice to me," Arielle said, "I could be very confused if I tried to absorb much more through my brain. I'm going to let my senses take over."

They headed toward the house. Ivy covered as if painted with thick green paint; white, many-paned windows on both storeys, roof sloping up to a flat top with chimneys on each corner. Formal. It stood in the midst of a sea of green lawn and the famous drifting amorphous flowerbeds, full of colour. Calm and natural.

They found a bench, in light shade amongst the island beds, giving a full view of a dry creek with the bridge over it. Flowers on different levels in full bloom pleased the mind as well as the eye.

It was as much a garden of leaves as of flowers and it had a very special charm.

Neither spoke for a long time. They knew each other well enough to enjoy silence. They were good friends, in spite of Molly being her mother's friend first. There was trust between Arielle and her mother, between her mother and Molly, and between Molly and herself. It was just there.

"You've never regretted leaving B-Man," Molly said.

"No," replied Arielle unemotionally.

"Are you lonely?"

"No, and yes," answered Arielle. "Are you?"

"Yes, and no," echoed Molly. "But I'm old, and a widow. When I feel lonely I don't know anyone who I would rather be with, so I just do something I've meant to do for a while and get on with it. I realize I'm mostly alone, rather than lonely. But you're young."

"Not all that young, and I stayed with B-Man at least five years longer than I should have."

"You weren't married so you could have left sooner."

"It was habit by then, and I was leading my own life anyway."

They slipped into silence as the breeze stirred the stands of ornamental grasses strewn through the flower beds.

Arielle let her thoughts drift. B-Man fell for her. A businessman whose wife didn't understand him. Arielle held that no one ever really understands anyone; that quite a bit has to be taken on faith. They lived together for eighteen years; longer than his marriage had lasted, but he'd never got around to the divorce he'd promised if she would move in with him.

As time went on Arielle was immensely glad that he hadn't. He thought they had a great relationship because she understood him. He basically never tried to get to know her as a person; to treat her as a person.

She finally realized she was only staying with him for convenience. He wasn't all that demanding, and maybe she might meet someone else. She wasn't too proud of that, but that was the way it was.

As with the first man in her life, she and B-Man had had great physical intimacy but once again there was no trust. No staying power. No glue.

B-Man always contended, "You can't trust anyone."

She queried, "Anyone?"

He said emphatically, "I repeat, you can't trust anyone."

She replied, "Maybe I'm not in the quote, anyone, unquote, category."

The comment went right over his head.

She also stuck with him to learn.

She had shifted from dance performance to music teacher and studio musician.

She realized that although she would inherit what her mother had, she really had to provide for herself. B-Man always bragged that he looked after his Arielle, but never added up that while he paid for the apartment, she bought all the food, and provided for all her personal needs.

She was also quietly tithing herself, putting money into retirement funds, building up savings. Diversifying, as she had learned while listening to the conversations of B-Man and his friends. Heard the words and discovered the concepts. Simply, not putting all her eggs in one basket.

He was always proud to take her places as she looked so good in her black and white. Once when he had shown her the invitation to a black tie affair and said, "Meet me there, honey", because business would keep him from calling for her at their apartment, she did the Flash Dance trick in a rented tuxedo, fixing a dress shirt complete with black tie into a halter. Caused quite a stir when she took her jacket off. Long hair piled elaborately for this occasion.

Their apartment. He always referred to it as his apartment. She had bumbled around for some phrase which would express their home, but was defeated at every turn. His apartment. Thin edge of the separation, going nowhere, wedge.

She did business entertaining for him at his apartment: cooking gourmet meals; learning from Julia Child, Elizabeth David and all the new cookery writers as they came along. She discovered Alice B. Toklas.

She had a particular problem with some of the haute cuisine as it contravened nutritional concepts which she thought she knew, and then started to explore further.

She watched with horror the new women athletes: the young girls in gymnastics, ballet, and figure skating. She started to look into proper nutrition for physical performance and became the expert in some circles, before the word Consultant was so easily used.

She had friends who were students, performers, teachers, coaches. She was part of a network and was consulted on a regular basis.

B-Man wasn't interested in anything she had to say about this part of her life. He didn't bother to take any notice.

Working with kids. Consultant. Nutrition. Life style. No qualifications. Just experience and contact with the scene. With teachers and performers. Cooked for them at her place, her studio.

She started to look at ethnic cooking when she began to explore Toronto's various communities, taking off on a long walk across The Danforth for the Greek stores and restaurants, Kensington Market for Portuguese, St. Clair W. for Italian, Spadina for Chinese. She discovered tastes, and produce, and fascinating worlds.

Off Chinatown one day, she found herself in The Art Gallery of Ontario looking at Still Lifes.

If it rained during her spare hours from teaching or performing she spent time in the Toronto Library with cook books, Gertrude Stein, Impressionist painters.

And then she discovered those stunning flowers painted by Georgia O'Keeffe, and her life with Alfred Steiglitz; and clothes exclusively in black and white.

B-Man was not the least bit interested, and their guests comments about the dinners she produced, didn't register.

It finally occurred to her that he hardly knew she was around. So each time she left their, his, apartment to go to her studio, she took a totebag full of her personal belongings.

None of the furnishings belonged to her. The whole place had been done by Eaton's Interior Decorating, and very nice it was. But completely impersonal. It could have been a hotel suite.

It took a leisurely six months over the winter to remove all her things. B-Man noticed nothing different. The last removal was on an evening he had arranged for her to join him and some business associates with their wives. It was really a power dinner at Truffles at the Four Seasons Hotel in Yorkville.

She dressed carefully in black dress, black boots, her black coat, and some simple pearl jewellery. All of it carefully chosen to display her body, which she knew was her role at these affairs.

She laughed at the last of her items left in the apartment: her best knives from the kitchen, and the egg beater; her nightgown, housecoat, track suit and jogging shoes from her closet. She carefully left a full row of empty hangers covered with drycleaner bags and a few empty shoe boxes; and lastly, her cosmetics and toiletries case from the bathroom. All into her large gold carrybag.

She gained the second floor of the hotel, deposited her things at the coatcheck and presented herself to the Maitre'd to join the party.

She was fashionably late, as expected, to create the impression with her black clad body that B-Man loved. He fielded any kind of comment his guests handed out as if he was the sole cause of what she was. She carried on in the usual manner, silently presiding as hostess over the dinner.

When it settled into men's talk, instead of sitting smiling and unspoken through the hour or so of business bravado, and often practising passages of music silently in her mind, Arielle quietly and charmingly said to B-Man that she would go home now. She would get a taxi.

Ever the dancer, she flowed out of the restaurant, collected her things from the coatcheck, and took the escalator downstairs. At the bottom, she looked out onto Avenue Road and saw a northbound bus pulling into the stop.

With a rare feeling of freedom, she stepped outside and caught it, and rode home to her studio apartment.

It was two weeks before she heard from B-Man.

In those two weeks two of his executive friends contacted her with offensive suggestions.

Why had she stayed with B-Man? Status. A two way street. Women get status by having a man. She knew she gave B-Man status because she looked good.

He had never been to her studio. He didn't know that she kind of lived there. He wanted no part of her life.

One Saturday she had sustained a leg injury when teaching a dance class at the studio in Scarborough. Tore a calf muscle and couldn't walk. She phoned him. Would he come and get her. She was in pain. He made all kinds of excuses. Then he asked her where she was. When she told him, he simply said for her to call a taxi, the driver could help her down the stairs of the studio.

Arielle had tried to adjust to men who didn't know who they were or what they were. Therefore she could never be right. The relationship always failed. They shifted ground. The problem was that she knew who she was.

So she had put men out of her life.

Finally, Arielle looked at her watch.

"There's a tea shop in the Garden Centre area. It's coming up to four o'clock. Shall we go for a cuppa?"

"Lovely," agreed Molly, and they made their way leisurely across the estate.

"What a surprising contrast," Arielle said as they approached the carefully constructed wooden fences of the Garden Centre and stepped through the gate.

He's just sketching this time, Arielle said to herself, when she saw Syd immediately inside the Garden Centre.

He was sitting on the little fold-up stool, working on his knee. Mr. Track Suit was behind Syd, watching him draw. Syd looked up briefly as Molly and Arielle approached.

"So did yous see the shapeless amorphous flower beds?" Mr. Track Suit spoke authoritatively to Arielle.

Mirth hit her.

Her eyes snapped to Syd's. Glee was dancing in them. A shared moment.

Arielle could feel Molly shaking with laughter beside her.

"Let's get to that tea room before I explode." Molly could hardly get the words out.

They settled at a table with their tea, looking out over the Garden Centre with its displays of packaged heathers and healthy shrubs.

"This Mr. Track Suit is too much," said Molly. "I'd half expected to see him riding that Merry-go-round way over by the coach park."

"Or maybe spend the afternoon on the train, or was it going? There seems to be a track around the place." Arielle suggested.

They were on the verge of giddiness.

"He spends a lot of his time hanging over Syd's shoulder, watching him draw," commented Molly. "I wonder if he's any kind of gardener. I can hardly imagine. But it takes all kinds."

"And all kinds come on a gardening trip, including me," said Arielle.

"Including the shoppers," said Molly. "I wonder if they're as tired as we are!"

"It'll be an early night for me," said Arielle. "It's been a wonderful day."

DAY 4: LONDON. PORTOBELLO ROAD. KEW GARDENS

"We can get off here for our visit to Portobello Road market. The coach'll be back at this same location at 11:30 am which gives you the better part of two hours for bargain hunting." Martin had the microphone. "Before we go, a reminder that there's a nice lunch room at Kew Gardens so you are responsible for your lunch here or there."

Grace stood up and stepped into the aisle. "Any of you ladies, or men too, who want to, can stick with me. I can help you avoid junk and get some real bargains."

By the time everyone had filed out, Grace was surrounded. "We'll go this way," she announced.

"Then we'll go that way," Molly said, and Arielle nodded in complete agreement.

Whether for the same reason, the others seemed headed in the same direction as Molly and Arielle.

Arielle noticed Syd had a large drawing pad under his arm instead of a camera or video camera around his neck, as most of the other men had.

Yesterday she had seen him at Beth Chatto's, camped out with the easel and stool he carried in that bag, painting with water-colours, then drawing at Bressingham, and had noticed his absorption and contentment with seemingly no reference to time.

Just the drawing pad under his arm today.

"The thing about antiques and bric-a-brac is that you really have to look at it," Molly commented absentmindedly.

"I'm not a collector or shopper," said Arielle. "My studio is small and functions as a work space for sound, but I like to look at way-out stuff, or stuff that's camp. Oh," Arielle had turned away from the brass bedsteads and old pottery, "look over there, Molly, second hand clothes ...." She drifted toward them.

On the edge of the pavement, a street boutique was set up, perfected by a chest with lacey antique lingerie spilling out of the open drawers, a vase of dried flowers, scarves, a hall-stand hung with old velvet dresses, jackets, and other bits of pre-Depression clothing and accessories. Some old worn high-heeled ladies' boots and shoes were lined up in front of the chest. A carved-back chair with a threadbare needlepoint seat was ready for milady to try on the footwear; and a standing full-length oval mirror angled to enclose the display, was ready for milady to consider the effect of the garments. A boudoir!

Molly followed Arielle to the boutique. There were fans and gloves to be looked at, tried on. Hair combs to consider.

Arielle picked up a feather boa, wound it around her neck and trailed it along her arm. It was moth-eaten and thin at one end. She glanced at herself in the mirror, and dismissed the boa, but over her left shoulder her eye caught the reflection of the back of Syd, bent over his sketch pad.

Arielle put the boa back and began rummaging through the rack of old velvet clothes. She picked up a long wine velvet dinner dress, bunched at the shoulders. Myrna Loy would have worn it in the movies. Arielle held it up against herself: hanger at her shoulders and pressed the dress to her waist.

Well to the side of the mirror, Molly said, "That's nice."

At the same moment as Arielle shook her head, she met Syd's eyes in the mirror over her left shoulder. He was shaking his head in agreement.

"No," said Arielle to Molly, "two against one."

"What did you say, dear?"

But Arielle had put the dress back and had picked up a black crushed velvet jacket with leg-of-mutton sleeves, and some exquisite beading on the shoulders above gathered pockets on each side of the bodice. It was fitted to the waist and flared around the hip. Arielle had a black charmeuse slip dress at home waiting for this jacket. She examined it for wear and found a few rends, and considered the size. Both conditions seemed adequate.

She held it up to herself and looked in the mirror. It looked fine. It was black. Her favourite colour.

Cautiously she slid her eyes over her shoulder in the mirror. He was looking. He simply nodded agreeably. She raised her eyebrows endorsing his judgment.

"I'll take this," Arielle said to the vendor. She looked around. Syd was walking away toward the Eliza Doolittle Flower Shop.

"You wouldn't want to buy any of those used clothes," Grace's voice was coming closer to Arielle. "Germs in them, and no style. You'd look like a bag lady in most of those old things."

Arielle completed her purchase. "Molly," she said, "there are some interesting food shops, and fruit and vegetable vendors here. I'd like to pick up lunch, kind of a picnic. I have my Swiss Army knife in my bag. I could serve a decent luncheon for six with it if I had to. Would you care to join me?"

"No thanks dear, I don't like to eat outside as you do. I'll take my chances on the facilities at Kew."

"You really don't mind that we're not always together, do you. You said that before we came and I feel it is true."

"Having that freedom means we both talk to other people on the tour or indeed locals wherever we are and we end up all the better for it."

"Let's head back to the bus," Arielle suggested as she put the few items she had purchased from the barrow along the way, having bought some bread, cheese and a bottle of water from the small deli at the end of the parade.

"All present and accounted for." Martin was speaking to the driver, with his list held triumphantly aloft.

Martin was on his feet as the coach stopped at Kew gates. "For those not familiar with Kew Gardens," he said, "I have a brochure to distribute."

Isobel was tugging at Martin's sleeve. He bent down for the whispered conference, then put the microphone to his mouth again.

"Before we de-bus, Ross and Barbara talked about staying here, Thameside, for supper. It's a lovely walk, with nice pubs. So anyone interested, meet with Ross and Barbara just inside the gate, after I've got us all admitted, and make your arrangements. For everyone else, meet us back here at this spot at 4:45 pm for our return to the hotel ... and you're on your own for supper, no matter what. I guess it's the turn of the folks on my right to get off first. Enjoy Kew."

Arielle and Molly moved into the aisle.

"I think it would be rather nice to join Ross and Barbara. I'm enjoying their company very much."

"Agreed," replied Arielle.

With brochures in hand the group filed through the main gate.

Barbara and Ross were waiting well along the path by the old glasshouse.

Arielle and Molly joined them along with Mr. and Mrs. Track Suit, Grace and a reluctant Jean, Syd with his easel bag, and Lorraine. Two other couples appeared interested.

"Maybe I can speak up for Ross and myself, and Syd," said Barbara. "We discussed this earlier. We've been comparing notes from our guidebooks. If you look at your brochure, west area, coloured blue, see The Brentford Gate. Out there are several riverside pubs. One of the most attractive is The Dove, a mile or so downstream toward Hammersmith and Central London, close to Kelmscott House where William Morris, the Arts and Craft man lived.

"Also a mile or so the other way, an attractive walk along Strand-on-the-Green to an eighteenth century river frontage. We think it's all pretty close to us here at the Royal Botanical Gardens.

"There's a row of small houses looking over the narrow towpath and the river. They're brick and covered with wisteria and roses. Would the wisteria still be in bloom at this time in early July? "

"I'd like to see some," said Lorraine. "I've read about it and seen pictures. It isn't hardy in Ontario as far as I can find out."

Barbara continued, "Two pubs along the riverbank, the Bull, and the City Barge, supposed to be nice in the summer."

"We'll join you," Molly spoke up. "Arielle and me."

"Me, too," said Lorraine.

"Count the wife and me in," said Mr. Track Suit.

"I don't suppose any of the pubs serve a club sandwich," Grace said hesitantly. "But the company looks good, so Jean and I will join you."

"I'd like to go," said Jean sounding stressed, "but how do we get back if the bus isn't here for us?"

"We're close to a tube station," said Ross. "Kew Gardens, or another one might be closer. Doesn't matter. It'll be on the District Line."

"I've never been on the subway here." Jean was timid, not difficult.

"Syd or I will help you. We'll all help you," said Ross assuringly. "We can always get a taxi, and catch the Piccadilly Line. Makes us feel close to our hotel."

"Sounds good to me," said Grace.

"When and where will we meet?" Lorraine asked.

Ross consulted both his watch and Syd. "How about 4:45 at the Brentford Gate?"

"Sold," said Mr. Track Suit.

There was a general muttering of agreement.

"Going to do some more painting?" Grace asked Syd sweetly.

He just nodded and fell into step with Ross.

Arielle took a step down the path. She could feel Grace's eyes boring into her. Out of a clear blue sky, and out of earshot of the others, Grace said directly to her, "You look divorced. You've got that used look about you. Divorced women can't make it. They're damaged goods. I can tell you're divorced. You are divorced aren't you, dear? Come on Jean, lets see if we can find something to eat in these gawd-awful English cafes." And she stalked off.

Jean gave Arielle a weak smile and followed Grace.

Molly had joined Barbara and Lorraine.

"This site's huge," Syd said to Ross as they sat over lunch in the Pavilion across from the Temperate House. "How many acres, do you think?"

"Hundreds. Barbara will have it exactly in her notes, but I'd guess two hundred at least and maybe three," Ross replied.

"Institutional gardening," said Syd.

"School of horticulture," said Ross, "library, collection of plants. Old royalty, you know. Mad George the Third. The buildings, or should I say structures, like the Temperate House, and the Palm House, are Victorian showpieces. Just look at that ornate iron and glass. A feat of engineering. Right up your alley."

"Well, it used to be. And while I appreciate it, and will take a cursory look at it, I'm making a conscious effort to move away from it."

"Burned out?"

"No. Dealing with retirement. Maybe you have some insight on the subject."

"Strangely enough, I don't," said Ross.

"But you said you retired five years ago."

"Stopped working as an accountant, but immediately went to work as a part-time student, downtown on the Subway to the university two or three days a week, and took my Bachelor of Arts degree in five years."

"That's right, you fellows in those days articled in an accountant's office."

"I always felt Barbara had something special from her English Literature and History degree, and I finally got around to it. It's wonderful to study history when you've been through so much of it."

"So, in many ways you haven't really retired."

"No," said Ross, "and I don't intend to. Just find another kind of work. Unpaid work, of course. But a person has to find that work."

"Being purposefully occupied," commented Syd.

"Are you ... purposefully occupied?"

"I think so," said Syd.

"Not sure? You strike me as having both feet firmly on the ground."

"I like to think so, but life made a big detour off the expected path for me."

"You're on your own on this trip. Not married?" Ross was hesitant to pry.

"Widower."

"Long?"

"About three years."

"Sudden?"

"No. That's what complicated it for me. Marjorie had been ill for a while. About ten years ago we made big changes. Sold the house. Moved to an apartment. Things to make it easier for her. She'd become a brittle diabetic. I took early retirement five years later. We had plans to travel, and enjoy life."

"And she got worse?"

"To the point I became the care-giver, which I was very glad to do. None of this was in the plan. And she died. And the emptiness was overwhelming."

"Going to marry again?"

"No. I don't think marriage is an answer. At my age, life becomes a minor odyssey. You know, everyman's hunt for himself. What do you say we get a move on."

"I want to spend some time in these plant houses," said Ross, "and have a look at those massive statues in front of the Palm House."

"Massive statues?" Syd questioned.

"Replicas of the Queen's Beasts. Lions, falcons, and griffins. That sort of thing. Created to decorate Westminster Abbey for the Coronation in '52."

"Queen's Beasts," said Syd with a sly smile. "Try that on Jack Track at the pub tonight?"

"Jack Track? Is that his last name?"

"No, but he and 'the wife' always wear track suits, so I've dubbed him Jack Track."

"Good enough. See you at the gate at 4:45."

On his own, Syd set down his canvas painting bag and studied the map.

I'm sure the collection of plants in any of these houses is spectacular, he thought. Fern House. Water-Lily House. Orchid House. Australia House. Cactus House. I may take a look. But they'll be just like the Allan Gardens glass houses in Toronto.

However, those magnificent trees grown in isolation, that great spreading one I saw on the way along this path. That's for me.

He passed a tall specimen pine, and came to his tree.

It was beautiful. In a bell shaped curve. The branches extending outward were supported by stakes. It was a pleasing sight.

He moved back and forth, side to side, getting the best perspective. He assembled easel and stool; readied his painting materials.

But first he started in a drawing book, making some preliminary sketches. The size was one thing to be reckoned with. The texture was another. For all its size, with solid branches in full leaf, there was a lightness through the leaves. Express it on paper, he said to himself. Somehow find some way to show the size of it: height and breadth.

Syd concentrated on the tree; on his page; on the tree. Ah, a figure. A person, hesitating in his view. Perfect to draw to show the comparative heights. He sketched quickly. Then she was gone.

He spent more than an hour. The tree was worthy of it. He was satisfied.

He reflected on his conversation with Ross. Lucky Ross. The continuum of the traditional Ontario life still intact.

For him, that traditional life had fallen apart, when Marjorie developed diabetes. It was shortly after her fortieth birthday that she was finally diagnosed. It was serious and much of her time was spent servicing her condition. Syd was, of course, supportive, but he secretly believed Marjorie was glad that the challenge of his job kept him busy with his life while she got on with her own.

Marjorie developed circulatory problems as a result of her condition, and by the time she was fifty she was having difficulty walking. She was short of breath and had to stop and rest her legs frequently. Food shopping became near impossible for her. She also was having difficulty with stairs and certainly up and down to the basement for laundry, or up and down to the bedrooms was curtailed. She just could not manage.

They didn't talk about the ramifications of her condition. Marjorie cheerfully and uncomplainingly carried on and Syd didn't want to undermine her courage by suggesting she was failing. Until one day he came home and she was sitting on the stairs in the front hall in tears.

He had gathered her up in his arms, carried her to the living room sofa and gently opened the subject that perhaps the time had come to move to an apartment. Flat, easy access. He didn't say anything about wheel chairs, or a smaller place for them to look after, or the household help Marjorie had always eschewed.

Syd wove some plans for retirement, how he could decrease work hours and how they could travel. Syd had invested in the real estate boom. Campeau. Reichmanns. Trizek. Templeton and MacKenzie Mutual Funds. The solid second stringer in his career and investments. He knew when to get out. He was well off.

That was 1983. They were about fifty-two years old when they made the move into the apartment. Syd had shied away from buying a condominium. He just couldn't buy something that didn't sit on its own hunk of land, in his own name. He had wanted to keep in the housing market and was able to buy a good older house just west of Avenue Road, off Chaplin Crescent.

It was a good buy: less than what he got for their Leaside house. He'd done the deal privately. A colleague was selling it. It had been his parents' home. Although it needed up-dating and modernizing, it was quite livable as was.

Steve, Christine and their baby, Samantha, would rent the house for a time while they made an effort to get their finances together and consider some job offers outside Toronto.

Syd and Marjorie's life gradually changed with the decline in Marjorie's health. Marjorie kept up with her children and grandchildren and took part in as much of church life as possible. Syd took early retirement and was finished with his work. He did keep up with some of his friends and colleagues from business, but gradually lost touch as they perceived his life changing. He retained his membership in the Professional Engineers' Association.

Syd hadn't expected to miss the outdoor work he used to do at the house. He had mowed the grass and tended the low maintenance landscaping. It wasn't a lot, but he missed the contact with the earth. And, of course, there was no garage, that domain of the Ontario male. The car didn't go in it, as it was too small for a car and the general machinery of the lives of the MacKenzies.

Fortunately Syd was able to transport most of the collection into the garage at the Chaplin Crescent property. It was in one of those great Toronto neighbourhoods that had a lane running through the middle of the block giving access to the garage from the back. It meant that Syd could come and go without interfering with Steve, Christine or Samantha. It was also a way of visiting them and have Samantha hang around with her Gramps in the back yard.

Syd often looked at the back yard space in terms of a garden, but had no idea what to do or where to start. Anyway he didn't live there and knew nothing of gardening. He did buy a book on container gardening when he spied it by chance in the bookstore in the concourse of his office building. Much to Marjorie's delight he got into it and filled the balcony of their apartment with bloom.

Syd often took Marjorie in her wheel chair to visit gardens in Toronto. They particularly liked the Allan Gardens in spite of the scruffiness of the neighbourhood. It was close to the Jamestown apartments in South Rosedale where Hughie and Heather lived. They were true children of the city and spent family time all over it, the Islands being their favourite haunt, always hoping they could move there.

Syd and Marjorie called for their three grandsons and took them to Allan Gardens. Everybody liked the secretness of the greenhouses and the variety of the plants. Or Syd played soccer with the kids in the big spaces around St. James Church. Sometimes they took a picnic with them.

Syd had never noticed plants before. They caught his attention and, much to his surprise, his imagination. He had read somewhere that reinforced concrete had been developed by a gardener in France in the late 1800s. The man had wanted to make delicate water basins out of concrete. Referring to stem and trunk structures, he had strengthened the concrete with rods of steel. Ever since he read that, Syd had looked at plants, even the tiny ones, to see their structure; to see what held them up and how. Specimen trees caught his interest.

And then Marjorie died. Circulatory problems and heart problems.

Syd was lost. He missed her very much. His whole life had ended up centred around Marjorie, family and church. And, Syd realized after Marjorie was gone, the ritual of it had been conducted by Marjorie.

But she was gone.

He had stayed in the apartment for a year and it nearly drove him crazy. He was retired. He was cooped up. He carried on with Hughie and Steve and their families. Get togethers were virtually the same, but they didn't fill time, nor were they intended to. Everybody had lives to live, but he found there wasn't much in his. He carried on at the church, grateful for the socialness of choir practice and the expression of Christian values during the church service.

But the emptiness was still there. The terrible emptiness. The nothing. It was devastating.

Syd knew he had to move on. His very survival depended on it. He decided to take up a new hobby. He got a lead on The School of Continuing Studies at the University of Toronto and ended up taking a course in Botanical Drawing.

He had spent his life drawing straight lines, well ninety-nine percent straight lines, or straight curves. He smiled to himself. Nature didn't function completely on the straight and narrow.

Syd liked this new experience so much that he took the summer course, Drawing in the Park. It featured trees, flowerbeds and landscapes. He liked the flowers best. And then he moved on to watercolour. He was hooked. Spent hours outdoors with his paints.

He wanted to get out of the apartment. He needed to move. He wanted to live in a house. He wanted to be able to step outside the door and be on the ground. On the earth. Outside.

He had become fascinated with flowers, had begun to read about them. He visited Garden Centres, and talked to people. He kept sketching garden layouts for the Chaplin Crescent house. Steve thought they were nice, but wasn't into gardening.

"As a matter of fact Dad, I've accepted a job at the TV station in Barrie, and we'll be moving at the end of the month."

The timing was perfect. The boys knew he had to move, and knew the house was right for him. Syd knew all this too. He also knew that when he moved from the apartment, his life with Marjorie would be over. He had never let on how apprehensive he was about that. Everything in the apartment had been collected by the two of them over thirty-five years of marriage. A collection of their lives together, or the treasured events in their individual lives. He knew he couldn't move all of it and not have Marjorie with it. He decided to take none of it.

With the blessing of all the family, Syd broke up home. Hugh and his family and Steve and his came to help. Syd said he wanted it to be another celebration of all they had been, and they could pick and choose, and trade and bargain, and have everything they wanted. The remainder could go to the Salvation Army store, to start someone else on their home, just as Syd and Marjorie had done years ago.

And so it was.

And here I am in Kew Gardens, London, England on this perfect summer day, he thought.

Time to move on. To what. Let's have a look at this map before I pack up my seat.

Decision made, Syd set off on a slow circuitous route past the Temple aiming to spend the last half hour before meeting time at Kew Palace itself in the Queen's Garden behind it.

He came by the Order Beds. He had to stop and think about them for a minute, because they looked like vegetable gardens. Plants grouped in parallel rows. Not done for design.

He read some markers: Compositae (daisies); Graminae (grasses).

Within an Order some were vegetables, but others were flowers. Of course, he thought, Order is one of the categories for classification. Like the flower nicotinia is part of the tobacco family or something like that, and related to potato, tomato, and eggplant, and deadly nightshade. All related. Have to ask someone.

Slight backtrack through the rock garden and stopped to note some tiny, exquisite flowers. They were alpines. Worth a moment to sketch.

He made more sketches in the grass garden, blown away by the textures, height and striated leaves. He was sure there were many of these in Adrian Bloom's garden at Bressingham, yesterday.

He decided to by-pass the Princess of Wales Conservatory with its progressively controlled climates and plant life, and give the Gallery a miss. He just didn't have time to do those paintings justice, and anyway he'd be in Paris in a few days with the Impressionists at hand. So on to the Palace and the Queen's Garden.

Syd walked around the easterly side of Kew Palace, into a pretty, formal enclosure.

It was enclosed and it wasn't. That wonderful teasing garden planners do.

Rectangular in shape. Sunken in the centre. Pink paved paths around the topside and parallel paths repeated at the bottom. Steps down to a path crossing the middle of the garden. Statuary. White.

All the plants. Green. Green is a thousand colours on nature's palette. Into the greys and silver. With yellow flowers and white. Some magenta and mauve. The same colours as Beth Chatto's Mediterranean garden. But different. Broad leaves and cut leaves. Unique.

The sign said early seventeenth century plants. Herbs, in the broadest sense of the word. Plants with domestic use.

A good place for a sketch, Syd thought. He sat on the step.

Something moved at the far diagonal. He couldn't see for the iron and gold structure surmounting the centre of the crossed paths. Movement again.

She stood up.

She fit in the garden. She belonged. Tawny brown clothing. Long, curly brown hair. The sun behind her in the west bringing out a burnish of gold flecks. She was observing the low plants making notes, moving a few steps at a time.

Syd sketched for a few more minutes, then dug into the pocket of his knapsack and to look at his watch. He packed up.

He walked along the path, noting plants until he was at the end near her. Arielle. That was her name.

"I think we should be on our way," Syd said as Arielle looked at her watch, "if we're to meet the others on time."

"I was thinking the same thing," she said pleasantly, and put her notebook and camera in her bag.

Syd let her lead the way to the gate as he struggled to keep his painting bag out of the plants, then caught up beside her.

Neither hinted at their exchange in the market that morning, although Syd was sure she was as aware of it hanging in the air between them as he was.

"Enjoying the trip so far?" he asked. Safe topic.

"M-m-m," she answered. "Better than I expected."

"How's that?"

"I'm not a gardener, but it doesn't really matter. There's plenty to see and enjoy and whet my appetite about growing things."

"Bad joke, to whet your appetite in the herb garden," said Syd. Marjorie and Syd had encouraged the boys with puns as their humour developed.

Arielle made an acceptable small laugh at his joke. "I'm glad you said herb and not 'erb."

"I always think 'erb sounds affected."

"It seems some kind of a North American habit of speech, as best I can find out in my culinary research."

Sounds like her job, thought Syd. But before he could ask, they were at the raised circular garden, straight ahead to the gate and the bus, or turn right to make their way to the Brentford Gate.

"Syd!" It was Martin. He was waiting on the east side.

"We're going to the pub. Not back on the bus."

"Righty-ho," said Martin. Then, "Would you like me to take that big bag of yours back to the hotel?"

"Thanks very much." Syd handed his painting bag to Martin.

"Have a good evening," Martin called to them as they strode along the path to the Orangery.

"Let's stop here and have a look at the map," said Syd. "We're here in the orange section ..."

"And we have to go into the blue ..." said Arielle.

"We've got it," Syd said and they turned off the path to the right.

They walked along in silence. Syd shortened his stride a bit, as he realized she was keeping up to his long pace.

Quite a while since I've walked beside a girl. Lady. Woman. He laughed to himself, wondering which Hughie would insist on. Actually, he knew.

She certainly can keep up, he thought. She looks so healthy. Nice. Like his daughters-in-law. They wear make-up that doesn't look like it. This Arielle has the same healthy glow. They're the fit generation of women, although she's older. He approved.

I'd like to talk to her, thought Syd happily, and I don't know what to say to her. Can't ask her about that jacket. Seems too personal. But that was a very personal exchange we had. We had the exchange. Can't make light of it.

"We're not in that much of a hurry," he said with no further comment on the statement, like let's slow down and get to know each other. "Want to see the Cycad House? It's on our right."

My god, Syd is that the best you can do, he said to himself.

"Cycads? It, or they were not on my list of must sees!" said Arielle lightly.

Thank heaven she picked up on it, thought Syd.

She went on, "What are they? Would you be able to give an enlightened discourse?"

"'fraid not. I have no idea what they are myself. We'll give them a miss."

"Good thinking."

Some easy banter. Nice, thought Syd.

"I see you drawing and painting," Arielle commented. "Is that why you came on this trip?"

Getting me to talk about myself. Charming. Very nice. And I still get to talk to her.

On time, they were the last to meet.

As they approached the group, a familiar woman's voice said, "He's dropped off the wrong bag."

No comment from anyone.

"I guess all's aboard that's coming aboard," Ross said lightly, and started out the Brentford Gate.

Ignoring signs for the carpark, the group followed the directions for Kew Pier. Arielle lessened her step to walk with Molly.

Then there was the decision as to which way to go. A huddle with guidebooks in hand: Ross and Barbara, Syd, Mr. Track Suit, and Grace.

"This way," Mr. Track Suit announced, arm raised downstream.

The group ambled along Thameside, enjoying the sights.

Grace was trying to break from the women, to gain on the men. She was aiming to walk beside Syd.

"I'm all out of puff," Grace said as she walked the rest of the way with the women.

They came to a pub, and all agreed it was suitable. Two adjacent tables accommodated everyone.

"I know this is a pub," said Barbara, "but I need a cup of tea first. And we are in no hurry to rush off anywhere."

"Make that two," said Marcia.

"About our finances," Molly spoke up. "I have friends who go to Florida every winter, and they eat out with their friends. There seems to be an unwritten rule that everybody goes dutch. Pay your own as you go. Then you don't have to keep calculating who you owe a drink to, or whether they bought you dinner and therefore you have to catch them to return the gesture."

"Here, here," said Leslie Phillips.

"I'll buy that," piped up Mr. Track Suit. "Come on, Syd, give us a hand. Tea for the girls, and pints of the best for the men."

"Dreadful little man," said Grace to Molly, as she watched the two men go into the bar. "Jack, I mean."

Syd and Jack returned with the beer. "They'll bring yous your tea, girls." Jack sat between his wife and Syd.

Silence fell over the group.

"Quite a show," said Jack nodding his head back toward the Botanical Gardens, making for a conversational opening. "Far too much work for me. I like annuals. They put on enough of a show for me."

Mrs. Track Suit leaned toward Lorraine and Molly. "Jack says annuals make the best show, without too much work," she said confidentially. "Their roots are shallow. We can pull them up quick in the fall."

There was a dead silence. Molly looked toward Arielle stifling a smile.

Lorraine's eyes were wide in amused disbelief. She looked toward Molly for a conversational bail-out.

Molly muttered something about "Royal Botanical Society," and "Collection of plant species," and "The world's most important collection of horticultural books ..."

"I went into the Princess of Wales Conservatory," said Grace, excusing herself to Jack as she drew her chair between him and Syd. "It's that new modern building which I didn't like. For her, they could have made something prettier." She addressed her remarks to Syd. She lowered her voice to engage him exclusively in conversation.

Others turned their attention elsewhere.

Grace went on, "It was swampy and ended up with cactuses."

Slightly taken aback by Grace's description of the climate controlled display, and making an effort to go along with her, Syd said, "There is a small section like that at Allan Gardens, at home."

"That filthy place. In more ways than one. Full of the dregs of society," responded Grace.

"Well, yes," agreed Syd, "but if you go during the day..."

"You actually go there?" asked Grace with some alarm.

"What I was going to say, to pick up on your visit to the Princess of Wales Conservatory, was that, it's a state-of-the-art structure designed to maximize energy conservation, for all the climatic zones in it. Likely all precisely controlled by computer."

Why am I talking like an environmental engineer, thought Syd. This isn't why I'm on this trip. I left all that behind. Now, quit it, he chided himself.

"You must still be in business in Toronto since your wife died," Grace said.

"No," answered Syd cautiously.

"Well, I thought Shirley said you were. She seemed to know all about you." Grace was settling into the conversation.

Syd shifted uneasily, rolling his near empty glass back and forth in his long fingers.

"So you're lonely. You have to be, now you're living alone," Grace said sympathetically.

"Not really," Syd said with still more caution. He wasn't prepared to have Grace define his lifestyle, particularly on the word of someone he barely knew, namely Shirley Wallace. Syd fretted inwardly.

"Another pint?" Jack Track asked, standing beside Syd.

"Sure," said Syd very quietly.

"Grace," said Jack, "have y' met the wife? Keep her company while I'm gone."

Syd turned his attention to Ross who was discussing the architecture of the Palm and Temperate Houses; that they were glories of Victorian engineering; that both had been recently restored; that they were there to house the many exotic species the gardens were accumulating; that everybody still liked to see the old favourites: palms, orange and lemon trees; and that they had climbed the spiral staircase in the Temperate House to the walkway running underneath the roof and look down on the mass of foliage and fruits below.

"Was there a Knot Garden anywhere on the grounds?" asked Lorraine.

"Not garden is my style, that's for sure," Jack arrived with the beer. In attempting to put it in front of Syd, he let a little bit drip on the back of Grace's chair.

"Y're in luck, Gracie, I didn't spill a drop on y'. Chair's a bit wet, slide over there beside the wife." Jack set the glass in front of Syd, with a sly smile, and then looked boldly at Grace.

He knows he's irritating her, thought Syd, and he's not going to quit. Not my problem.

"What is a knot garden?" Arielle asked.

"It's a very formal flowerbed that has twisted designs formed from dwarf evergreens," said Lorraine.

"I was in the Queen's Garden behind the Palace, and while there were herbs ..."

" 'erbs," corrected Grace.

"I think they are called herbs," said Arielle, "and there was no formation such as that ..."

"Everyone who knows, knows they are called 'erbs," insisted Grace.

"Don't get yer shirt in a knot, Gracie," said Jack. Then he burst into song: "You say tomaeto, and I say tomahto ...."

"Oh, Jack, don't be silly," said Mrs. Track Suit.

"As you wish," Arielle conceded the herb discussion. "But there was not a Knot Garden, to tie down the first point. Now," she went on, "what is a pleached alley. Or what's the meaning of pleach?"

Lorraine spoke up again. "It's a technique of interweaving branches of well-spaced trees to form an alley. You walk through a kind of tunnel."

"That sounds like too much hard work for me." said Jack authoritatively. "Believe me. I was in maintenance at Transit Head Office, until I took the golden handshake. That's when I said to the wife I wasn't going to do no more hard work. It's play time. Yous retired?" He included all the men with one sweeping glance.

Jack carried on, "I figured you was, Syd, because yer clothes are with it. I said to the wife that we was gonna to throw everything out, even good polyester suits and not look like Senior Citizens. We went down to Eaton's when the sales was on and got us gussied up. We're havin' a ball. Anybody for a drink?"

"We should ask for the menu as well and put our order in," Barbara spoke up.

There was a general babble of agreement and organizing.

When they had all settled down, drinks in hand, food ordered, Leslie Phillips said, "I may sound as if I'm taking the floor so to speak, but I'd be interested to have a go-around the group to find out why you came on this gardening trip. We don't get a lot of time to socialize when we're walking about, but I'd like to get to know you a bit better. We do have eleven more days together." Turning to his wife, he said "Marcia, hon, you start, and then I'll say a bit."

"We just think landscape is an important part of our home, and this looked like such a quality tour without too much time spent going through stately homes. I liked the pressed flowers at Kew."

Leslie said, "And I liked the scope of the trip, going through Europe. I'm no gardener, but our house has acreage around it which we've had landscaped and which has to be maintained and I thought these would be interesting."

"Leslie and Marcia," Grace smiled at them approvingly. "Your place sounds wonderful."

"Barbara will speak for both of us," said Ross.

"I'm the gardener in our family," said Barbara, "and I do as much as I can to keep the beds around the house done up. I confess to quite a few annuals, mostly impatiens at the front where it is quite shady, but in the back I have a border, in the Gertrude Jekyll sense, which constantly keeps me reading about gardens. I guess I'm more of an armchair gardener. And then I read all the novels Victoria, you know Vita, Sackville-West wrote, about Knole in the Edwardians, and All Passion Spent, the one about being yourself when you're really old! I don't want to bore you, but we have done a kind of literary tour of the great houses here in England, and decided this garden tour was a bit more leisurely, but put us into real England which we both love. Ross just graduated from U of T this June with an arts degree in history. The garden tour does a bit of everything for us. Syd."

"Yes, Syd," said Grace with devoted attention.

"I've become a gardener. Read mostly about the gardens, although a bit of the life-styles of Vita Sackville-West and Harold Nicolson.

And, of course the paintings of Claude Monet. Whether any of it has translated into my effort at my new place, well it's not for me to say. Your turn Jack."

"Me and the wife," Jack paused and looked around, "yous all know the wife, Ev? We like a nice show of annuals. Lotsa petunias. 'sides they're not too much work. We're here to meet some new people, for the nice scenery and do Eurip without all the boring history. Gracie, tell us about yerself."

Grace bristled visibly.

"My name is Grace," she said, throwing a visual dagger at Jack. Immediately pasting a gracious smile on her face, she addressed Syd. "I just love flowers, and I guess I just arrange them, since I don't have time away from all my committee work in Toronto, to get my hands dirty. My late husband arranged for a property management company to keep up our Forest Hill home. I wanted to meet interesting people, so I came on this trip."

There was silence. Grace said, somewhat shortly, "Speak up Jean."

"I sort of said on the bus yesterday," said Jean shyly. "Anyway, Grace persuaded me to come so she didn't have to pay the single supplement. I hope we get back to the hotel all right."

Leslie made some soothing sounds.

"Don't worry about it Jean," Jack spoke up. "I was in maintenance and did more than sweep the floors. Hadda look after all them 'xecutives, keep their lifes straightened out. Me and the secretaries. I'll look after yous."

"My turn, I guess," said Lorraine. "I spoke up on the bus yesterday too, and being a librarian I have access to all kinds of gardening books which I've read with great gusto ... yes with gusto! I have a townhouse and have developed a garden, planned and landscaped in a space ten feet by twenty feet. Keeps me very busy, and it's my favourite place in all the world. I must admit some of the gardens on our trip are going to run it a close second. I've never been to Europe before, and this trip looked good."

Everyone looked at Molly.

"I've been a gardener all my life. I spent all my summers in my garden as an adjunct to housekeeping which the women of my generation did. My husband and I lived ordinary lives. He was in Insurance. We raised our two children. He died ten years ago. I live on my street in my neighbourhood where I'm friends with Arielle's mother. Arielle and I are friends, too. I found out about this trip, and wanted very much to come. Arielle's mother wasn't well enough to come, so she volunteered Arielle to accompany me. We're having a lovely time."

"The food's coming," someone said.

"Plenty of time to hear from Arielle."

"Do we have to?" Hardly audible, but for those tuned, it was definitely Grace's voice. The same voice that commented on dropping off the wrong bag.

"I'll be brief. I've been cooking with herbs ..."

"'erbs," Grace corrected.

"... for some time. Done a lot of reading, and been to Rickters, in Goodwood, east of Toronto, on the way to Uxbridge. Herbs ..."

Gesticulating disgust with a wave of her hand, Grace intoned a matching "Hmph."

"... give wonderful flavours." Darting a questioning glance at Grace, Arielle continued, "I'm learning more about cooking vegetables, the pulses, you know, peas, and beans and lentils, so ..."

"Dreadful food to serve to luncheon guests," Grace said derisively.

Syd watched Arielle keep her cool.

"... that Order Garden to-day was very interesting," Arielle finished calmly. Then she added charmingly, "Allow me to announce dinner, as the food is here."

DAY 5: DEPART LONDON. AFTERNOON AT SISSINGHURST CASTLE. DOVER OVERNIGHT.

It's check-out and good-bye to London," announced Jack Track to the group gathered around the coach at the side of the Regent Palace Hotel. "Always better to see yer bags loaded before y' step on that bus."

"Good advice," said Syd with a friendly smile.

"Not takin' yer paint stand inside?"

Jack Track doesn't miss much, Syd thought to himself.

"No. Not allowed inside Sissinghurst garden. Sketch book in here." Syd patted his knapsack.

Most of the group who had eaten at the Thameside pub the evening before had clustered together, waiting to depart for the drive southeast to Sissinghurst Castle Garden for the afternoon, and on to Dover for the night.

"Special part of the trip for me," Ross commented to Syd.

"Me, too. I've read a lot about this garden, and the making of it. I've actually tried to follow the basic principles they developed and used. These people were, well, something else, for want of a better comment."

"That's more what I mean than the garden," said Ross. "Harold Nicolson was old King George Fifth's official biographer. As well as reading that, I read Harold's diaries for background to my European history studies for the first half of this century. Three volumes. Full of references to the garden. The diaries went on until 1962."

"Must have made a difference to read history after you've lived through it," commented Syd thoughtfully. "I always relate history to my perceptions in high school ... that being a year or two ago!"

"And Barbara took to reading everything Vita wrote. The poems and novels, and some of Virginia Woolf's works. We've had quite a spirited preparation for this trip. Got into the Bloomsbury group. The book the son Nigel, Harold and Vita's, wrote about their marriage ...," Ross gave a little laugh.

"That's the extra one I read ... but I didn't have anyone to discuss it with ...." Syd's voice faded off as he was unexpectedly struck by the deep loss and emptiness he had felt when Marjorie died.

I thought I had conquered those feelings with the acceptance. The acceptance that she was gone. Died. The acceptance that I have to build my own life.

"All aboard," called Martin to the last few standing with Syd and Ross.

Carrying his knapsack carefully along the aisle, Syd hesitated beside Molly, acknowledged her with a "Good morning", then addressed Arielle who was sitting beside the window. "If you keep watch on the countryside close to the road, you might see some allotments. They're garden patches allotted to people in cities so they can grow food or whatever as they wish. An old Act of Parliament, out of the industrial revolution."

"Interesting. Thanks," said Arielle, "I'll keep an eye."

"God, I hate vegetables," said Grace in a too loud voice, that made a direct hit on a moment of dead silence in the coach. "They ... are ...," she was flustered, "so green ..."

Everyone laughed.

"What I mean," Grace was clearly annoyed at being laughed at, "trying to make lovely arrangements with them is just impossible." She sat back pleased with herself for having smoothed out awkward people.

"A lovely arrangement with vegetables is about the last thing I'd try," said Molly dryly.

"M-m-m." Arielle expressed agreement, as Grace made the mistake of darting looks back, with a weak smile hesitating on her lips, to see how everyone had accepted her explanation.

Syd watched Grace turn a glare in the direction of Molly and Arielle, then shift to surprise at making eye contact with him. Instantly, she settled a beaming smile on him. Syd looked away quickly.

Dangerous, he thought to himself with some surprise. More surprisingly, a feeling of unease spread on top of that moment of grief.

A feeling. I haven't been conscious of a feeling since the numbness set in after Marjorie died. Three years ago.

Not true, he corrected himself. I feel that same unease about everything concerning Grace, as that phone message. Hopefully that's not the limit of feelings for the over-sixties.

He knew it would take time. He had faith he could change, make adjustments, dig deep into himself, prepared to move on, was moving on, hoping to get some feeling and find a balance. Get emotionally fit and survive. But unease? That's all?

Don't be daft. There's a non-with-it word Hughie would have me eradicate from my vocabulary. I feel good about my house and garden and painting. Setting some goals and doing something always makes me feel better. That's why I did them. Drifting would be destructive. I came on this trip.

I felt good this morning, maybe borderline great. No idea why. Something yesterday? I do have some feelings, except today they are bouncing all over the place!

"Some people've traded seats," Grace said accusingly to Martin, while looking at Leslie and Marcia Phillips who had traded with Ross and Barbara. They now sat across the aisle from Syd. "You said we would all trade around."

"We will," Martin assured her. "Some people've just made their private arrangements."

"Good enough for me." Grace pulled her crossed hands tight to her body in determination.

"No, I don't mind if you sit across there with Syd. Nice for you two to get to know each other. I may doze anyway," Barbara confessed, "... south London, again. Kent is another matter."

"The Weald of Kent." Ross made it a statement. "Never could get a satisfactory answer about that word, weald."

"Other than it is wooded and fertile land, but so are other places," commented Syd.

"I guess we just take the Weald of Kent on faith."

"It's the garden basket of England with plants special to Kent, and they grow all of them at Sissinghurst. Every season. Lavishly. And then some."

"Profusion." Ross added.

"She, Vita, was the plant expert," Syd went on, "roses and vines climbing through each other. This business of under-planting with ordinary old-fashioned plants. I tried to do it at my place. Crowded everything in. It's supposed to look lavish and secretive. My grandchildren think it's a secret garden, and my daughters-in-law say it's romantic, so I guess I achieved it in some small way."

"Harold was the master designer," said Ross, "for all she was the poet, he was no-nonsense with straight lines, classical formality which he had to impose on a seven acre site already full of irregularities. At least it was flat."

"Just boils down to formal planning, informal planting in a private sort of way," Syd summarized.

"Complemented each other," Ross said impressively. "Quite a pair. But still individuals."

They rode in silence. Syd's mind drifted.

He had really studied this garden and the Nicolsons who had made it. More correctly, Syd reminded himself, it was two individuals, Harold Nicolson and Vita Sackville-West, who also coincidentally were married to each other, who had designed and developed it. A tribute to two talents which completed and complemented each other. I should be so lucky.

That's not correct either, Syd chided himself. He had found his completeness in Marjorie for a long time and he knew, yes, knew, that it was the same for Marjorie.

"They, Harold and Vita were from prominent upper-crust families," Ross said simply but implied the whole of the English Establishment.

"Un-huh." A faint sound of understanding from Syd. A far cry from my upbringing.

Syd's family was very proud of him. His father and mother had both been born in Hamilton, Ontario. Their fathers had worked in the steel mills, as did Syd's dad. Neither of his parents had had an education, but they had encouraged their only son to go to university and had backed him financially all the way. His sisters, like his mom, had gone to business college and all three had worked in the office of the steel company until they were married. Syd's mom had later worked for Revenue Canada at tax time, for her pin money, she always said.

Marjorie had grown up in a small town north-east of Toronto. Her father had been in Insurance and her mother had done volunteer work for the Red Cross during the war and always in the United Church. The church had been a very important part of her family's life. She had gone to Victoria College for that very reason.

"They met at a formal dinner party before a play. Manners all in place, as only the English can exercise them." Once again Ross's comments implied the rituals of a highly structured society.

"Un-huh." Syd understood.

He and Marjorie had met at university. He was in engineering at University of Toronto in the Little Red Skule House, as the Engineering Building was called, implying a complete lack of the fine points of education in engineering, on the crescent across from University College. Marjorie was at Victoria College, taking her general B.A. They had met at the dance at the Drill Hall after the football game in their second year.

The game and the dance were de rigeur for everyone on campus, but it had taken Syd until second year to go. The Tea Dance as it was called then was what's called today a meat market. Girls standing along the side and the guys three deep drifting past, eying the best looking. All the guys from Devonshire Place went. It was one of the few places they had any contact with girls. It seemed Marjorie and three of her girl friends from her residence, Annesley Hall at Vic, had decided to forego the arts types around Wymilwood and be adventuresome at the Drill Hall.

Syd hadn't asked anyone to dance. He was a gangly six-footer and had no confidence in his social skills. He could dance. His older sisters had seen to that. With a partner who could dance as well as they, he was pretty good. He had been going to the game and dance all that fall. He went with guys from his year. Ken in particular was his saviour. Marjorie was one of Old Kenny's discards.

Syd usually had at least one dance with the girl and then either she would thank him and move on, which usually was the case or as happened twice, he had asked her to go to the Hart House dance that night.

The first girl had been nice but had gone with him just to go to the dance. He felt she could have been with anyone. The second was Marjorie.

She could dance. Ken had muttered something about "Maybe she can dance with you" as he left. And she could. Syd had always wondered about Ken as a dancer. It seemed he mostly kept time to the music as he chatted-up and looked-over his partner.

For Syd, dancing with Marjorie was like dancing with his sisters. She could even jive, and when they got their feet or arms tangled, they fell about laughing, just like his sisters did. Then they would stop, work out the move and dance on. Even that first day. His buddies stopped and watched him, them, giving some appreciative hoots and claps. He and Marjorie beamed at them and each other.

That was it. They were a couple.

Syd felt very comfortable and secure in his memories.

"She had to give up Knole. It was a house. They developed a garden."

"Un-huh."

"He was a diplomat. Never had much money, but they were always able to buy a country house, fix them up, and have gardeners. Long Barn first and then this ruin."

"Un-huh."

Silence again as the coach made its way along the A21 which would pass between Knole and Long Barn on their way to Sissinghurst.

Marjorie had graduated with a B.A. at the end of Syd's third year. Then she went to Ontario College of Education during his fourth year and she qualified as a High School English and History teacher. At the end of the school year, when Syd graduated from Civil Engineering, they were engaged. It was the spring of 1954.

Syd was employed by a construction company in Toronto. Marjorie was hired by the North York Board of Education to teach in one of the new collegiates.

Toronto was booming. Unlike other young couples who moved into a new apartment in one of the high-rise buildings sprouting all over Scarborough, they bought an old house on Alexander Street in downtown Toronto. Mortgaged, yes, but building up equity. Something to have when they were ready to move up. They furnished it in Early Miscellaneous and Late Salvation Army and settled into marital bliss.

Syd's talents and solid work ethic put him on the crest of the wave of success.

Marjorie taught successfully for two years, earning her permanent teaching certificate and a permanent contract with the school board.

They planned for her to teach for two more years at which time they would buy a house in Leaside, decorate it traditionally from Eaton's College Street store, and start a family. All went according to plan.

Syd and Marjorie moved into their house on Bessborough Drive. Marjorie transferred her church membership to Leaside United and Syd joined. He had been brought up close to the Presbyterian church in Hamilton, but his family had not been faithful churchgoers. Baptism, marriage, and funerals, with Christmas and Easter services attended occasionally.

"They settled into their unique life-style as they developed the garden and buildings at Sissinghurst. He back and forth to London. She writing and gardening. They had two boys."

"Un-huh."

Within the first year of their move to Leaside, Syd and Marjorie's first son was born. Traditionally, family names were used, naming the son after his father or grandfathers. Syd was named after his uncle whom his dad had left in Nova Scotia when he came to Upper Canada to work. Syd and Marjorie discussed it and in deference to offending anyone had named their first son after Syd's father Hugh and Marjorie's father Douglas. Their second son was born two years later and they felt free to choose his names. They picked Stephen Andrew for him.

Syd, Marjorie, Hughie and Steve also known as Sammy as a result of his initials spelling S.A.M. were a good family. Their life centred around home, job, school, and church.

"They each made something of themselves."

"Un-huh."

Syd was a solid performer. He worked his way up the ladder into management, while the church became Marjorie's work outside home.

During the early years, Syd was treasurer of the Sunday School and he joined the church choir. He had had enough vocal music through compulsory classes in elementary and secondary school in the Hamilton system that he could sing bass and could read music. It was something he enjoyed. The practice was at eight o'clock every Thursday evening which he could fit in with his work schedule and he was at church on Sunday morning anyway. As he spent more time on his career, he continued to keep the choir. It was one of those things. Two to three hours a week. Not a big commitment. A small indication of his steadiness.

"They certainly gave each other freedom for their affairs."

"Un-huh."

According to their son Nigel their marriage was a harbour. Marjorie and I had that. Trust, friendship, and affection, as well. Often, in quiet moments alone, sliding into reflection, Syd wondered about more. As he grew older, he thought of intimacy. Sharing his deepest being with someone. That someone should be Marjorie. But somehow there was a block.

Their physical love in the early years of marriage had been cautious but satisfying. But Marjorie shied away from any change in his physical approach to her, and she gradually but definitely ceased to make any approaches toward him. They hadn't changed, just touched less and less. Only in the usual familiar ways.

Then Syd realized they didn't explore new ideas.

Marjorie was content.

Syd often wondered what the women Marjorie associated with, her friends and acquaintances, talked about regarding their husbands. The men he knew joked about the little lady or the nag. That's no lady, that's my wife was the in thing to say in those days. It was superficial and stereotyped. Some he knew were hostile in their relationship with their wives. No one spoke of intimacy. Syd often joked to himself, what would Sean Connery say?

"They were more unconventional than their kids."

"Un-huh."

Not only were Marjorie and I conventional, we're pretty small potatoes compared to the likes of Harold and Vita, and the kind of lifestyle they had, Syd mused. That's strange, it worked the other way around with our kids. Perhaps more normal.

Hughie and Steve had applied themselves at school, attended Sunday School, and played sports. They grew through those normal activities, absorbing what they had to teach them.

Hugh had gone into law and became involved in store front justice. He had a practice on Queen Street East and thrived on municipal politics. Jeans all the way.

Steve had been a sound nut from early on and had his own D.J. business through high school: had gone to Ryerson Tech for broadcasting and then worked for CityTV. He liked the way Moses Znaimer dressed.

Syd had looked in awe at both of his sons with long hair and ponytails.

Hugh and Steve commented on Syd's short back and sides hair cut, and that the only change in the jacket and tie department was the width of the tie which Marjorie bought him every Christmas and Father's Day.

Hugh and Steve had teased Syd, still long and lean in spite of moving to a desk job off the construction site, that he would look better in jeans than either of them. "Over my dead body," Marjorie had said. Terrible quirk of fate.

Both boys had finally married. Both families were traditional for their generation. More IKEA than anything else.

Hugh and Heather had three boys.

Steve and Christine had a little girl. They had married one month before her birth, having lived together for a two years. Syd had found this a sexual turn-on.

Syd flinched physically a second before the coach lurched over a some rough road.

I've never admitted that to myself before. I damned well knew it; felt it. He was surprised and shocked by this reaction. He was conventional. He just hadn't had to think otherwise before.

He did now. He had made a choice, and had to admit sometimes he questioned how wise he had been. The boys liked the outward signs: long hair, beard, jeans, Eddie Bauer gear. But there was the whole person inside.

He was faced with all this leisure. Gentlemen used to work to have leisure. Now leisure is destructive. These great stretches of time.

He couldn't go back. There was no back. He had retired from his job. His work. He must find his new work. Not paid work. It was his painting and gardening. Marjorie was gone. No going back there. There would not be another Marjorie. Conventional choices. Step into the role Shirley Wallace or Grace had vacant since their husbands' deaths? No. A terrifying thought. But the safe known way. No.

"You O.K.?" Ross said with a slight rise in his voice.

"Sure, sure," said Syd confidently.

"You kind of jumped," Ross said.

"Nothing at all," reassured Syd. The coach bumped on something on the road.

Nothing at all? Just an absolute terror of what you could find yourself caught up in if you waffle on your decision in any way. And you know in your deepest heart that you want to move on, into the unknown, whatever that is, and how hesitant you might imagine yourself to be. Besides, Syd grinned to himself with some relief, there may be nothing there. Nothing! Oh my God, emptiness? That terrible emptiness you felt in the apartment after Marjorie died. Only if you let it be.

At least he felt alive; his emotions were unleashed in some different way. Maybe it was thinking about Marjorie and comparing their lives to Harold and Vita; maybe it was because of being on this trip, away from everything routine and familiar.

The fact of the matter was he felt something. He had some feelings, and although he couldn't put his finger on it, it wasn't all bad. Something yesterday? Like this morning: good, nearly great. I'll buy it, he thought.

"There's the sign for Sissinghurst." The first time Martin had spoken since they had left London. "It's a village. We go on to the

Castle, off to the left.

"As you de-bus, I'll hand you your ticket for entry. It doesn't open until 1 pm. Isobel will hand you a boxed lunch. There are facilities in the farm part, at the oast-houses, I believe. You'll see. And a tea shop and a National Trust shop. Please make your way back to the Carpark about 4:30 for a 5 o'clock departure. Anyone who wishes to have some guidance regarding this garden, stay at the bus and we'll plan when to meet and how we'll go about it to fit your needs. Have a nice day."

Approaching Sissinghurst Castle, Syd found himself as excited as a child on Christmas morning.

Through the winding lane on the curve, then came the Victorian farmhouse itself, with chimney, a group of oast-houses, the Elizabethan barn and white weatherboarded granaries. A complex that now housed the tourist facilities: shop, restaurant, tickets.

Syd fully expected men on tractors and herds of cows in the fields. Yes, the cows were there. Real business. This is no stately home with imposing gates and a long sweeping drive. Just a beautiful collection of mellow brick buildings with mossy roofs in the middle of fields. Very inviting. Friendly and unpretentious. More of a manor house than a castle.

Not really a castle, yet there is a tower.

These mature trees, thought Syd as they drove past the avenue of poplars leading up to the entrance, positioned perfectly, but not formally. Part of the planned planting, he knew. There would be another avenue of poplars leading away from the garden somewhere at the moat. He knew this garden. And the pair of lime trees at the entrance. More in the Lime Walk. Pleached.

Arielle had asked about pleaching. Yes, Arielle. Good feelings.

The Lime Walk. The most formal planting in Sissinghurst. It was Harold's planting alone. Not touched by Vita.

Syd's excitement heightened. He had an inexplicable jumble of feelings. I don't know what got all this "hepped up" feeling going, but I am hepped up, he thought.

The coach stopped in the carpark.

There was the usual general confusion as the passengers collected gear to take with them.

As Syd stood waiting to get off, he heard Arielle say to Molly, "I don't want to study Sissinghurst, I want to feel it like a work of art. Like hearing a piece of music for the first time."

Wow, thought Syd. I've never heard anyone make such a unique comment ever before. He studied Arielle seriously. She certainly is different. Makes me feel good. Wow. Hughie would approve of "Wow"!

Syd purchased the Castle Garden booklet from the shop for a reference to carry around with him, in case he missed something.

With it in hand and sketch pad under his arm, Syd walked toward the archway in the long stretch of mellow pink brick Tudor buildings which the guidebook indicated housed the Long Library and Main House. He hesitated on the paving stones in the Forecourt, savouring the magic of his first step into the garden.

Already, the formality of plan was announced by four bronze urns with satyrs head handles in each corner of the court pathway. He idly wondered what a satyr was.

He stepped into the arch and inched forward to see the right bend the walk took toward the Tower. How an amateur, Harold Nicholson, pulled this site full of endless irregularities together to form a masterpiece is nothing short of genius. And what's more, he made a formal plan of it! Brilliant. Syd shook his head in disbelief. But seeing was believing.

Only a few steps inside and already he was overcome with the specialness of the place. The overview from the Tower was still to come.

He turned to look through the archway. Of the four Irish Yews which, as always described, stand sentinel in the Front Courtyard, only the lefthand ones could be seen. Two steps took him to the other side of the archway and he followed the paving between the yews to the archway of the Tower. Syd turned to the left to follow the path back around the Front Courtyard to observe the purple border.

Nobody, but nobody would see this enclosure, Syd said to himself, as an irregular shape. A quadrilateral. Period.

It was here: formal structure of enclosure and profusion of informal planting. He knew he would see the same theme over and over. Very satisfying to the eye, he thought. Spurs my curiosity.

He was going to take his time and enjoy every step of the way and then go around it again and maybe again.

He cast his eyes along the so called purple border on the north wall of the Courtyard. Not completely purple, reds and purples, and blues. Monet would be impressed, Syd thought, then smiled at his own pun. He could give Hughie and Steve a gotcha on it.

Harold and Vita certainly liked to work with colours, and to find plants to be true to the purple range without ever sliding over the fine tone line into yellow was genius itself. Not a hint of bright red let alone into orange, and blue flowers are blue. Yellow could never touch them. Vita saved it for some other place. She did manage some green flowers. Solomon's Seal, a green rose, a couple of others. But not found in this border.

Roses were certainly not just confined to the Rose Garden: the beautiful red climber was over the arch; a purple one and a mauve one on the north wall. Harold and Vita had mixed them in with herbaceous plants which you expected in a border, and Syd knew that in the rose garden, herbaceous plants were mixed in there. Double double.

Syd noted friends or relatives from his own garden: clematis, specifically jackmanii; silver-leafed lambs' ears with tiny touches of purple on the flower phallus, which he had started from a package of seeds from the hardware store; salvias; cranesbills; the deepest dark purple delphinium he could never have imagined. Beautiful plants with beautiful textures.

The jackmanii was covered with buds. He loved the structure of them. They were long and pointed like a bird's beak. As each and every one started to split open, each petal point formed a hook. He had painted them in his own garden. From the point of view of spectacular nature, they were nearly as interesting as lavatera buds which were corkscrews unwinding. Perfect and beautiful.

I've been in this garden about fifteen minutes, he thought, and I'm hardly beyond the front door. At this rate, I'll have to stay for a week, he chided himself.

Syd deliberately walked the centre path of the Courtyard to the arch of the Tower to the top of the steps overlooking the Tower Lawn. Only one planting, a catalpa tree placed informally to the left. Not a perfect lawn. Obvious weeds out, but pretty little daisies, and any nice volunteer would be welcome.

He stood between the pair of bronze urns with sphinx handles. Sphinx, not satyr. He wondered at that and then dismissed it from his mind. With certainty he looked straight ahead, through the gap in the row of yews on the far edge of Tower Lawn, into the distance just at the far side of the Moat. And there he was. Dionysus. The statue that marked the first main structural feature: the focus at the far end of this major axis. Precisely and deliberately placed.

Feelings welled up in him again.

There were other statues. Most of the names slipped his mind, but he could remember Dionysus. Maybe because he was such a kingpin in Harold's plan.

With great anticipation, Syd climbed to the top of the Elizabethan Tower. That's correct, he said to himself. The long stretch of buildings at the front are Tudor, but the rest of the buildings, the South Cottage and the Priest's House, are Elizabethan.

He walked out onto a kind of rampart to make his first observance of the countryside, and then close to the edge to see over into the garden design and their relationship.

He stood motionless. He was overcome with the beauty of it. This emotion, this welling-up. I must control it. Fine for my head to say that. It's my heart, my solar plexus that seems to have a mind of its own.

A glance within gave an impression of the formal structure of the garden; a glance without gave an impression of the crazy quilt patchwork which was England to him. Woods to the south; single ancient oak trees; towers of village churches off in the distance.

The planting of the garden, melded easily into the open country, with avenues of poplars linking the two together. Away over to the right, the hornbeam hedges behind the limes holding off the pasture, acacias on Sissinghurst Crescent, just past the South Cottage, making an informal break midway.

Tall yew hedges for Yew Walk. Lower yews for the demarcation of the Rondel in the middle of the Rose Garden.

A feeling of satisfaction came over Syd.

He turned his attention back to the structure of the garden. Straight ahead, Dionysus. Looking to his right, Syd could see into the Rose

Garden, and knew if he looked left he would see the White Garden. But don't look yet, he cautioned himself. It may be the second main axis, but it will wait. Save the White Garden until the right moment.

Facing Tower Lawn, the Rose Garden was square to the right. Square to it to the east, the South Cottage and Cottage Garden. That makes a big rectangle, all things considered. Almost tangential, if it is possible to take poetic license with geometry, the Spring Garden and Lime Walk! They knock off the far corner of the Rose Garden and take a slice off the corner of the Cottage Garden.

From the Lime Walk straight down the Nuttery into the Herb Garden, at the extreme right corner where the moat should end but doesn't. Have to go north through that precise grid in the Thyme Walk to the moat for Dionysus.

But drawing his eye from Dionysus, kind of parallel to the Nuttery, Syd could see the Moat Walk. He knew it used to be a third arm of the moat. Up some steps to an ending at a crescent, Sissinghurst Crescent, to be exact, but named as an urban planning joke by Harold and Vita. It blocked out the Cottage Garden, held focus by a Lutyens bench.

The big open space, the Orchard, scattered with interesting things, including dog graves.

All the irregularities were skillfully camouflaged by Harold to make a formal garden patterned with straight axes leading to focal points. I'll bet dollars to donuts, wouldn't Hughie give me a time about that archaic expression, that this geometry is nigh onto impossible to detect from the ground. Likely a person would be aware of some plan of paths, but it would surprise you at every turn.

Syd looked back at the garden, and started to study it bit by bit. It was easy to do, being divided into rooms, which had been accurately described in every book or article he had read about it.

He attended to the details: the South Cottage and its brightly coloured flowers; the Rondel so perfectly formed by the clipped yew hedge; the Lime Walk looking bare after the spring flowering; farther away to the Herb garden; and, the Moat.

He found all the focal points Harold Nicolson had so carefully positioned. Not that they made complete sense from up here, he knew, but deliberately placed to be seen for emphasis when in a garden itself: to look ahead from some position in the garden and have a statue or a garden object right before your eye.

A stunning triumph. Plants tumbling everywhere; a profusion of colour and texture, and even from up here, contrasts in heights and shapes. Vita's work.

Syd was ready to savour the White Garden. It did not disappoint him. Left, square to Tower Lawn, and through Bishops' Gate. He was impressed with how many of the details he could recall.

He could feel emotion welling up in his throat; a tightness in his chest. All was beautiful around him.

And she was there. Arielle. She was in the White Garden, at the far extreme, facing the gate that looked out into the countryside. She walked back to the centre under the rose-covered canopy, around the Ming jar, toward Bishops' Gate which led onto Tower Lawn. She stopped and looked beyond. Stopped and turned back toward the Ming jar, crouched down to see under the Rose canopy, swivelling around, still crouched, looking toward the countryside.

I think she's discovered that axis, Syd thought to himself. Very impressive. Very impressive. A feeling of joy washed over him.

Syd watched Arielle walk back to the Ming jar, turn right along the path to enter the Yew Walk. She disappeared.

Syd watched the gap in the yews, opposite the Tower steps. Arielle appeared in it. She stopped, took one step onto the Tower Lawn, looked one way to Bishops' Gate, the other way toward the Rose Garden, stepped back into the Yew Walk, and looked left, then right.

She's discovered that axis too, and knows it's parallel to the first one. Amazing. A broad approving smile crossed his face and danced in his eyes.

Syd saw her disappear into the Yew Walk and watched for her to reappear in the Rose Garden just beyond the Rondel. Yes she's there. He watched her walk into the Rondel.

She's tall, he thought, maybe as much as five foot eight. No more. There's a golden-pink glow to her, he thought, in this gentle English sun. It's in her brown hair too, he observed. Silver and gold. That long curly hair, making a cloud around her head.

She was wearing a long crinkled skirt of East Indian fabric in golden-brown shades much like her hair, and a loose tawny sweater, cowled around her neck and falling to mid-thigh. Clothing that denied the body underneath, but which surely was there.

Strong. Fit. Slender, but not skinny as she likely was when a kid. Defined, in spite of the soft clothes.

Her whole look was one of softness, crinkle lines and curves. But her movement swung a posture that told it all.

Even standing, now concentrating on a flower in the garden, you knew. Back straight in the lean, head inclined, body weight appearing unbalanced, but contained on sandalled feet. She shifted her weight. There was an extension of body as she did it. Hands were clasped behind her back holding the big canvas totebag from sliding off her shoulder. She was still.

She started to walk the long axis of the Rose Garden through the Rondel to the semi-circle of grass with another Lutyens bench as the focus at the end; back to the Rondel taking the path to the right to look at the statue at the end of the path which she had seen from the White Garden. She took a cursory glance down the Spring Garden and Lime walk, but turned back to the Rose Garden.

Syd watched Arielle as she made her way back across the Rondel to the low rose-covered arch in the brick wall into the Tower Lawn, stopping to look at hedged beds in the sunken garden. Magnolias, the blue poppy, and alstroemerias. She continued to Bishops' Gate and stopped to look at the plaque mounted on the brick wall.

She walked back into the White Garden, taking Syd with her.

She walked. She paused. She walked. Then paused. She looked one way, then another.

She studied it as a choreographer might. As if studying a background, a stage. The paths. The resting places. The tall plants. The low hedges that defined edges and limits. The statue of a virgin, under the window of the Priest's House.

It became a dance as she moved about the garden as surely as if someone had composed it for her. She seemed unaware of any performance as her concentration was complete.

Other people were in the garden. They were observing, taking notes and pictures. Talking. They appeared not to see her. She appeared not to see them.

"I think she's pretty damned good to look at, too."

Syd pulled himself together as if caught with his hand in the cookie jar.

"Oh, hello," he said to Jack Track. "Wonderful garden," Syd said absently, hoping to head off any other comment.

"I don't mean the garden, I mean her," Jack said it emphatically pointing toward Arielle.

I know damned well what you mean, Syd said to himself, but be damned if I know what to say about it, because she is pretty damned good to look at. He could feel himself almost glowing.

"Want me to fix things up with her for y'?"

No! Syd was feeling a bit confused. Trapped was more like it. Because yes was really the answer. But no, he didn't want Jack Track to even entertain such an idea. But yes, she certainly looked nice. His feelings were bouncing around within him like a cork on a waterflow.

Get a grip on yourself.

"What do y' think?" Jack was pressing.

Right now I can't think. I don't want to think. I've got a ton of feelings all jumbled around. And they're not all bad, Syd thought to himself.

Time to move on.

"Nice day," Syd said as he headed toward the stairs for his own walk through the garden, and he was still going to save the White Garden for the end. So turn right, along the walk on the edge of the Tower Lawn and right again into the Rose Garden.

He could smell the roses before he could see them. Heavenly scent, or heaven sent. Both. The making of a bad pun.

He wondered how long he could continue to catch their fragrance, so walked through the Rondel toward the statue. Now he remembered. A Bacchante. Means fun, I think.

He knew much of the garden accents like statues and most urns were not expensive except the two lead urns at the curve at the head of the Rose Garden, and the ones he had passed on the way in. Harold and Vita were never really rich, and put their money into the planting rather than the embellishments.

A brief look down the Spring Garden and Lime Walk showed the bloom spent. No surprises there.

Syd could feel the sense of privacy already.

Lawns and hedges were very English. The idea of linked enclosures was Tudor. Native yews and those lovely big trees beyond the limes were hornbeam. Native to Kent. Surely not, Syd said to himself peering at the bright scarlet hit and miss among the hornbeams. Definitely nasturtiums. Just tucked in to keep your eye sharp.

Back to the Rose Garden, and into the Rondel. Syd stopped.

Rondel. That's a neat concept and name. A developer's dream, Syd thought, harking back to his construction days. A local word, rondel; with a local meaning. The circular hop-drying floor in an oast-house. All it is, is a circle of grass. The focal point of the Rose Garden. Not a statue, not an urn. A flat circle of grass. The Rondel. Vita's imagination.

The shimmering soft blue covering the curved wall at the raised end of the Rose Garden captured his eye. A clematis. Multiple plantings around that curve. Syd stood motionless.

"Have you ever seen such bloom?" Barbara asked almost rhetorically of Syd. "That clematis is Perle d'Azur. Don't know what the dark-leaved vine intertwining it is." She and Ross were there. "Colour everywhere. Those black dahlias!" There was wonder in Barbara's voice. "I thought I knew something about roses," she continued, "but I've never seen such a collection or display like this, and I hardly know how to look at it. Shrub roses, for starters, and then ramblers against the walls or hedges."

Lorraine had caught up to Barbara and Ross. Syd listened to them talk.

"I know this is the Rose Garden," said Lorraine, "but take a look at its composition, if you can see the forest first and then the trees. Not only thick planting, but interplanting, underplanting, plants intertwined. Abundant beauty. Creates the so-called romance."

"Yes," agreed Barbara, "pansies, fern, iris. Have you noticed the iris leaves all over. They must have had a show of them in June. Then peonies, taller delphinium and even Eremurus Robustus, you know, fox-tailed lilies. Then small creeping plants like acaenas, you know, burr plants and dwarf campanulas. Somewhere around there have to be the smaller indigineous plants like primroses and violets. Gives all these different textures, right off the bat!"

"But then they picked the tall plants close to the dark green yew hedge so their colour would be pronounced."

"Plants appropriate to Kent," said Syd. "I took their advice at home. Ordinary, old-fashioned plants, like peonies, iris, hollyhocks, foxglove, lupins, sweet william. Mind you, their ordinary plants are of the more outstanding cultivars than what I've figured out."

"No bare soil to be seen," put in Ross.

"And while I certainly expect climbing roses, take a look at the climbing things, grow into and through one another and not just on the walls. Through roses as well. Very few stakes, they don't nail climbers too tight to walls," Lorraine commented.

"Deep purple clematis jackmanii, it grows like a weed for me. Its six-petalled flat face is all over," Syd said. "The only other one I can identify is Nellie Moser with the mauve petals and dark bar down the centre. I've seen a red one too. Growing naturally. But that one on the crescent. It's almost a silver blue. Can't stop looking at it."

"I understand," Ross said with an appreciative grin, "they wouldn't prune at all if it would threaten a bird's nest!"

"Helps keep the wild overgrown look," Lorraine commented further. "Vita wanted it to be Sleeping Beauty's garden."

"Once you do look at the roses, it's the colour that strikes you first. Did you see the group of deep purple roses together? Stunning. Most people would dot them around thinking it the best way. Definitely not so." Barbara was surveying the plantings in each rectangle between the paved paths. "Then you start to look at the variety of cultivars, species ..., Lorraine." Barbara knew she had a fellow rose fancier.

"Vita loved roses," said Lorraine. "Loved them. But they had to smell like roses. Old roses were Vita's choice. Top quality. She said to grow only the best. Shrub roses and climbers: musk, damask and cabbage roses, rugosa, especially Blanc Double de Coubert, bourbon, and gallicas, China roses and the Rose de Provins, and many species roses. Rosa Moyesii. Very few hybrid teas or floribunds but the odd one." Lorraine was speaking, but really for all of them. "She, Vita, returned Rosa Gallica to cultivation. Its interesting that when they found this place in ruins, a rose was in the orchard. The clump of Rosa Gallica. Not another plant to be found. Except weeds."

"I could stay and listen about these roses all afternoon, and keep looking at that blue," said Syd, almost apologetically, "but I'd never see anything else. I saw the red and purple ones in Purple Border in Front Courtyard, and know there are white ones waiting for me in the White Garden."

"Circle of little scotch roses around the classic altar in the Orchard. Hedge of the musk rose Penelope dividing Delos from the farm lane," said Barbara, looking at her notes.

"Climbers all over. South Cottage smothered with creamy Mme Alfred Carriere and Mme Edouard Herriot; scarlet Allen Chandler on entrance plus yellow Gloire de Dijon," said Lorraine.

Ross turned to Syd. "You've really read about this place. The so-called rooms. So private. Have you ever seen a hedge like this? And walls. Only the English can do these walled gardens."

Ross was pointing to the circle of yews, so precisely clipped; the straight wall on the north side covered with roses and clematis; and the bare crescent wall on the west. A setting for something theatrical, Syd thought, and Arielle popped into his mind. I wonder where she is. The thought of her both surprised and pleased him.

"More metal vases. Lead? In front of the crescent. Gives some sense of calm," Syd said.

That's almost Freudian, he thought. But I do feel calmer. Mustn't let myself get feeling too much. But you were numb before, a small voice said in the back of his head. Maybe feelings get a jump start. A big surge. Okay. Okay. But how do they get expressed? What do you do with them? Finish your walk around the whole garden, then find yourself some different spots and do some sketches.

"I know this garden from books, but standing here, it's not completely evident how to get to the South Cottage," Syd said.

"That's part of the charm of this place," said Ross with great respect in his voice.

"Just take a look," said Syd holding out his map, "if I approach the South Cottage Garden from here, here being in front of the Lutyens bench, I have to make my way to the axis through the Rondel and right to the Bacchanate, then through the Spring Garden and Lime Walk. Anything else is a dead end."

"Actually, no," Ross pointed out. "There seems to be a minor path parallel to the Lime Walk, but it wouldn't be very interesting, I should imagine."

Syd nodded in agreement.

"I'll push off for the Spring Garden and Lime Walk. See you later."

Syd headed for the Rondel and realized there were poplars flanking each side of the yew hedge as it led into the Spring Walk. Another touch of unity.

He stopped beside the Bacchanate, a goddess. With a cymbal. Then looked the full length ahead. Another statue in the Nuttery was in direct line. A man. He looked at the statue beside him. A woman. These two were a pair. Playing up to each other through all that distance? So far apart. Never to get together. He recalled a fleeting image of Arielle in the White Garden when he was up on the rampart. Syd shook his head. Pay attention to the garden. Look at the large basin-type planter at the far end. That would be the centre of the Herb Garden.

Save that one, check this part. Definitely a different character, even with the bloom past. Not a lot of interest except the intertwined branches of the lime trees planted on either side of the central paved walk. Pleached. Arielle had asked what pleaching was. Somebody could show her. Maybe even me.

This was Harold's garden. Syd remembered a silly detail. Harold referred to it as M.L.W. My Life's Work. I know how he felt, Syd thought. My garden, the lot which my house stands on in Toronto would be about the same square footage as this, and it is now my life's work. Nice. Nice feelings. Feelings. Calm. Good.

Syd walked to the entryway to The South Cottage, and took a couple of steps into the garden. Another set of four Irish Yews on guard here, too. Echo of the past.

Now here is colour. Planned as precisely as the White Garden. What a contrast. An obvious scheme of all the bright flame colours. Very cheery. Vita did this one for Harold. His study, work place was in the South Cottage, as well as their bedroom. Done with cottage plants, whatever they are. I suppose plants which ordinary people could buy or exchange, and would grow easily. I'll make a mental list, thought Syd.

A vigorous white rose climber covering the cottage wall right up to the eaves; a yellow climber as well; dark crimson tree peony; strong yellow broom; strong shades of reddish columbines; brown and gold pansies; potentillas; nasturtiums; feathery achilleas; dianthus. Don't call them pinks. But they are red pinks! Looking around the perimeter, Syd noted gold evergreens. Looking back to the cottage door, Syd saw a pot of black-eyed Susans. Great touch.

Strong. Bright. Cheerful. Another mood again. Strong feelings.

The Spring Garden had had its show; the Rose Garden was at its prime now, but would not last; the Cottage Garden and the White Garden would bloom from June till the end of summer.

Syd noticed some of the people from the tour. He didn't want to look closely to see exactly who it was. It did register that Arielle was not there. But Jack Track was. And he doffed his cap to Syd. Steer clear of him, Syd cautioned himself. He didn't want to get side-tracked in idle conversation.

Syd consulted his map. There was a devious minor route back to the Tower Lawn, but he didn't want to go that way. There was also a minor route to Sissinghurst Crescent, just a stone's throw away, but it would spoil the major focus of the Moat Walk, which should be approached from the other way.

This garden is work, he laughed to himself.

Back the way I came into the Lime Walk and go into the Nuttery and see the man standing there, and how his woman looks from his point. Lots of foxglove here: deeper maroon colour than what I got from the packet of seed from the grocery store, and not quite so tall. It grows wild here in England, I know.

He observed the spent plants, feeling relief to pull back from the endless beauty of this place. It's still strangely attractive, but a rest from full bloom.

Syd made his way on the leftish path to the Herb Garden, right to the centre to the marble bowl resting on three lions. This was one of the treasures Harold and Vita had brought back from one of Harold's work stints abroad, early in their marriage.

The bowl was planted with houseleeks. Semper... something. Syd smiled. Hens and Chicks. He had established a big patch at the corner or the house where only weeds would grow. Did the trick. They formed a solid mat no weed could get through. His were a common variety. These were different.

Syd started to turn slowly and let his eye extend gradually outward over the dozen or more small beds divided by paths, in an ever-widening circle. He smiled at the living garden bench, either made of foliage or covered with it. He could only guess at the number of different kinds of plants.

There would be sages, rosemary, fennel, garlic, and mint. He carefully touched some leaves to transfer the aroma onto his fingers. There were plants collected from all over the world. That blue one was special. Couldn't remember its name. But for sure the tall yellow one was evening primrose.

There were textures: coarse leaves, feathery ones, upright sticks. There were heights: plants clinging to the ground to tall bushes. There were colours: foliage from densest green to silver, and flowers of orange and blue and pink and white.

Syd had a flash of memory from the Queen's Herb Garden at Kew. How many days ago? Just yesterday?

He looked up and around. I wonder where she is. Arielle? His mind called.

Syd moved to the stone bench in the Herb Garden. He looked at the details again, and surveyed its position in relation to the rest of the site. He picked up a scent that teased his memory and then was gone.

The beauty of it all overwhelmed him again. I'm not sick, he said to himself very sternly. But these emotions are flooding me. They're not bad. Actually they're joyful. And I'm not becoming some kind of a nut. I am in control. Let them happen. Run their course. There's a certain release, he admitted to himself.

Just sit for a while, tucked behind the hedging. Out of sight. Still lots of time to see the rest of the garden and do lots of sketching. He felt he could start with that big bowl in the centre. Exactly at eye-level.

Come to think of it, he'd noted many pots, troughs, sinks, urns, and coppers all over the garden. Beth Chatto had lots at her place. Close to her Mediterranean garden. Maybe some kind of influence. It did put plants at eye level, so you could look into them. He liked that for painting with watercolours. The structure of a single flower was staring you in the face. Must do that at home.

People were moving in and out amongst the herbs. They spoke in soft voices. He didn't tune into any of the conversations.

"There you are. I was hoping to catch up with you sometime today. You can do me a big favour, and help me put in the time." It was Grace. She came and sat beside Syd on the stone bench.

He slid too quickly to the extreme edge, as a feeling of near panic stuck him. Stop that, a voice within him yelled.

"You don't mind if I sit down with you."

And if I do will I be chased off into another part of this garden I'm not ready to see? Because of you? No thanks.

"The whole afternoon seems a lot of time to give to this place when you can see it all in half an hour." Grace was on her own sure ground.

Anger flared in him. I haven't got around once yet, but be damned if I'm going to try to communicate anything like that to you, you old bag!

How do I get out of this without spoiling my time? I'd like to get to some sketching, go calmly about my calming business of sketching, but not with you, you old biddy, hanging around, making me feel anything but calm.

Maybe I am crazy, with conversations with myself going on in my head!

"Aren't you going to say anything?" Grace asked sweetly.

I'd like to say, Buzz off. Except Hughie would tell me that's old-fashioned. Something more graphic is said nowadays! Syd almost laughed to himself.

So say something. What? Then cautiously he said aloud: "I'm enjoying every minute of this."

Oh my god, she'll think I'm talking about sitting with her.

"You know, the wonderful planting ...," he bailed himself out.

"It's all crowded in so close, you can't see what they've got." Grace's voice had a hint of a whine in it. Her habitual tone when being critical? She went on, "Personally, I think they should have arranged the plants in a more orderly way, organize them. Make the flowerbeds look tidy."

I wouldn't be surprised if Vita descended from wherever to smite Grace for that comment, Syd thought. If I could call down spirits, I'd give a shout!

"All that stuff in the Rose Garden spoils it. I want to be able to see the roses. I like bedding roses. The ones you can cut for arrangements. Like the florists."

Syd walked to the centre of the Herb Garden. Grace followed him.

Syd was mulling over some kind of a reply to Grace's impossible comment, when he heard a very loud "Psssst" coming from the other side of the Thyme Lawn.

"Psssssssst". It was almost a stage vocalization.

Syd looked over his shoulder. It was Jack Track standing at the edge of the moat.

Jack shook his head dramatically while pointing at Grace.

Syd focused back on the herbs.

"Grace!" It was a sharp bark.

Grace looked around. She turned back to Syd. "That horrible little man." She ignored the call.

"Grace!" The bark was louder and sharper.

"I'll just ignore him," Grace said sweetly to Syd. "Now we were saying how much nicer these flower beds would be if they were better organized and planned."

Syd was at a loss for a comment, but was saved by Jack calling again in a much louder voice.

"Gracie! Come'ere!"

"How dare he shout at me like that," Grace bristled. "Everybody's looking at me! How dare he!" She was practically huffing. "Pity there isn't a train ride or an amusement park to keep him busy."

Hate to think what Harold or Vita would say to that one! Maybe they could have worked a Ferris Wheel into their design!

Grace had her hands on her hips and turned to look at Jack severely.

Syd watched as Jack caught her eye and waved his arm frantically, motioning her to come to him.

"I have no idea what he wants, but I'm afraid he is going to make a scene if I don't go." She was angry. She took a step toward the Thyme Lawn. "He's spoiled our little visit. I've been so looking forward to getting to know you."

Syd made no reply.

"Surely you won't be taking much more time in here. I'm going for a Coke in that restaurant after I see what he wants." Grace was her charming best. "Please join me. We have so much to talk about."

With great relief Syd watched her go. I don't know what Jack Track wants either. Maybe her friend Jean needs her. Who cares. But I'm eternally grateful for being rid of Grace. Lucky timing by Jack.

Time to move on, into the thyme garden. Thyme to move? Another bad pun. His boys had been incorrigible with them when they were preadolescents.

The Thyme Lawn was an interesting tapestry of textures and shades in spite of being just thyme. Magentas, blues, silvers. Something of that Persian influence that Harold and Vita responded to, having worked and lived there in their early years of marriage, career and gardening awareness.

Now, Syd said to himself, walk over to the far side of the moat to Dionysus and see what he can see.

Syd stood beside him. You can see your handsome reflection any time you want, you lucky devil! My goodness Syd, he said to himself, you are becoming near reckless in your thoughts. Watch your actions!

Iris. That's water-iris. Water-iris along with the water-lilies. Trust Vita.

Syd then looked straight toward the Tower arch. He had to wait a moment for some other visitors to clear the view. Arielle was on the step looking directly at him. No, at Dionysus. She must have seen him over that long distance, for he was sure she acknowledged him with the briefest of waves.

She's found this axis too!

Syd felt goose bumps and a shiver up his spine.

Is it seeing this perfect line Harold has drawn, or the fact that she has discovered it, or that I like to think she has made the discovery? The feeling became a little thrill which caught him unawares.

Arielle stepped toward the Rose Garden and out of his line of vision.

Syd shifted his view to his left, to the Moat Walk: that stretch of grass, taking his eye up the steps rising to Sissinghurst Crescent to that beautifully designed and positioned Lutyens bench. An invitation to sit and enjoy this vista.

Syd promised himself to accept that invitation.

The overwhelming feeling of beauty stayed with him. He brought his eye back down the grassy walk to the calm water of the moat directly in front of him.

I don't think I'll ever be the same after this experience at Sissinghurst Castle Garden.

That's what I've been trying to do. To move on. Not easy.

Syd consulted his map. Go up the Moat Walk and see those urns on the wall, make my way past the South Cottage to the Yew Walk. Take it to the White Garden.

He hesitated in thought. I don't remember really looking at the White Garden from the Tower. Then he smiled to himself at Jack Track catching him at Arielle-watching. Not girl-watching. Arielle-watching. That was surprisingly clear in his mind. He felt really good.

It was a lovely stroll between the Azalea Bank on the left and the moat wall on the right. Between the spent azaleas, lilies bloomed. A few white flowers lasted on the wisteria, which hung from the moat wall. Small-flowered clematis were climbing in and out. Some sharp yellow spurge gave colour around the buttresses at the base of the wall, where tall, mauve asters were beginning to bloom.

Syd climbed the steps and paused at the Lutyens bench which was occupied by other visitors. Maybe from the tour. He wasn't quite sure. Engrossed in their own conversations.

He made his way to the path that should lead directly in front of the South Cottage. It did. The scent from that white rambling rose filled the air as surely as the rose filled the wall of the cottage. Heading around the shrubs at the west side of the cottage, Syd came face to face with Arielle.

They both stopped. Neither said a word for a long moment.

"It's magical," Arielle breathed in a near whisper.

"Yes," agreed Syd simply in a low quiet voice. Then, "Vita called it Sleeping Beauty's Garden."

"Yes," said Arielle in a moment of knowing, as they both moved off on their separate ways.

With a spring in his step, Syd turned left on the edge of the Orchard to the Yew Walk.

It was close and secretive between the two rows of dark green. He felt close and secretive.

Bright flaming red nasturtiums climbed through the yew, giving signs of life. Certainly makes me feel alive, Syd thought.

He stopped briefly at the gap in the yews to look left to the Tower arch, and right to Dionysus on the other side of the moat. Did you expect the axis to move? He laughed to himself.

He continued through the yews toward the classical statue forming the focus at the end. An armless woman, green foliage around her feet. It almost had the air of a religious shrine in a grotto.

The next gap would give him a view of the Orchard to the right or let him into the White Garden on the left.

The Orchard can wait. Its wildness, unkemptness, will be a welcome rest after the beautiful White Garden.

Syd paused before making the move into it, almost being inducted. He had that same high anticipation he experienced arriving at Sissinghurst.

He stepped forward. He was in the White Garden.

Tall yews in straight lines behind him. Low box hedges at right angles in front of him and to the right, holding in their plantings. To the left beds with greenery spilled onto the paths.

Dark green and white. Silver a transition.

Syd didn't move. He was momentarily transfixed.

He would start his sketching here. It was the only way to appreciate white and green and silver.

If there were roses throughout the garden, there were only white ones here.

If there were delphinium throughout the garden, there were only white ones here.

White lilies.

White campanulas low to the ground.

White snapdragons. Mass plantings.

Silver artemisia.

Silver lambs' ears with the touch of purple florets.

The beauty of it washed over him and settled to a feeling of calm. He walked slowly to the Ming jar in the centre of the garden and took in the majesty of the single rose climber that covered the metal frame and crowned this focus.

Syd stooped to go under the rose and around the jar to the statue of the virgin. Originally she was standing under a weeping silver pear tree. He didn't know if this was the original tree now, but she was in place. All was well. Her back to the Priest's Cottage? A bit Freudian, that!

He was ready to sketch. He had a cache of pencils, coloured pencils and crayons.

He sketched. He moved about the garden. He saw flowers. He sketched them. He saw walls and hedges. He sketched them. He saw Arielle. He sketched her.

He lost all track of time. He was absorbed. He was happy and at peace.

He was in the Orchard, by the Greek altar when he looked up to see Arielle standing in the gap in the yews at the White Garden.

She waved to him and pointed to her watch.

Syd fished into the pocket of his knapsack for his watch. Four-forty. Couldn't be.

He followed her through the yews.

She was taking her time through the White Garden, a last lingering look, focusing on plants.

Syd understood completely as he watched her again, and took a leisurely last look at the garden.

They each made their separate ways to the coach.

It was a silent ride to Dover.

DAY 6: DOVER TO CALAIS FERRY. DRIVE TO PARIS. EVENING TOUR OF PARIS LIGHTS

"Are you awake?" Molly asked cautiously.

"Just," said Arielle. "We're in Dover, aren't we?"

"Yes."

"Could be anywhere, from the style of the room." She folded the duvet back and tucked it under her chin.

"Our last morning in England with this most civilized of customs of having tea makings in the room. Let's enjoy every minute of it. We'll not find it on the rest of our trip."

"It's early."

"Not yet six o'clock."

Arielle listened to Molly moving the tea things. She'd been very, very tired, and knew she'd withdrawn into herself as deeply as before she came on the trip.

It had been a long mindless ride from the beautiful Sissinghurst Castle Garden to this hotel which looked over the harbour. Someone had said something about the White Cliffs, but mostly everyone was thankful for the waiting dinner and an early night.

Molly and Arielle had gone to their room and with scarcely a word had settled into bed with a book in Arielle's case and diary in Molly's.

Arielle hadn't read a page although she looked at one for a long time. Molly had scarcely asked for a verification of some event of the day. Both their lights were out by ten o'clock.

Sleep didn't come. Arielle's mind was sifting over unrelated things.

She retraced her steps through the garden, over and over again. A feeling of enchantment had settled over her upon entry and had still not left her this morning.

Bits from her past life flashed through her mind.

They were all caught up in the depth of herself to which she had retreated.

"That garden yesterday was a very special place," she said at last.

Arielle sat up as Molly handed her a cup of tea.

"It made me feel wrapped up as I used to feel in a dance or when I'm playing a piece of music. The long ones, where it becomes part of you, or you cease to exist except as a part of it. All afternoon. I was a part of a piece of art. Right into it. Detached from reality, except the feeling of communicating with an audience. You know the people are there, but you don't perform to them. In performing arts, you perform for them."

"But you were not performing. I saw you. You were just walking around the garden when I saw you."

"Good. I hoped that was all anyone saw. Because I hesitate ...," Arielle did hesitate, " ... hesitate to say that I felt sometimes as if I was being watched. No, not watched ..., maybe observed, as if I was in performance." She thought for a moment. "Just fleeting. And only for short times. It was nice."

"There's plenty of tea, and plenty of time before breakfast. We leave for the ferry at eight-thirty." Molly consulted the itinerary.

"Funny you asked about B-Man. When. Two days ago? Three."

"Three. At Bressingham."

"He's been rattling through my mind. Not him particularly, but his strange attitude toward me. I had no idea our relationship would go, I hesitate to use the word develop, the way it did.

"I don't think he knew who I was at all. I don't think he had any idea what I did all day long in spite of the fact that he would tell people that I had piano and violin pupils. Never asked me how my practicing was going. No concept that I actually had to learn a body of work, practice at home, preparing for symphony performance. Still taking lessons myself."

Molly was listening intently giving Arielle silent encouragement to talk on. Molly knew Arielle's mother had been concerned about the depth of Arielle's withdrawal and the length of time it had been going on.

"He would sometimes come to a concert when I was playing and never comment about it, in spite of the fact that he knew something about music. Then he would discuss the piece at some social occasion with others, me at his side, as if I wasn't there!"

"But he would make some reference to you being in the symphony," said Molly.

"No! That's just it! He wouldn't acknowledge even my presence, let alone any expertise. Within my work I have expertise and authority which is recognized. If I were to dance a part I had to do it skillfully and sincerely. Convincingly. Courageously.

"If I'm to play my violin part in a selection, I must be courageous, correct, a member of a team to be counted on.

"When I teach, I must have knowledge; understand my pupils; work with them so that they learn. With music there's no hiding. It's obvious if learning has taken place or not.

"When I was out with B-Man, I was seen to be dumb, mindless, something to be seen and admired. My body. Nothing more. My body is my body. Lucky me.

"It took me quite a while to figure that out, as no one takes you aside and tells you that because you are a woman you know nothing; not even to have a few ideas about Bach or Beethoven, let alone F. Scott Fitzgerald, or a simple investment plan, or the cash in your own bank account.

"I finally realized I was trying to communicate with another person whose sole concept of me was some idea in his head that has nothing to do with the person I believe myself to be. Not me at all.

"I am going on," Arielle apologized to Molly, "but I'm clarifying some things about myself and that relationship which I hadn't put altogether.

"B-Man kept making 'you' statements: 'you don't want material things', when something came up about buying a special piece for the apartment, our home; and then 'you don't want babies', when we had specifically discussed that when we first got together and had decided to have a child. It was to have been a love-child. We both wanted one. At least at first.

"I later found out, he'd had a vasectomy without telling me. It came up in a conversation with some business associates' wives, in the ladies' room at a very fine restaurant when we were at a dinner party.

"I was stunned. No wonder I wasn't getting pregnant.

"I challenged him that night when we got home. He'd had too much to drink, fine wine, of course, to even comprehend what I was talking about. Said that he didn't think I really wanted a baby and he'd had it done one 'business weekend' a few years back. What with my biological clock running out, I might have a mental defect, and he didn't want to have to take that on!

"I even picked up the challenge in the morning when he was sober. He said he remembered discussing it the night before and it was a closed subject.

"Molly, you don't mind me speaking out like this. But I feel better for it already. That was the first concrete demonstration of lack of trust."

"Why did you stay on with him, dear?" Molly had shared her mother's concern.

"By default, I suppose. Knowledge of the vasectomy was final. I wasn't so desperate to have a baby that I was going out to find a man for that specific purpose. How tacky! And we got along all right. I realized the relationship was going nowhere, but it became a habit. A convenience. It hasn't clicked until now, although I guess I intuited it, that he liked the fact that he had no responsibilities toward me. But strangely, he still had feelings of responsibility toward his wife and children."

"Did he not divorce?"

"No. That was another promise that just slipped away. He was always so busy with his job. Senior executives in big business seem to be far too busy for any other aspect of life. Every social thing we did was business related."

"I see, for want of a better comment," Molly said.

"That's just it. There was nothing there. I thought I had as good a chance of meeting someone else by keeping in the swim, but I must confess I was bad. Do you know that for the last five years, I made no effort, quite on purpose, to broach any subject of conversation with him. Frankly, I was completely indifferent to him. I heard him say that our relationship was perfect.

"All you have to do is be a great girl. Anything else was considered depressing, and he didn't have the time for me. A woman could not be considered thoughtful, serious, or have a brain in her head."

"And that certainly isn't you," said Molly as she patted the duvet where it covered Arielle's feet.

"Think of the men on this trip," said Arielle. "Except for Mr. Track Suit, they're all the executive type who would think the same as B-Man, I'm afraid. All of them Grace's type." And Arielle laughed out loud. "Except for the one who's changed his outward style. It's neat. But I'll bet it's the same old person inside." Arielle was quiet for a moment, then suspended judgement with: "But he knew about the garden."

As she started to pack her case, Arielle softly hummed the Shaker tune in Aaron Copland's Appalachian Spring, then broke into the words, "I danced in the morning when the world was begun, and I danced in the moon and the stars and the sun ...".

Pulling the big tawny sweater around her body for warmth over her cotton-knit wedge dress, Arielle sat on the open deck at the back of the ferry and watched the White Cliffs of Dover disappear in the haze, and said good-bye to England and things English.

She wasn't in any mood to inter-act with the other people on the coach, particularly after all the fuss Grace had stirred up about where everyone sat.

Nothing to do with me, Arielle said to herself, bathing in the sea air, settling down to enjoy the lapping of the water behind the boat and the sight of the other ships on the channel, and thinking of more things about B-Man than she had told Molly.

Arielle was sure two of his buddies were in cahoots with each other to be so exact in what they did. She'd known both of them socially but didn't think either had the courage to act alone.. Each in turn, immediately after she'd left B-Man, had, by chance, met her outside The Royal Conservatory Building at the University, on Bloor Street. By chance. Two Fridays in a row.

Arielle usually did chores on a Friday and often it took her to music stores, library, or she dropped into the Conservatory.

Did she have time for lunch? Or at least a drink? Or coffee?

With the first one, she agreed to have lunch. No, thank you, not at the hotel, why not something simple. CULTURES, her favourite salad bar? But he would like something better. Okay. A not-so-little restaurant in Yorkville. A drink? No thanks, not even a glass of wine. Wine makes me sleepy. I have things to do this afternoon. No, I'm sure about the wine, just mineral water. Hindsight told her it was a leer at the mention of being sleepy.

He drank his double something, as they ordered, and they would have a litre of the house wine, perhaps the lady would change her mind.

Arielle was beginning to be a little uncomfortable.

By the time they were half through their lunch he said he had the afternoon free to go somewhere and that he'd like the things she did to B-Man in bed.

He was specific! B-Man had actually told someone about their intimacies!

Disgust and repulsion, for this creep and for B-Man, washed over her.

She deliberately set her fork down, quietly picked up her purse, rose to her feet, and walked out of the restaurant.

She was shaken to the core that B-Man could have broken what she could only think of as a sacred trust. She found she was past disgust with him. She realized what a shallow and empty man he was. A hollow man. He had destroyed the memories of their relationship.

Hindsight again, but she had begun to pick up vibes during those last years that she was considered to be a lesser person. Face it. They, B-Man's friends thought you a fallen woman, a loose woman. A woman of easy virtue. In spite of the fact that you had lived with him for a long time. It was subtle. It was primitive.

When the second man appeared on the steps of the Conservatory the following week, not having any real reason except suspicion, she turned him down for lunch. No thank you, not even coffee. His persuasion almost turned into pleading: Oh come on, give me the good time you gave So-and-so last week. I'll even pay you for it ...!

Nice friends B-Man has. Says more about him and them than about me. Certainly couldn't trust any of that lot.

None of them were worth any more of her time or thoughts. Forgotten and dismissed.

Trust. M-m-m-m-m-m. One note neutrality.

As the ferry plied on, Arielle moved to a better position to see Calais, her first glimpse of France for a long time. There were French port officials and truckers as well as private cars and coaches. A busy place.

Not hard to tell they're French, she laughed to herself. As if they'd look like anybody else.

She stayed aboard and waited for the bulk of the crowd to land, since the view of the activity was so good from her vantage point. She also knew she could keep herself isolated from her fellow travellers for a while longer.

When she caught up with Molly at the appointed place to board the coach, Grace was about to make an announcement.

Looking directly at Arielle, Grace started by saying: "So you finally got here."

"I'm not late," Arielle whispered to Molly. "The coach is just pulling up now."

"I know," said Molly. "Just grin and bear this!"

"Martin said that it was the policy of the travel agents that we rotate, or change," Grace gave a winning smile as she corrected herself, "our seating arrangements. That gives everybody a chance at the best views, and also for us to get to know each other better." She made this last statement directly to Syd. "So think about that as you get on. Have a nice day. I am."

Grace turned from her audience. "Syd," she called.

"Gracie." Jack Track was right beside her.

Jack winked at Syd.

"Get away from me, you horrible little man," Grace hissed. "Get away."

Jack Track stepped to her side, precisely blocking her path to Syd.

Syd wasted not a moment. Molly was two steps closer to the coach than he. He was beside her in a jiffy, forget it Hughie, and with his hand lightly but firmly on her elbow, said, "Come and sit with me," as he steered her to the steps of the coach.

A cry of "Shoppers to the back of the bus" was tantamount to a latter-day tally-ho and resulted in the pack swarming toward the vehicle.

Syd gave Molly a hand, as Lorraine caught up with them.

"I was hoping," she said to Molly, "that we might sit together and talk about the roses at Sissinghurst."

"Do join us," said Syd. "I'll sit on the window side and you two can talk across the aisle to each other. I'd like to hear what you have to say about roses."

Syd followed Molly onto the coach, and they settled into the third row of seats with the big expanse of glass. Syd was safely on the window side as the shoppers filed past, already full of chatter about the hunt, the quarry, and the catch.

Arielle had watched this manoeuvre in wonder. A bit of comedy, she smiled to herself.

"I'm going to have the next pick of the seats." It was Grace. She pushed herself to the front of the queue brushing Arielle aside, and mounted the steps of the coach in a flurry.

No problem for me, thought Arielle as she followed Grace into the coach and saw her take the seat directly in front of Lorraine. I'll just sit here in the seat Grace has given up. Can't understand it. It's one of the best in the bus.

That was a close call, thought Syd. Thank heaven for Jack Track again. Timing dead on. Stop. Think about it. It can't be that much of a coincidence. He's deliberately interfering with Grace. Running interference for me! I think he's figured out that Grace's making a play for me. Face up to that one. That's what all the talk of Shirley was about. Another one. Here on the damned trip. Damn's not for the trip. It's for Grace and all those foolish women. Damn.

And bygad, Grace has plunked herself down in front of Lorraine. Unless I keep well to the window and pay attention out of it, I'll be in eye contact with Grace everytime she turns toward Molly.

Play this carefully. Listen with your eyes closed!

He did.

The subject was roses. He let the words drift past him.

Wild roses: a dog rose and a climbing musk rose, and the deep pink of Rosa gallica with perfumed petals.

Damasks, Gallicas and Albas in all the shades of clear pink or bluey pink between white and purple.

Damasks. Fragrant. From the musk rose. From Damascus. Crusades. Single or double petals with flat faces and puckered petals in red, pink or white. York. Lancaster is white with a red stripe. War of the Roses.

Low bushes with thorns. Albas have smooth pale foliage.

Autumn Damasks. Well-scented and twice flowering.

The Dutch rose of a hundred petals: the Cabbage. Heavy heads are better in a vase or painting.

"For arranging," Grace contributed.

Syd had opened his eyes and had been watching the countryside go by, watching the terrain change. Definitely not England.

He had been letting his mind drift over the discussion of roses, thinking of the next garden they would be visiting the day after tomorrow. Monet's garden at Giverny.

Monet grew and painted roses. Simple, single ones. Part of the move away from the traditional painters who captured the likeness of those big ones.

Syd could visualize the arches over the Grande Allee in front of the door of Monet's house. Photographs always showed it specifically.

Molly and Lorraine were still talking roses.

Traders brought roses from China.

Roses sporting. Mutating. Pure chance. Chance that someone recognized it. Sported to produce a dwarf bush. Continuous flowering.

Lorraine was speaking. "All this has brought us to today's Hybrid Teas and Floribundas. Rose breeders and horse breeders are cut from the same cloth. And still the modern breeding goes on."

"More than I want to hear," put in Grace shortly.

"Unfortunately there is more," said Lorraine expecting nor taking any short-shrift from Grace. "Shrub roses, those self-sufficient plants were nearly forgotten in developing the China characteristics. But people saved the old roses. Gertrude Jekyll. Vita. Graham Thomas made a case for them and catalogued all he could find. Wrote his book The Old Shrub Roses."

"In my younger day," Molly said, "there was the Japanese influence. Big interest in Japanese things, like the Mikado dishes, and Gilbert and Sullivan! It was the Japanese who reawakened interest in the lovely, simple single flower."

Syd turned to Molly. "That may answer a question for me. I never could find out why Monet had so many Japanese prints in his house, or why particularly the Japanese bridge in his waterlily pond."

Lorraine consulted her notes; "Japanese Rosa multiflora brought profuse cluster-flowering; another Asian R. rugosa, brought recurrent-flowering combined with extreme hardiness and splendid foliage; R. wichuraiana ...." Her voice faded out.

They both slid into the focus of their notebooks and silence.

"Maybe, Syd, you'd be better company for me than these two." Grace swivelled around in her seat and craned her neck to look past Molly and get Syd's attention. "Not a lot to see out that window on this endless bus ride."

"Just the changing countryside."

"Bor-ing."

"We are driving through some interesting farm land."

"If you like farms."

Is there no way to introduce something this woman could or would pick up on? "And I find the highway construction pretty interesting."

"I've heard everything. He comes to France and wants to talk about roads! I've heard everything!"

Well, Grace, thought Syd, here's your big moment. You carry the conversational ball and engage me in something riveting.

"You're living on the edge of Forest Hill, in Toronto. Done up an old house, I hear."

Grace, Syd said to himself, you didn't come all the way to France to talk about Toronto, did you? Syd said nothing aloud.

"Planning to sell it?"

No, Grace, I'm not planning to sell it. Interestingly enough, I'm planning to live in it. Syd said nothing aloud.

"I didn't catch what you said," said Grace, leaning well into the aisle.

"Grace must be uncomfortable," said Molly. "Perhaps I could

change seats."

Don't do that, a voice shouted in Syd's head.

"Lovely," said Grace.

At that moment, Martin stood up with microphone in his hand, "We're just minutes from pulling into our lunch stop. There it is."

He sat down while the coach navigated the off ramp and swung its way past the complex of Ibis and Novatel hotels to L'Arche, in the eating and service centre.

"We're going to take a full hour break here," said Martin. "The coach'll be right here. Please feel free to sit in whatever seats you wish for the ongoing trip. Enjoy your lunch."

"No sense trying to beat the rush to get off," said Molly to Syd, "unless you are in a hurry."

"Fine," said Syd agreeably. "I'm in no rush. Happy to be the last person off, if need be."

L'Arche was a modern complex for the traveller. Benches outside under carefully planted trees, washroom facilities, shop, and a very attractive cafeteria.

Syd joined Barbara and Ross at the end of the line.

Jack Track and the wife joined them.

That's interesting, thought Syd, I'll bet Grace doesn't join us with Jack in the crowd.

When she came along, she took one look at Jack, and sweetly asked, "Has anyone seen Jean?"

"Just look for the Tilley hat," said Ross, nodding up the queue.

"I'll join her," Grace said, all sunny. "Nobody minds if I go ahead."

"Part of the plan." Syd heard Jack mutter under his breath.

Syd turned his back on the food counter to look out at the complex. Molly was making a purchase at the cash desk of the news kiosk while Arielle was waiting just outside.

"The wife says that's a tube dress." Jack was looking at Arielle. "I say that's no tube, if y' get my drift."

Syd considered the dress Arielle was wearing. She was standing straight on with one foot in front of the other. An inverted isosceles triangle defined by the shoulder pads with the vertex at her bare knee-cap. She made a quarter turn and the triangle righted with the vertex at her shoulder and the base a straight line across the hem stretching from one knee to the other.

"That's quite a dress," said Syd still studying the mechanics of the dress in motion, "more of a wedge."

"Look what's inside." There was a note of exasperation in Jack's voice. "Are y' blind, man!"

Syd was looking; had been looking; was still looking.

Jack said, "Marilyn Monroe was fat."

"You make me laugh," Syd said to Jack.

"I finally got a reaction outta y'. I was beginning to think y' were dead!"

"Not quite," said Syd, as he felt a familiar, but long forgotten twinge low in his body. Deep in the groin.

He watched Arielle, standing beside Molly at the end of the food queue, tuck her hair behind her left ear, and by touch skillfully thread the shank of her hoop earring through the pierced hole.

That's the sexiest thing I've seen a woman do for a long time. Ever. What a turn-on. She is gorgeous.

He must have swallowed or something for Jack Track said, "So y' finally noticed her. Nothin' wrong with y' after all. 'cept that Gracie's watchin' y' like a hawk."

Get ahold of yourself. Those emotions that were flying around yesterday. That was yesterday, and today it's simple pleasure. Nice feelings.

Okay, but keep your distance. You have no idea what she's like. This is a trip. Your lifestyle at home's okay. Don't complicate it. Besides, she hasn't shown any sign that she's even noticed you.

"Well isn't this fancy," said Jack. "The wife doesn't put up a lunch like this at home."

"Oh, Jack, be quiet," said Ev, the wife. "This is your French cooking."

"Actually it's one of the most attractive buffets I've ever seen," commented Barbara. "At a service centre, too. Look Ross: a basket of endive, whole ones, slice them yourself, for salad; that round chewy bread and Normandy butter; chicken fricassee; pate; two quiches; and those small whole cheeses. They must be local, one pear-shaped, the other one square ..."

"Wine by the half-bottle. But also beer. Very nice," agreed Ross.

"And sixteen franc for a cup of coffee. The wife better drink wine."

"Oh, Jack!"

"Today seems to have been hotel rooms or coach riding," said Arielle as she stretched out on her bed.

"By definition that's what travel is!" Molly tossed the comment out.

"I'm glad we have a free day tomorrow. It will be good to stretch my legs and move the bod, and see Paris to boot." Arielle laughed. "I haven't made a pun for years! Or seen Paris for years. I was too young before to get that much out of it."

"We'll split as planned," Molly said. "I'm going with the group to Versailles. It's a local trip. They pick us up right here at the hotel. There was some talk of all going out to dinner together and some entertainment, if we can figure what to do. I'm kind of hobnobbing with Jean tomorrow. Grace seems to have abandoned her. I don't think they're particularly close friends. Barely acquaintances. Jean's a bit timid, but good company. We'll have a nice day."

"That was a beautiful outing tonight," said Arielle. "Isn't Paris known as the city of light? If it isn't it should be."

"The illuminations allow the features of the city to stand out boldly, with the minor structures disappearing into the woodwork, so to speak."

"By starting at the Ile de la Cite and the sombre Notre Dame, then working the Seine both ways, gave me my bearings for tomorrow. I know where the Louvre is in relation to the Cathedral, then comes the Jardins des Tuileries," Arielle pronounced this with a very passable Parisian accent, "into that hauntingly beautiful Place de la Concorde."

"I felt it too," said Molly. "Maybe it's the mood of the night, but that flat open space in the middle of a bustling city ..."

"... where the guillotine ..."

"... and all that history ... emanating from those government buildings ... and the mobs ..."

Both Molly and Arielle drifted off in thought.

"Then up the grand," Arielle was talking enthusiastically, "and it really is grand, Champs Elysee to the Arc de Triumph. Beautifully lit up, but oh so solid compared with the Eiffel Tower. The light making it lace. It was stunning, in contrast to all those classic building, and then to see the new pyramid in the courtyard of the Louvre puts you smack into the end of the twentieth century."

"I liked the little, winding, hilly streets toward Montmartre," said Molly. "I certainly couldn't do that on foot."

"Past the Moulin Rouge. I used to think that was an exotic name, when I first learned of the lifestyle that went on around it. Toulouse Lautrec and all that. Of course Moulin Rouge is simply a red windmill!" Arielle laughed.

"Nice to see where the fashion district is. The Faubourg St-Honore. And speaking of fashion," Molly asked slyly, "did you happen to take note of Mr. and Mrs. Track Suit?"

"I didn't dare look at you when they came onto the coach." Arielle was laughing. "Perfectly dressed for an evening in Paris!"

"Matching black and white parachute silk track suits!" Molly was howling.

"And the hats!"

"Baseball. But what sport or team?"

"Black, white and silver! To go with their outfits. I took a close look! Los Angeles Kings!"

"And she had on ersatz diamonds ..." Molly was holding her sides, "matching earrings, necklace, pin and bracelet."

"Too perfect, as the kids would say." Arielle wiped the tears streaming down her cheeks.

"In all fairness," Molly had control of her voice and sides, "she's very sweet. A good travelling companion."

"And he, seems to be everyone's friend. I can understand his association with the men on the trip, but I can't figure why he and Grace seem to be together, well not exactly together, well, together off and on."

DAY 7: FREE DAY IN PARIS

Arielle made her way out of the hotel entrance and through the arcade of shops that led to the Boulevard de Bonne Nouvelle. They were in the Opera district.

She was ready to see Paris, handles of her tote bag and purse over her shoulder, map in hand on top of Paris Walks, a guidebook she had found at Britnell's Bookstore on Yonge Street in Toronto. Not your average guidebook, but one which took you on detailed walks of choice. She had decided on the Left Bank. The St. Germain des Pres area.

Having to make a quarter turn to get her bearings, she lined the map up, and traced her finger to the Metro station she thought she wanted, then turned the map over to the Metro map, found the station on it, and traced her finger along the route she wanted muttering in perfect Parisian French, circa Toronto 1950, "*Here, Bonne Nouvelle. Where is St. Denis? Cite. Four, colour pink.*"

She stepped back to get a better view of a street sign and made an electrical contact with another person. Syd! She knew.

"Excusez-moi, s'il vous plait." Arielle's French teacher at Havergal had been from France. Educated at the Sorbonne.

"Me, too. Excuse me. And Metro line four, stop at Cite."

As they sprung apart Arielle turned at the familiar sound of Syd's voice.

Looking over her shoulder at her map and book, he met her gaze with a gesture of shared possession as he held up the same guidebook.

Arielle thought she saw an L.A. baseball-hatted man. Jack Track Suit? He disappeared into the hotel behind them.

"*Same thing,*" she said in French hoping not to betray the feeling of being unnerved. She smoothed her hair up to the clip on the top of her head and fingered the band that held her hair in a pony-tail, as much to smooth her feelings as her hair.

He's very attractive, she thought. The cropped beard for sure, and the loose collar-length hair just caught behind his ears. Not tied at the nape of his neck today. No! Put those kind of thoughts out of your mind.

Apparently considering the French phrase, Syd said simply, "Yes, I'd planned to go on walk one, two or three." He almost mugged at the silliness of the choice. "Left Bank anyway. St Germain des Pres. I thought Cite and Notre Dame would be a good decision making point."

"*Me, also,*" said Arielle, responding to the silliness of the choice with a warm smile.

Hearing French again, Syd paused. Then cautiously he said, "Shall we go together? ...Unless ...?" Syd granted an out.

Trapped, thought Arielle with panic. I don't know if I want to. Yes, I do! To spend how long? I don't know this man. This nice man! That thought surprises me! But he is nice.

Not sure at this point if I want to know any man. He's on the tour. Well, okay. We can split when I've had enough company. Hey. Think. I've got it. Good way to curtail too much conversation. He'll tire first.

"Yes. D'accord. Okay," Arielle gave a friendly nod of her head.

"Metro ...to the right?" Syd asked.

"Un moment." Arielle stopped. She looked at him. "You were going to do this on your own, so you're not concerned about the language." She was making a statement.

"I can get by, I think. Barely. High school French to get into University Engineering which nobody would believe these days, and then an executive's crash course back in the seventies when we were all to become bilingual. But how good it is ... well, I'm game to try. But you seem to be able to say something fairly on time."

On time! Arielle laughed to herself. Most people would mention fluency or something, but on time! A quick response maybe does indicate skill! Never thought of it that way. "Bon. We will speak French today. Nous parlons francais aujourd'hui," she said with daring.

"O.K. .... That's French," said Syd quickly with a sly look and implying agreement. Then hesitantly, "Maintenant, you know, 'now'" he looked at Arielle with smart-alecky tone, "Metro. Stazion?"

Both were consulting the map.

"*Here is Boulevard de Bonne-Nouvelle. Metro line nine. Citron.* No. Green. Lime?" She pronounced it leem. "*D'accord? D'accord* means O.K." Arielle was reading the map.

Pointing left, Syd said cautiously, "A ...gauche. Strasburg - St. Denis. Ligne quatre," with four fingers in the air, "a St Michel."

"*Wait a moment,*" said Arielle. "*Perhaps we should plan a little. I would like ...*"

"Um-m-," Syd was thinking, "ah, lentement, s'il vous plait."

"*Yes, I'll speak more slowly,*" Arielle said pleasantly. "*I'd like to go to the food store. Fauchon. Near Madeleine. The food is haute cuisine. To look, not to eat. It's a work of art.*"

I wonder if he'll want to negotiate any plans.

"O.K. Pardon. D'accord! Madeleine? Sur le plan ...," Syd was turning his map over and over, looking for the Madeleine building and then the Metro stop. "Difficu...," Syd stopped short and changed his pronunciation to "Difficile."

"*It's not far from here. It's easy to walk,*" Arielle offered.

Syd looked down at her feet.

Arielle looked down below the hem of her wedge dress at her bare legs and feet ensconced in serious sandals.

She looked at Syd's feet below his jeans.

She looked directly at him as she indicated her feet and said: "Clarks."

He looked directly back at her and said: "Eddie Bauer."

Syd pointed to his map and said: "A l'Opera."

"*Straight ahead,*" said Arielle.

They set off along the wide Boulevard. Paris was still coming to life and there was a freshness on the streets as shopkeepers and cafe owners sluiced down the pavements outside their premises.

Arielle felt good to be walking and she was comfortable with Syd striding along beside her. The forgotten B-Man wouldn't put one foot in front of the other. He had a prestigious car, and had no interest in going places by any other means. Her mother and Molly had ceased to do any serious walking. Often Mr. Dog accompanied her in Toronto, but half way wanted to be carried.

It was still cool enough to leave her Indian cotton shawl wrapped around the scooped neck of her wedge dress. The sleeves were let down to elbow length. It was July and Paris had been having lots of sun and daytime temperatures in the mid twenties.

Arielle noticed Syd was wearing a light denim shirt with the sleeves still buttoned at his wrists. He had his knapsack over one shoulder.

They negotiated the universal traffic light and crossing just before Boulevard Haussmann, to take the street to the front of the Opera.

Arielle stopped to look at it.

"Ca va?" Syd said hesitantly.

"*Very well, thanks. The building, there.*" Arielle pointed. "*L'Opera. I'd like to look at it. It's beautiful.*"

"Oui," said Syd, "tres beau."

"*On the facade,*" Arielle was pointing to the sculpture, "*the dance,*" she said. "*This building is the home of music: opera and ballet. Nijinsky and Pavlova danced here ... Richard Wagner.*"

"Tu ..." Syd was stumbling for a verb.

"Non." said Arielle, wagging her finger like a schoolmarm. "Not, tu. Vous."

"Mathematique?"

"*Singular and plural. Vous, for ordinary use. Tu is for intimacy.*"

"Intimite?" Syd repeated her French pronunciation.

"Intimacy, in English," answered Arielle.

Syd was quiet.

"*You wish to speak?*" Arielle sensed a change in Syd's mood.

"Vous aimez la musique?" he asked finally.

"*Yes. I'm a musician, and I teach it.*"

"Le professeur. A l'ecole?" Syd was handling basic vocabulary with ease.

"*Not at school. Private.*" Arielle turned back to the building. "*Very beautiful.*"

"Oui," said Syd. "Peut-etre au mileu de neuf, non," he was mumbling some numbers, "dix-neuf cent." He laughed at himself as he tried to expand his comments. "Je essayerai encore: dix-neufieme ..."

"*Century. Nineteenth Century. Well done.*"

Syd snapped his finger in accord.

"*Histoirian?*" Arielle asked him.

"Non, construction." Syd gave the pronunciation a French twist. And with equal bravado as he pointed down the street, "Continuez? J'ai ... need, ...oh, yes, besoin de rester mon francais."

"*You can rest your French,*" Arielle said agreeably.

Exactly what I want. Some company, but minimum attempt at communication or getting to know him.

But considering him from what she had observed so far, for a construction man he's taking this really well, Arielle thought. I would have guessed him terribly macho. Stereotypes all in place, dear? she asked herself. Lighten up. He hasn't done or said anything out of line. Actually, very good-humoured about it. That's fun.

"*The map,*" said Arielle waving the paper. "*We're here in front of L'Opera and we wish to go behind,* derriere la Madeleine." Arielle stopped with foolish alarm on her face.

"Derriere de Madeleine! Where is ..., I mean, Ou est Jack Track quand j'ai, ... need... besoin de ...him! ...him?" Syd got the thought out.

Arielle watched Syd's face try to hold back the laughter dancing in his eyes. It slid its way across his mouth and finished in the dimples in his cheeks which joined the line under his chin. Evident under the clipped beard.

"*Who is* Jack Track?" Arielle asked suspiciously.

"Tu ... excusez, vous savez Jack et Ev qui, uh, wear ..., ah, ... portens le meme ... track suits"

"*Oh, yes.*" Arielle was laughing, "*... and hats! L.A. Kings!*"

"Adrian's Foggy Bottom et maintenant, derriere Madeleine. C'est un haut voyage." Syd mocked the last phrase.

High class trip indeed. Laughing, Arielle used her finger to make a circle on the map behind the Church of the Madeleine. Clearing her throat theatrically at the same time said, "Derriere de Madeleine."

"Oui," agreed Syd. "Marchez ...!"

Arielle smiled as they negotiated the lights to cross the spokes of the wheel which made up this intersection as well, to gain the other side of Boulevard de la Madeleine, heading for rue de Seze which would take them into Place de la Madeleine.

Immediately on the left was a covered flower market. Green grill work with glass at the end letting light in. Yellow plastic buckets held wrapped and bunched flowers. Under trestle tables were large florist cans.

Syd stopped. Arielle hesitated.

"Les fleurs. J'ai besoin de regarder. Un moment?"

"D'accord. *We've plenty of time for you to look.*"

"Les marches des fleurs ... la couleur est important ... non clair et sombre ..."

Arielle appeared to be looking at the banks of flowers, for there were at least three if not four sellers. In reality she was observing Syd. He's in construction, she said to herself, but he needs to stop and look at the flowers.

She watched him open his knapsack and take out a small sketch book and a few pencils. He looked closely at the flowers, squatting on his heels sometimes to turn their heads; on one knee sometimes to prop his book and make some swift sure strokes on the page. Completely absorbed. She had seen him like that at the various gardens they had visited, but didn't expect him to be so absorbed by individual flowers.

She made a few surreptitious peeks at his sketch book. She saw taut geometry in the man-made awnings, umbrella poles, and pavements in contrast with the random delicacy of the flowers.

Fifteen minutes later he simply said to her: "Merci." Then pointed to one of the shops with food in the window.

This was Fauchon. Fresh fruit and vegetables, meat, poultry, game, fish and other seafoods were in the store on the right side of the street across from the flower market.

Arielle walked to the display windows. Syd followed her at a comfortable distance.

"*Attractive,*" was all Arielle said in a quiet voice. She was grateful that Syd wasn't attempting to make conversation. Maybe he was sensitive to her need to look at this beautiful display of food, as she had realized he needed to look at those flowers. Nice to have understanding exchanged.

Remembering the incident in the Portobello Road, Arielle hesitated to sneak a look at him in the glass. Then she grabbed her courage and let her gaze drift casually toward him. He's quite a nice looking man, she thought with approval.

He was looking at the food.

"Voulez-vous!" Syd's eyes lit up. "Le vieux, voulez-vous! Serieuxment, Voulez-vous en aller? Moi, aussi. Oui?"

"*Yes, I'd like to go in and am glad you'd like to, too,*" responded Arielle, leading the way to the doors.

They entered at the produce end and wound their way past displays of apples of different shapes and shadings; oranges, lemons, citrus of different shapes and shadings; berries and cherries; pears; melons as she had never seen before. Peasant baskets of aubergine; mushrooms, deuxelles, champignons, chanterelles; green feathery fennel, white celery and knobbly rough brown celeriac; lettuces, endive and escarole; garlic and garlic of different shapes and colouring. She took it all in. She stopped and turned to Syd.

"*They paint ...,*" she hesitated at Syd's questioning look, "*still lifes. I'm so happy that artists see the beauty in food....*"

"Ah, oui. Monet, Manet, Cezanne, ..."

"Oui."

"Tu ..., excusez, vous... ne fait pas la erreur encore. Vous etes une artiste?"

"Non. *Not an artist.*"

"Un jardin...i...er?"

"*Not a gardener. I like to cook. Real food. But attractive.*"

Syd nodded in understanding.

Arielle led the way to the counters with prepared food of individual servings: mushrooms a la greque; gnocchi in a creamy white sauce; salade nicoise; quenelles; things en gelee; things au gratin mornay; things florentine. The fresh fish and seafood counter with mullet, moules and eels. Past the poultry and game. Past the meats and cheeses. Beautiful food, beautifully presented.

"*Enough,*" said Arielle.

"Oui."

They emerged onto the street.

"*Another store, there.*" Arielle was pointing to her right, and across the street running at right angles to the street they were on. "*Let's just look in the windows. Cakes and chocolate.*"

They worked their way past gorgeous displays of every confection.

"*Perhaps it's my age, but these aren't as appetizing as at the other store.*" Arielle indicated the first store.

"Mon age aussi. D'accord."

They walked away from the display windows and stopped directly in front of the large windows and door that led to the spiral staircase down to a coffee counter, eatery and food shop.

"Un zoo," Syd commented.

"*Cafes are better outside,*" said Arielle.

They turned away from the store, and opened their maps.

"*Next?*" Arielle asked.

"Rue Royale devant Madeleine." Syd had his little finger on the church and his index finger on Notre Dame.

"*Rue Royale. Straight ahead to the Place de la Concorde,*" Arielle said with interest.

"Allons sur rue Royale a Place de la Concorde, trouver une cafe ..." Syd was struggling with his French.

"*Agreed. Find a cafe and rest your French,*" Arielle said lightly, "*Have a cafe au lait, look at the maps and guidebooks, and watch the world go by ....*"

"Exactement," said Syd.

They headed toward Rue Royale.

"Premier croix?" Syd had his finger on his map.

"*The crossroad,*" said Arielle.

"Faubourg St. Honore."

"*Everybody is here,*" said Arielle. "*... fashion,*" Arielle was speaking slowly and enunciating clearly, appreciating that Syd's linguistic receptors were flagging. "*A cafe, there, in the shade.*" Arielle was pointing to the other side of the street. "*I don't wish to shop.*"

"Doute, ici, aussi belle que Portobello Road noir."

Doubt, here, as beautiful as the Portobello Road black. Bad French but crystal clear meaning, thought Arielle, with a warm glow rising in her, remembering the connection their eyes had made in the mirror and the absolute understanding.

Afraid to steal a glance at Syd in case she revealed too much of the interest she was feeling about him, she simply made her one note comment, "M-m-m-m."

They crossed the street and made their way through some tables to a central position.

Arielle watched Syd set his maps on the table and open his knapsack to sort through some sketch books until he chose a smallish one.

Arielle set her maps and guidebooks on the table, took her shawl off, folded it, and stowed it in her totebag. Purse on her lap, she set her big bag under her chair and sat down. She watched Syd set the knapsack under his chair as he sat not quite opposite her but not quite beside, either. The chairs were facing the street.

Arielle watched him reach for his left cuff. He's going to announce the time, she thought ruefully. But he just unbuttoned his cuff and started to carefully turn his sleeves up. Wrist bare of anything except fine hairs covering muscle-defined forearms.

He is not wearing a watch! I don't believe this. Maybe he's left handed and wears it on his right arm. No, she thought he's right handed. I saw him drawing.

Syd looked at her suddenly as he turned back the right cuff.

Arielle felt caught. Embarrassed at observing him so closely. She spied a different looking ring on the little finger of his right hand.

"*Your ring,*" she was indicating on her own hands. "*Differente.*"

"Oui." Syd settled back in his chair. "Permittez de penser." He gave her a sly look and said, "je pensing en English!"

"*Thinking in English is permitted!*" Arielle said back with equal slyness.

Syd sat forward and started to present: "Universite. Engineer, on-jon-ee-r-r ...capish? Non. Non, Italien."

"Capish!," Arielle said prissily, with tongue in cheek.

"Graduation," said with the French twist, "Toute a donne, un bague?"

"*Everyone was given a ring?*"

"Oui. ...Ir-ron ...ah, ... fer, pour le petit digit ....non.....rougie?....le rosie?" he was holding up his right hand with little finger, the pinkie extended, "sur le main travail. Un ceremonie." And he sat back in his chair.

"*I understand.*" An iron ring for the little finger of the working hand. Interesting. And Arielle sat back.

That's enough, she thought. With my pupils I always know when they've had enough, and with any more push at that point, I know I'll lose them. He's doing very well. He's also not about to quit. I know that. How? she asked herself. I just know. He could have managed on his own quite nicely. But I'm glad he didn't.

Arielle's reflection was interupted by the waiter.

He said, "Monsieur?"

Syd looked at Arielle.

"Cafe au lait, s'il vous plait." She looked serious.

"Deux," said Syd holding up two fingers.

"Petit ou grand?" asked the waiter.

Syd looked at Arielle.

"Grand," she said with repeated seriousness.

"Deux. Grand," Syd said to the waiter.

Arielle slid her sunglasses from the top of her head onto her nose. Both sat quietly. Comfortably, although there was a little itch in Arielle's brain.

"*The waiter and others,*" she spoke slowly for she wanted Syd to understand her point without undue fuss, "*today, will defer to you because you are the man. In order to pay could each of us, you and me, put, say one hundred francs in the breast pocket of your shirt, and you pay the bill here, or buy tickets if we need them. It makes others more comfortable if the man pays.*"

Syd had been listening carefully.

Oh my god, thought Arielle wildly. I've just made a commitment for how much of to-day? Maybe I was wrong. He would like to split. I don't want to. Face it, you are having a very pleasant time with this man Syd.

"Oui," said Syd patting the left breast pocket of his shirt. "Le

Treasurie." He took a money clip from his jeans pocket, and peeled off a one hundred franc note and put it in the shirt pocket. He looked gleefully at Arielle and held out his hand.

She laughed and fished out a similar note from her purse and placed it in the waiting hand.

The waiter brought the cafe au lait. Deux. Grand.

This was Paris.

Arielle listened to the sounds as much as watched the action. She watched Syd open the sketch book and saw his pencil moving, watched him look at the street, look at her sometimes, and draw again.

Finally Syd picked up his map. Arielle watched him, as she turned up the sleeves of her dress far enough to make them into cap sleeves. It was going to be a more than warm sunny day. She picked up her map.

"Ou?" Syd asked.

"*Here.*" Arielle brandished her copy of Paris Walks as an answer. "*I like walks numbered two and three. Special, St Germain des Pres. Rive gauche, certainment.*"

I hope he doesn't think I'm speaking pigdin French, and is insulted. If I was too expansive we might lose communication.

"Place de la Concorde, travers a Les Jardins des Tuileries, et passe Le Louvre ..." Syd was thinking outloud, in French.

"*Not enough time to go in the Louvre... do you think?*"

"Non." Syd was shaking his head. "Pas de temps. J'ai besoin de six semaines. Plus de pluie."

"*You need six weeks and rain?*" said Arielle with a slight frown and thinking of her own excursions to the art gallery or library on rainy days. "*I don't understand ... the words or the idea ...*"

"Tard - er," Syd, at a loss for the French comparative, pronounced as in English. "...oubliez! La promenade ...."

"*Finish at Notre Dame?*" asked Arielle, patiently.

"Oui," said Syd.

The waiter arrived with the bill, and with nary a glance at Arielle, Syd reached into his shirt pocket and produced some money.

Arielle had opened her bag and was taking out her jogging shoes. She had kicked off her sandals and was putting on the sturdier shoes.

"*For serious walking.*"

With her plain knit wedge dress, sleeves rolled up and runners, she had a completely different look. Daytime summer.

Arielle slung her bag over her shoulder, Syd did the same as he clapped his no-name baseball hat on, and they set off for Place de la Concorde.

They crossed to the Place itself, ignoring the traffic scrum surrounding it. Arielle found it a haunting place even in daylight. She must have looked strained as Syd said again, "Ca va?"

She pointed to the eastern end, to the fountain and said: "*Gillotine.*"

They wandered at will. Arielle walked to the edge and looked up the Champs Ellysee to the Arc de Triumph, then crossed over to the other side to look at the Jardins de Tuileries. Syd was moving at his pace, stopping with his sketch book.

Arielle was at the exit closest to the Jardin, when Syd waved at her. He pointed to his wrist. She looked at her watch and nodded, then flagged him to come.

They escaped the rush of traffic around the Place to the relative quiet of the Jardin de Tuileries.

"*Do you have a watch?*" Arielle was pointing at her wrist.

"Oui," replied Syd. "Dans la petite poche de mon sac. La poche emergencie."

"*Why don't you wear it?*"

"La liberte sans it."

They walked through the centre of the gardens. Arielle was aware of the deliberate and classic structure of it.

"*You're a gardener,*" she said to Syd, "*Tell me a fact about this one.*" Arielle posed the statement in an inquiring way.

"Le designeur est Le Notre. Tres fameuse. Aussi Versailles." Syd answered. After a bit he said; "Vous n'etes pas une jardiniere, dites un chose au sujet de it."

"Catherine de Medici, of Italy, commissioned it. She also introduced the Renaissance cuisine of Italy, which has become the high cuisine of France. She's very interesting. I've read much about her and the de Medici family in Italy."

Syd stumbled on something. Quick on his feet, he hopped on the stumbled foot, regaining his balance and threw in a step behind as a flourish to his neat recovery. Arielle saw his easy footwork and thought of him as doing a bit of Agnes de Mille's choreography in the Aaron Copland Rodeo.

If he was wearing a cowboy hat and high heeled cowboy boots it would be Rodeo. But with the baseball hat and mountain shoes, it's got to be Appalachian Spring.

Her mind drifted to the quartet music she was working on. An arrangement of Tennessee Waltz. She found herself humming it.

"Tennessee Waltz," said Syd. "I never could waltz," he said absentmindedly, French forgotten for the moment.

"Likely nobody told you to step forward first," Arielle said, bypassing French.

With that comment still on her breath, she stepped in front of Syd with a turn to face him, put her left arm on his shoulder and extended her right hand for dance position. Without missing a beat, she stepped back on her right foot as she counted one, with a heavy accent, two, three.

"Forward, side, together." She was calling Syd's steps as she went backward. "Forward, side, together."

Syd was right with her, in step and in rhythm.

"Turn," and she made them pivot on the first long step, "side, together. Turn, side ..." Syd's knapsack swung around and landed a soft blow to Arielle's side.

They stopped in a tangle, laughing.

"Non, non," a French voice called out. "S'il vous plait, continuez!"

They looked about to see a man with a camera. "Encore. Encore!" He was brandishing his camera.

Syd and Arielle looked at each other laughing.

"Non, non," they chorused together.

"Americans?" asked the man. "I put your picture in the journal ... the newspaper?"

Syd and Arielle laughed again.

"Sure, sure," Syd agreed with Arielle's approval.

"Tell me about yourselves," the man had a notebook in his hand.

Arielle looked at Syd. "Tell him we don't give interviews, we just perform!"

They walked on enjoying the park and noting a few sculptures dotted about.

"*Shall we go through the courtyard of The Louvre?*" asked Arielle. Syd nodded his head in agreement.

They passed the other Arch de Triomphe, and made their way into the courtyard to see the pyramid by I.M. Pei.

"La Louvre est trop grande pour a visite petit," Syd commented.

"*Leo Stein, the brother of Gertrude, passed the mornings here.*"

"Oui, oui," said Syd with lively recognition. "Que je dit avant. Je passe plus de jours plui dans l'AGO en Toronto. Les jours je n'est pas dehors."

"*That's what you meant about the rain. You go to the Art gallery too when the weather's bad.*" Arielle was nodding her head in understanding.

"Leo Stein, Gertrude. Picasso. Les collections d'Impressionists! Vous savez de them?" There was a certain level of awe in Syd's voice.

"*A little. It began with Alice B. Toklas brownies back in the sixties. No, I didn't eat them but I heard of them. She had cooked for Hemmingway and everybody in Paris at the atelier of Gertrude Stein. One thing and another, the cook, the people, the writers, the painters. Then I went to the AGO, and discovered Still Lifes. Flowers by Georgia O'Keeffe ... then life styles ....*"

Arielle felt she was making connection with her companion in spite of abbreviated conversation. He knows what I'm talking about, she thought, and what's more I know what he's talking about. Nice.

"Et nous allerons chez Monet, aujourd'hui ...son jardin," said Syd.

"*Yes, ... tomorrow, ... Monet's garden, ... his table. A beautiful book about his life style ...*"

"Je ne sais pas ..." said Syd.

Their conversation was halted by their walk through of the courtyard of the Louvre, wending their way out to the street by the Seine toward the Pont Neuf to the Ile de la Cite.

They walked along the left side of the Ile toward Notre Dame, non-verbally questioning each other on the turn onto the road to Notre

Dame, agreeing to pass it in favour of the stretch of book and poster stalls formed by green painted lockers unfolded onto the street.

They browsed at their own pace, Arielle feeling comfortable with the attention span of her companion. She heard a soft, "Ca va?"

It was Syd. "Juste verife-checking. Tres grand ville." He said a bit sheepishly.

"Merci," Arielle said reassuringly. That's nice. He's just checking. B-Man wouldn't bother. Syd and I are together. I'm not lost or kidnapped! I'm being looked after. Gratitude touched her. He did that so naturally and easily. Part of being a nice man.

Syd had moved to the river edge of the street, and was leaning on the balustrade, Paris Walk guidebook open. Arielle joined him.

"Nous sont pres de Walk deux. Page ...soixante-onze."

"Oui," said Arielle opening her guidebook to the same page. "*I'd like to have lunch in St. German de Pres at the cafe Les Deux Magots.*"

"Pardon!" said Syd. "Ou?"

Arielle laughed. "*A famous cafe on the Left Bank. Artists frequent it. Outside.*"

"Comme vous dites! Conduiez!"

They crossed on the Pont au Double to the Left Bank.

"Pres de Pont St Michel, il y a un market des fleurs qui a les oiseaux chaque dimanche ... oubliez." Syd was looking down a side street.

"*Let's go toward Huchette Street which runs in St. Michel ... here.*" Arielle had her finger on the guidebook map.

Syd leaned over her shoulder to look at the same. Concentrating, he said, "Rue St Andre Des Artes would take ...oh, excusez. En francais. A St Germain de Pres a votre maggots ... pres de ...."

"*Let's go,*" said Arielle, saving Syd from his knotted French.

They worked their way along the old streets that seemed hardly changed from the middle ages, except for the influx of Greek immigrants who had a restaurant in every shop. Further toward their destination were shops, and street markets with breads, and fish, fruit and vegetables, butchers and chartuceries, flowers. They wandered among the stalls, stopping to consider and point out unique items to each other, feeling part of the commerce of the street.

"Ah," started Syd with absolute confidence, pointing to some overhead signs. "LOTO et Coca-Cola!"

It was after one o'clock when they sighted Les Deux Magots. They took a table outside, under the awning on the Rue Bonaparte side looking across to the garden of church St. Germain, and settled to a silent contemplation of the busy corner, the menu, and their memories of the morning.

The waiter took his time before attending to them. Finally, Syd ordered "La pression, Heineken, cinquante centilitres"; Arielle ordered "Buckler, en bouteille."

Syd questioned, "Non alcool pour vous?"

"No and yes. My second will be a draft. I'm thirsty. We're not in a hurry, are we?"

"Je n'ai pas presse."

"Look at the prices. Divide by four for Canadian dollars. My beer is $9.50! For a quarter litre!"

"Non problem," said Syd patting his shirt pocket. "Plien ... je pense!"

Both settled into the menu. Finally Arielle said: *"There are markets to buy fruit and some water later; now, I'd like one of the classics, un Croque Monsieur. Ham, not chicken."* She laughed. *"Croque Madame! Same thing with an egg on top. Figure that out!"*

Syd caught the joke. "Croque Monsieur pour moi aussi."

Arielle listened as he gave the order to the waiter, with a degree of confidence in passable French. She was impressed with his easy style.

They sat for the better part of two hours, resting, watching. Syd took out a sketch book and worked leisurely, turning to a new page now and then. Arielle listened to the sounds of Paris. She had reviewed some composers before she came: Ravel, Debussy, Faure.

I wonder what he's like in real life, at home? Can't be married. But those two young men at the airport had to be his sons.

Arielle, she chided herself, you've given up on men. Forget about him other than spending a pleasant day in Paris. Put your mind to something else.

At home along with Ravel and Debussy, she had found a tape of an accordionist playing the songs of Paris. She thought she could hear one now. Playing somewhere off in the market. Likely a buskar. She felt an incredible peace. A comfort she hadn't felt for a long time, if ever. I like being with him, she thought. I feel good when I'm with him. He's nice. Nice. I always think of nice with him.

They entered the Museum d'Orsay. It had been an old railway station. Now an art gallery for Impressionists. Syd had said that he specifically wanted to see Monet's work, not for them to be wandering aimlessly about and miss what he wanted to see. Mind you he had said to her, if there's something good, well, it's all good of course, let's take the time.

They found the Monets. Arielle watched Syd come to a dead stop in front of a painting entitled Gare Saint-Lazare. Minutes passed he didn't move. He stared at the shimmering blue that appeared to be a locomotive just beyond the purplish lines that gave the impression of the high metal struts of a building. Touches of yellow and orange gave it a glimmering of life.

"For an construction man ...," Syd was speaking more to himself than to her, "... I thought Monet just did flowers and rural ... he's painted my stuff ... touched me, ... and now I'm trying to paint his flowers ..."

Arielle moved away toward the decorative panel The Lunch, leaving Syd entranced with the paintings.

Time was lost. Arielle was caught up in what she saw. She had really only looked at the still lifes before, but the few comments Syd had made about Impressionism interested her. She was attentive to what was on the walls.

She heard the now familiar voice, "Ca va?"

He's just checking to see where I am, and am I all right. A little thrill moved through her. I like that. He hasn't smothered or demanded all day. But he has checked on me. I like it. I can trust that he's there. Trust. She felt emotion flood her.

All she could manage was a little smile and a nod.

They finished what they had planned. Agreed they had seen what they wished and exited at the main door.

They had their guidebooks in hand.

Arielle reached in her bag for the large bottle of water she had purchased at the market.

Syd pulled out the same from his bag. He indicated the steps as a seat.

"Buvions un toast a Paris," he said, in his fractured French.

They raised their plastic bottles, clicked them as best they would click, saying: "A Paris."

They sat in a comfortable silence. Arielle had no thoughts of going back to the hotel, but she just realized they had done what they said they were going to do. They had run out of plans. She didn't want to leave him.

"*We've had the best overview of Paris, today* ..." Arielle said for want of something better.

Syd was quiet for a moment. Then he said, "Je sais ou il y a un meilleur ......"

"*A better view?*" She translated.

They both said together: "The Eiffel Tower!"

"Metro. Allons," said Syd on his feet and he reached his hand out to pull Arielle to hers.

The Metro was crowded as only such systems can be at rush hour. They navigated their way through the rabbit warrens to get the correct train, reaching out a hand for the other when needed.

They finally became part of the jam on a car. It was so tightly crowded, that Arielle could feel Syd slide his hand across her back, as much to steady himself as her, for she had a hand hold on a rail and she didn't think he did. His hand stopped at the middle of her back, with no hold at all. She felt his body contract and heard what she thought was a stifled laugh.

"Coded language," Syd said. He was containing laughter.

On a Paris subway car, English could be a code, Arielle considered. But what was so funny?

"We're packed in here so tight," Syd was fighting laughter, "that when I slid my hand across your back, two of my fingers have slid inside this man's shirt."

Both of them were twitching with laughter.

"It's so tight, I can't pull my hand back to get them out." Syd could hardly speak, but he was leaning toward her ear.

The train took a curve. Syd grabbed Arielle's shoulder with the other hand to steady himself.

"As near as I can figure, the man doesn't have an undershirt on."

Arielle nearly guffawed.

"I'm afraid if I move my hand, I'll tickle him."

Both were nearly in hysterics. Arielle tightened her grip on the rail. Syd tightened his grip on her shoulder.

The train slowed for the next stop. They stayed the course.

Syd shook his hand as the transit-rider formation changed at the stop, and they regained their footing and their sensibilities.

Two more uneventful stops took them to the Eiffel Tower.

The view from the top was magnificent. They circled it; stopped; pointed out and named landmarks; consulted their maps; disagreed about details; followed the Seine up-stream; followed it down-stream.

"*They say that the view of Paris from Sacre-Coeur, there, is different, but special.*" Arielle was looking out over the central part of Paris.

"Trouvons. Et nous avons manger le diner quelque part," Syd tossed the comment out.

"*Find Sacre-Coeur?*" Arielle was repeating to tell him she understood, and was that what he meant. "*Montmartre? Dinner?*"

"Pas pourquoi? Du restaurant la? Regardez cette guidebook ordinaire," he said.

"D'accord," she said surprisingly happily. "Fait accompli."

They made their way to the elevator.

"Le Metro encore?" Syd asked.

"*Again,*" said Arielle, "*but watch out for your fingers.*"

They both laughed.

They decided on the scenic route, taking the green line to Charles de Gaulle, change to the purple line to Pigale.

Gaining the street and walking left along the Boulevard de Clichy, Arielle pointed out the Moulin Rouge, as they made their way up the hill toward the Abbesses. Some careful comparing of maps prevented overclimbing or backtracking through the winding streets, until they came along Rue Tardieu that brought them to the foothill of Sacre-Coeur.

The positioning of a carousel in all its spangled glory and the efficient funicular of space-age design was spectacular.

It took Syd and Arielle a trice to decide to ride the funicular up to the church.

The view out over the city as the sun was dropping in the west was as good as that from the Eiffel Tower. Again they pointed out and named landmarks; consulted their maps; disagreed about details; followed the Seine up-stream; followed it down-stream. Paris was still the same, but different.

"Les artistes," said Syd.

"*Around the church. There's a square ..., called, Place du Tertre.*" Arielle had turned her back on Paris. "*Left.*"

"Oui."

They worked their way out of the churchyard and peered into the shops full of cards, posters, souvenirs, and other tourists.

The shops changed into cafes and they were in the square.

Artists with large drawing boards were approaching Arielle to do her portrait. Syd fell a few paces behind.

Arielle brushed off the approaches. However one artist was particularly persistent. He even started to draw her. She tried to discourage him, darting a look toward Syd for help.

Syd, she noticed had pulled a larger sketch book out of his bag and was selecting a pencil. He's not going to help. Well, why should he.

She turned back toward the artist. In truth she felt there has been more than a little flirting in his approach to her, and her responses could easily be misconstrued as playing hard to get. Get out of this gracefully, she thought.

"Non," she said very firmly and walked back to Syd.

He closed his sketch book before she could see. They started to walk around the square looking at the artists' displays, in the fading light.

A quiet was descending over the square. Arielle felt it settling over them.

"*Let's stop for an apertif. Pastisse?*" Arielle suggested.

"Oui," said Syd quietly.

"*A table in the middle of the square?*" Arielle asked.

"Non. Ici." Syd was pointing to the row of caned chairs at small round tables along the edge of a cafe. "Nous vuons toute la monde."

They sat side by side, nearly touching elbows in the crowded space. The waiter came for their order.

The pastisse was served and they watched the clear liquid turn cloudy as the water was added.

They just sat and sipped their drinks as the night fell and the sparkle of the lights filtered through the trees.

At length Syd said, "J'a faim."

"Moi, aussi," said Arielle.

"Mangerons ici?" asked Syd.

Here? she thought. Arielle looked at the cafe, then she looked down at her jogging shoes. Then she took out her all-purpose guidebook.

"*Tourist menu here. This is Montmartre,*" said Arielle. Then she spoke slowly and deliberately: "*Would you care to have dinner with me in one of the little restaurants that we passed on the walk up here? Each put more money in your pocket. True French food.*"

"Oui, merci." Syd sounded pleased.

Then Arielle said mockingly, "*I usually dress for dinner, and do my hair.*" She passed her hand over some tendrils which had escaped their moorings.

"Moi, aussi," said Syd, dusting off the thighs of his jeans.

"*I have an idea. After we choose a restaurant and pay the bill.*"

They looked at the guidebook for Montmartre, and zeroed in on a street, Rue des Trois Freres as a likely place for a selection of restaurants.

Syd settled up with the waiter and they rose to leave.

"*Come,*" said Arielle leading Syd along the sidewalk to the most vacant corner of the square.

"*First, here are more francs.*" They looked at the guide book, estimated one hundred and fifty francs each, and put in two hundred each.

"*Now, I will make* ma toilette!" said Arielle. "*Back to back. Twenty paces. Make your preparations, turn, and wait for the other, then walk together.*"

"Un duel!" Syd laughed. "D'accord."

They turned back to back and set out: "Un, deux, trois, quatre, cinq, six, ...", letting their voices fade out.

Arielle stopped. She set her bag on the pavement and pulled out her sandals. Balancing one foot and then the other, she kicked off her jogging shoes, stripped off her socks, and slid her feet into her sandals.

Then she rooted about in her tote for a cosmetic bag, and took from it some towelette fresheners, like the airlines hand out. She used one to freshen her face and neck. Another one to repeat the same and around her ears.

She released the clip which held her hair in a pile on top of her head and the black stretchy-satin band that had held her hair in a pony-tail.

Carefully brushing her hair loose, she smoothed the curls back from her forehead and ears, as best she could and secured it with the same black band, leaving the rest to swing down her neck and shoulders.

She then took a small bottle of lotion and smoothed it over her face; pulled out a brush and smoothed her eyebrows; a small case opened to produce another brush and she applied some of the contents to her eyes; another little case and brush and something went lightly on her cheeks; a tube of dull lipstick, and a light spray from an atomizer of scent and she was finished.

Arielle deposited the cosmetic bag in her tote, shook out her shawl and after unrolling her sleeves to elbow length, draped it loosely over her shoulders.

She picked up her totebag and assembled her things, paused to consider whether she was finished or not; knew she was put together. He's ready too. He's watching me. A familiar feeling. I know it. How do I know. And she turned toward Syd.

Standing beside a large water spill on the sidewalk, and the empty plastic water bottle in hand, there he was forty paces away looking at her.

A smile broke on his face and she smiled back.

Gone was the baseball hat; his hair was slicked and tied at the nape of his neck. His shoes were clean and still wet. The sleeves of his shirt were neatly buttoned at each wrist and he was wearing a tie! Burnt yellow with coin dots of some kind.

Syd lifted his eyebrows as Arielle nodded and they walked toward each other.

Syd extended his arm. "A le diner."

Arielle took his arm and they set off for Rue des Trois Freres.

There were a number of restaurants along the street. They read the menus in the windows. Agreed. Disagreed. Backtracked and finally decided on Le Petit Chose.

It was rustic. Bare pine, blue cotton curtains. Two levels. Four steps up to a back platform containing six or seven tables. Mostly for two. Some pushed together for four.

They were early by French standards.

The waiter let them chose their table up the steps.

They worked over the menu, Syd questioning Arielle on the meanings. They settled for: Veloute des legumes; Estouffade, Moutarde de Meaux; Tartine Poilane rotee; Magret a l'ananas; Pase de saumon a la va peur sauce generoise; Confit de canard; Cafe liegeois; Coupe charentouise; Fouisselle aux anandes grilles. They let the waiter chose their wine.

It was a lovely dinner. They ate in the quiet bustle of the restaurant, only now and again making a French superlative, but in complete communication.

As they were finishing, Syd said in English, "At the Musee d'Orsay, I didn't want the day to end."

"Neither did I," replied Arielle, in English.

They found a taxi at the main thoroughfare, and rode to the hotel in silence.

At the door, they could see into the lounge area. Ross, two other men from the tour, and Jack Track were having a drink in the reception area which doubled as a bar.

Arielle stopped and turned to Syd, and extended her right hand.

He took it in both hands. Then saying, "Comme en Rome", leaned forward to kiss her on one cheek, the other, and the first again.

"D'accord," she said, looking into his eyes, and then walked through the doors into the hotel.

DAY 8: MONET'S GARDEN AT GIVERNY

"Everyone had been accounted for for yesterday except you and you," said Grace, pointing to Arielle and then to Syd, "until we all saw this." Grace was brandishing a newspaper in front of them, showing them in dance position: Arielle, in her jogging shoes, stepping backward with a gracefully arched back, and Syd, baseball cap determinedly square across his forehead, stepping forward with a deep knee bend. Knapsack and totebag swinging wide.

Grace sounded very angry.

Syd looked around at the rest of the group. Everybody had broad grins on their faces.

"'Americans in Paris', is the caption," said Ross. "Article goes on to say that Paris has been invaded by tourists and fortunately my French isn't good enough to read the editorializing." He was quietly chuckling to himself.

"What were you doing?" Grace demanded.

Syd looked straight at her and said, "Waltzing. Having a lesson."

This drew a good laugh from everyone.

That had been as they were embarking for Giverny to spend the day in Monet's garden.

Syd stood in the garden just out the front door of the house beside the island bed of pink standard roses, under-planted with red pelargoniums and bordered with silver-leafed dianthus. One of Monet's carefully planned colour shadings.

He'd taken a walk around the garden for a cursory overview before he went through the house but he hardly knew where to start.

He'd known before he came on the tour, because Sissinghurst and Giverny were the two places he really wanted to see and had prepared for.

But once more he had this jumble of thoughts and feeling within him, with some feeling of guilt, which had never been there before. Was now. About what?

Dancing.

Not with Marjorie.

Feeling disloyal to Marjorie, or at least the memory of Marjorie. Why?

Because he'd had fun dancing those few foolish waltz steps. With Arielle.

Arielle.

She was still in the house.

Be careful. We're on a trip. No reality.

"There you are," said Grace. "I'm sorry I sounded a bit abrupt over your picture in the paper. It's just that I didn't think it was dignified for a person of your professional standing in our city ...."

"Ah, Grace," said Syd non-commitally.

Swiftly changing the subject as she moved around to face him, Grace said, "Now there's a nice home." She surveyed Monet's house. "That lovely dining room, with twenty chairs. Yes I counted them. To be able to have the whole family and friends as well. I really like that. That's my style."

"Oh," said Syd. Then, "so those Japanese prints with ordinary people doing ordinary things would be to your liking."

"I'd as soon he left those off the wall, and bought some Mikado china. All that blue and yellow is too heavy. Personally, I don't care for yellow."

Syd was thinking of his experimentation with shades of yellow in his house with the effects of seasonal lighting. Grace's comment brought him up short.

Grace darted a glance to the front steps of the house. A frown creased her brow.

Ah, thought Syd, Arielle has come out of the house. He knew where she was. On the top step.

Smiling gamely, Grace made another conversational quantum leap. "We've so much in common, I'd like to spend some of our free time together and get to know each other better."

"Well..., I... I...," Syd was lost for words. No he wasn't. But he just couldn't fire them out to this misguided stranger. He knew damned well they had nothing in common except the fact that he had been in business, as her deceased husband had been; that he was a widower and she was a widow; and that she had an empty role in her life, husband, which she likely wanted to fill. All of which had nothing to do with himself as a person, which Grace had either ignored, or wasn't capable of considering.

He took hold of himself. "I've come to do a lot of painting," he stated.

"Of course, d...," she said with understanding charm.

Grace had clipped off the last word which Syd was certain was to be 'dear'.

Syd squirmed.

He set his easel case directly in front of him, and at arms length, extending the space between himself and Grace. He saw an image of a halo of gold speckled brown hair and a ruffled skirt pass behind him.

Grace must have sensed this distancing, physically, for she smiled sweetly and said, "I must get on with my tour of the garden. This one's easy to get around with it's straight paths and nicely lined-up flower beds. Have a nice time painting. We'll catch-up later."

No we won't, Syd said to himself. She hasn't clued into the fact that I've shown no interest in her at all. I don't find her the least bit attractive. Those awful, cute hats! She just represents the traditional life style we've all had, and that's the extent of the personality of Grace. She sees no farther than her own self, on a life path that has no questions, no growing.

Grace and her life is exactly what I don't want. I know that now, and I'll put her out of my mind. She's as the boys would say, 'Dead meat'. What an expression! I'm not sure I want to be completely with it! But it certainly describes my position on Grace! Period.

The realities are, he thought to himself, that I have to put a stop to Grace, in spite of the fact that there is nothing to stop except Grace's expectations. That has nothing to do with me, except, I, mygawd, am the chosen! It's going to take a bit of finesse, and one sure way not to do it is to latch onto Arielle and make a spectacle of both of us, and, more importantly destroy what might be.

I don't want to stop Grace because of Arielle. I want to stop Grace because of Grace. I don't want her.

To see if anything develops between Arielle and me is quite a separate matter.

Do I want something to develop between Arielle and me? I told the boys I was a reconfirmed bachelor. That was before I met Arielle. A little bit has developed between us. If I'm honest, I do want more.

But the guilt about Marjorie lingers.

Damn Grace, he thought. Here I am with this analytical thinking ... on a subject I don't wish to analyse. Here in the great Impressionist's garden.

Grace is not going to spoil my trip, Syd said emphatically to himself.

Ross and Barbara came down the steps from the house.

"Great view down the Grand Allee, from here," Ross commented to Syd, as they joined him.

Syd knew Arielle had walked down the Grand Allee and had turned left toward the morning 'sunrise' garden.

"Nasturtiums just nicely started," Syd pointed to the growth at the sides of the path under the arches of roses.

"Can you imagine this life compared to the corporate one we lived?" Ross asked.

"Before I retired, I could never have conceived of a purposeful life as a gardener and painter. The fact of the matter is, that's exactly what I am. Now, it's okay."

"You've got your easel there, I see," said Ross. "Going to do a lot of drawing?"

"And painting. Don't look for any masterpieces. It's the inspiration and the glory of colour that's here."

Ross trailed after Barbara toward the side beds with the 'sunset' borders.

Syd had decided to do the Grande Allee first, then the sunrise borders with their cool restful colours of lavender, mauve, pink and blue. He couldn't have been at them as early as Monet, who was painting by first light, but Syd could do the sunset ones with their hot colours of lemon, gold, deep red, and orange with the sun behind them as Monet planned.

It wasn't a difficult garden from a design point of view, but chock-a-block for a painter.

Spend the afternoon in the water garden across the road after he had his mind marginally tuned to Impressionist colours and effects.

That's a laugh, he thought to himself, you've barely got yourself off blue-prints and computer-plans onto nature's precise structure, and you fancy impressionism? I don't know if I'm capable of it, but it's the next step in moving on. Setting sail on a course of discovery. Never to be the same again. Not now the man Marjorie knew, which also accounts for some of the guilt.

At least I've got my linear thinking straight, and it's in a line too! The boys would work that one over!

In a better frame of mind, Syd took his time walking the Grande Allee. He stopped to look at the individual structure of the single roses Monet favoured because they transmit light better. Up on their trellises, brilliant red, silvery-pink and clear yellow, putting colour up and over. Cineraria, hollyhocks, dahlias in mauve and blue with white nicotinia sparkling down and beside.

At the end he looked back. Pink into mauve into blue. That grouping of colours to intensify the impression. The shimmering effect. He had seen it in paintings, or pictures of the paintings.

Syd settled his easel at the end of the Grand Allee looking toward the house as Monet had done. Arielle was still in the sunrise flowers. She had her camera in hand.

Unlike his day at Sissinghurst when his emotions were all over the map, Syd was ready to settle into sketching and painting.

When painting masses of flowers and foliage, he had learned, plan the hard and soft edges carefully to create effects of delicacy and crispness. Use many big blurs. Pick a few flowers to lend accuracy.

Growth, and pain to change. Random thoughts all over the place. Guilt over Marjorie, which surprised him since he never had it before. But maybe because of his growing interest and attraction to Arielle. Feeling disloyal to Marjorie. But he was not being disloyal. She never wanted to control him from the grave. He'd just never been attracted to anyone else before.

The day speaking French with Arielle fit in with his philosophy of less is more. He discovered a lot about her.

Spending the day with Arielle.

Really, Syd didn't know when in his life he had felt better. He had been smiling on the inside all morning and he knew the cause of it all was yesterday. All day yesterday with Arielle. She made him feel good.

He knew she was still there. He didn't need to look. He could feel her presence. He knew she took a picture of him. Maybe two.

He started to do some preliminary sketching and let his mind wander.

I think I've become a new person. No, not a new person but a person who has grown. I have this horrible feeling that we're to be forever teenagers, with emotions and personality growing all our lives. I suppose a person could be scared to death of that and build a careful little structure, or high wall around yourself and cling precariously to what you think you are and want to stay. Safe, I would think, but very, very fragile if something came along and upset your applecart. Something like your wife dying. And trying to hang on to something that is no longer there, or finding someone to fit the mold. Not for me. I'm not looking for a replacement for Marjorie, and I've avoided being the prop that fits someone else's void. Grace doesn't know that.

No, I've moved on and spending the day with Arielle yesterday is part of it. It was me. Syd. Not Marjorie's widower, nor Hughie and Stevie's dad, nor Gramps. Me. Syd. In Paris, with a new person who happens to be on the trip, with no expected structure, except to enjoy the day in good company. And I certainly had all of that and more.

All this thinking. Linear thinking. Thinking in a line. A straight line. The shortest distance between two points.

He let his pencil move freely on the page.

Two points? Zero in on a point and think straight until we come to another point? How tidy.

Not with these flowers.

But which direction do we go? Up? Down? Left? Right? East? West? Forward? Backward? East by Northeast? It sounds like Stephen Leacock's man who jumped on his horse and rode off in all directions.

Can't do it horseback riding, but you can drawing flowers.

Forget about the old world functioning at its most efficient, its best. The analytical left brain of Homo Sapiens in charge of planet Earth.

And a wonderful thing it is too. We have goods and information coming to us and going away from us at a rate of knots. All in a straight line.

The sketch was showing life and form.

The straight and narrow which perhaps is the reason we no longer need religion. Each person on his or her own linear thought. And what with the uniqueness of each individual no one can connect.

Do we end up at cross purposes with only one shared point on each others lines? And we certainly couldn't be going in exactly the right direction unless we got parallel to someone. That would be nice but for how long? Just one thought parallel with one other person's thought.

Maybe some thought on its path might become congruent with someone else's thought. A oneness.

That's that intimacy.

Pure chance.

Chance meeting with Arielle on this trip.

Impossible.

Genes and ecology being what they are.

How much do Arielle and I have in common?

Doesn't matter, we both had a wonderful day yesterday.

But even if one did get that close to another human could there be more than two of us who could do that?

Don't need more than two, except that I'd like her to like my boys and their families. Her family?

Would thoughts be going in the same direction? And surely one thought is not enough to sustain us together for any length of time.

Relationships are impossible unless you grow up in one.

Syd was drawing some hints of detail.

Einstein, he reminded himself, said a line is a curve. The shortest distance between two points is really a curve!

Nice to have an escape; to be released from the straight and narrow and go off on a tangent.

Syd took out his paper, and started to organize his watercolour kit.

Curves. A stroke of the brush. Colour. Connecting.

She walked along the path close to the road, toward the sunset flower beds.

Syd was in a focused world of his own in unreserved happiness.

DAY 9: DRIVE FROM PARIS TO LUCERNE

Out of the corner of her eye Arielle had watched Syd all yesterday at Giverny. He'd been a study in concentration, once everyone left him alone. She'd taken at least five pictures of him, because he seemed to be in the right place at the right time for the light on the flowers. Admit it to yourself that you thought he looked nice and you wanted a picture, pictures, of him.

She felt a little silly about it, but no one saw her, and pictures are private unless one wants to show them.

She was trying to figure out what it was between Grace and Syd. At the pub, that very first night in London, Grace had announced that he was hers.

And Grace seems very hostile toward me. I've experienced this from women before who seemed envious of me. Usually because at my age I seem to have hung onto my body.

But I've kept my distance from Grace and then she fires off at me as at Kew. That dreadful remark about looking divorced, and again when boarding the coach after the channel crossing. Completely uncalled for.

Grace had almost been possessive in her anger at seeing the picture of the two of us waltzing in the park, and Syd's blunt comment back to her had almost a husband-wife sureness.

Then Arielle had seen them talking beside the garden in the front of Monet's house. Grace had walked away with a smile on her lips, and a spring in her step. Arielle couldn't get a read from Syd at all. No expression on his face. No body language.

That nice body. She had briefly brushed his firm thighs, and hit his kneecaps with hers when they were dancing. And no paunch to navigate, as she had had to do with B-Man.

Poor old B-Man. He was going to pot and was definitely in denial. She had never mentioned a word.

She was glad to have those pictures of Syd. She was smiling, experiencing a happiness she hadn't felt for a long, long time. Nice trip, she thought.

The coach was well out of Paris on a broad, sweeping, superhighway.

Arielle saw Grace move out of her seat to confer with Martin and Isobel.

Martin took up the microphone. "Grace, here, has commented that this's a long boring drive to Lucerne. Any suggestions for some amusement? Some local talent, here in the coach? Singing songs? Telling jokes? Any suggestions?"

There was a somewhat shocked silence.

Hanging on against the movement of the coach, Grace rose from her seat behind the driver and with her best winning smile took the microphone from Martin.

"What I meant was, we're no longer going through that nice farm land that Syd liked so much on the way to Paris. Driving takes a long time to Lucerne, and perhaps we could amuse ourselves. Syd, what do you think?"

Grace was beaming her smile the length of the coach at Syd, and stretched her arm toward him in the expectation for him to contribute.

The passengers shifted to look toward him.

Syd, in his seat by the window, remained still.

There was a pregnant pause, as everyone waited for him.

Syd slowly pulled himself to his feet, and with head bent under to storage bins, he said deliberately: "I commented to Grace on our drive to Paris that I enjoyed the changing countryside and that to me we were passing through some interesting farm land." He paused, obviously carefully considering his next words. He continued: "As a person lately come to gardening, I'm fascinated to watch things grow. It takes time, but that's not a drawback. I'm seeing the countryside give way to hills and am interested to watch the terrain become mountainous. Driving through this changing landscape is fast compared to plants growing. I'm enjoying the drive and expect the rest of the trip into Italy will be just as interesting."

Arielle looked at Grace. She was obviously crestfallen.

"Why don't I just hand the mike over to Martin, and he can get on with some of the entertainment he thought would be nice for us all."

"Martin wasn't promoting entertainment, as I recall," Molly said to Arielle.

"That's another one of those bizarre bits of behaviour I've seen from Grace. I can't figure her out."

"You can't? I thought it was as plain as the nose on your face. She's making a big play for Syd. Syd is a widower. You know that don't you?"

"No, I didn't know that." replied Arielle truthfully. She hadn't given any thought to his circumstances. She just enjoyed him as a person, at the given moments. "Molly, about Grace. You're not one to conjecture up gossip about people."

"If I'd said it before Paris, it would have been an unfounded opinion, and I did think it."

"What makes you sure now?" Arielle was curious.

"Well, after Versailles I spent the rest of the day with Jean, in Paris, leisurely seeing some sights, having lunch at an outdoor cafe, a little shopping at Au Printemps, which was in our price range, while Grace strolled the Champs Elysee looking for bargains, or at least something to take home from Paris.

"Jean's sharing with Grace, but Grace has virtually abandoned her. Grace told Jean that she wanted to do more of the fun things than just look at the same flowers over and over again."

"Why did she come on the trip?" asked Arielle.

"Because Syd was on it and she's decided he's going to be hers. Don't you remember that first pub supper in London when she announced he was hers, so hands off?"

"Does she know him?"

"Jean says Grace has a friend in Toronto, another widow, who has virtually landed Syd, and that she, Grace decided she wanted him, and has come on this trip to do the job."

"Sounds horrible," said Arielle wincing. "I think Grace is awful. Supposedly the perfect lady. But pushy and manipulative."

"She's more to be pitied," Molly said.

"You're wonderful, Molly. You can always see another side, or find some good. It's nice that Grace has something to redeem her. Tell me." Arielle was sincere.

"Jean said that Grace was a wonderful wife, mother and grandmother. She created a wonderful home and always had family and friends around. A true chatelaine. Then her husband died, and it's not the same. The family's not centred on her, and she believes if she can marry again, it'll all be the same as it was before. She's so lonely and lost without a man to take care of. And she's decided Syd's the man for her. And Jean said most emphatically that Grace always gets her way."

They rode along in silence.

There had been some small attempt to have people take the mike for jokes, or reminiscences, but it had petered out as passengers watched the approach to the mountains.

Martin made the best of it by drawing everyone's attention to the window boxes of geraniums on Swiss chalets. Often single colour. Just red or just pink. "But," Martin noted, "you have to admit when they put a touch of a second colour in, like some pink with the red, or orange with the pink, it's a much better show. Did anyone know why?"

"Ask Monet," Syd called to Martin.

"Ows fart," came the loud voice of Jack Track from the back of the bus.

"Jack!" scolded his wife Ev.

"Look for yerself," Jack said, pointing to the road sign which read Ausfahrt. "Gracie, how's that for entertainment?"

"That's another pair I can't figure out," said Arielle. "What's the connection between Grace and Jack. Frankly, they're not of the same socio nor economic strata. What in the world do they have in common?"

"If you'd been watching, you'd know," said Molly wisely. "Think about it."

Arielle let her mind drift over the events of the last few days. The only thing that came to mind was an impression of a black and grey L.A baseball hat receding behind Syd as they made their plans to spend the day in Paris.

Arielle let it go, and watched the suburbs become old city, as they drove down Alpenstrasse to their hotel near Lake Lucerne.

It was dark when dinner at the hotel finished. It was included on the tour, so everyone sat down together. Martin announced, "We've a free day tomorrow, and I'm sure all of you have some idea of what Lucerne has to offer, but in case you want some reassurance, the hotel people here have given me a list of suggestions. Of course, there's shopping."

Patti and Peggy and cohorts whooped in delight.

Martin gave them a warm smile. "There are some coupons with the brochure in everyone's room. If you didn't get one, I have some more."

There was a shuffling as if to get up from the tables, but Martin held up his hand. "More to come. There are some hotels along Lake Lucerne that have special lunch and special entertainment, local folk traditions, Swiss Bell Ringers, yodelers, that kind of thing. Very popular. And of course there's the cable car to the top of the mountain." People were starting to stand up. "And we are," Martin said in a raised voice, "just a few blocks, short walk to the Lion Monument, which is particularly beautiful to see at night. Let's meet outside the hotel in twenty minutes, anybody who wants to go together."

"Might as well go," Molly said to Arielle.

"Of course," Arielle replied. "Twenty minutes to freshen up and also take a look around the main floors of the hotel."

They made the street in plenty of time to join most of the tour. Certain groups had formed. The couples inevitably were together and Syd stood in general proximity to Ross and Barbara.

"Come on Jean," Grace instructed her friend, "come on over here where the nice men are." Grace walked well around Jack Track and the wife toward Syd.

"Grace's making her move," Molly commented. "I'll bet dollars to donuts she walks up the street with Syd and sticks with him the whole time."

"Interesting," replied Arielle.

Martin gave the signal to go, and the group moved up the street, past antique shops and mini-supermarkets situated at street-level of apartment buildings. Multi-purpose buildings with the European efficiency in using space.

"You're on your own for crossing," Martin waited at the light as people went across, or waited for the next light. Grace had skipped ahead to be with the couples on the first crossing. Jean joined Molly and Arielle. Arielle detected a comfortable understanding developing between Molly and Jean.

A street off the main road, turn to the left, twenty paces brought them to the edge of a pool in front of sheer rock fifty feet high. Chiselled into the rock face was a lion in agony. Concealed lighting emphasizing his hurt. Silence descended on the group. Anything was said in a whisper, unheard above the splash of water streaming down the wall.

This was the famous Lowendenkmal, to commemorate Swiss soldiers who died in the defense of Tuileries in Paris in 1792.

Arielle walked around the pool to the right. A rise in the land. Nicely landscaped. A completely different view of the lion. The members of the group looked like shadows in a light breeze, shifting one way and then another. A voice stood out, then silence. Grace had moved to Syd's side. They were directly across the pool from Arielle.

Arielle made only a cursory glance to take in the physical dimensions, arrangement, plan of the park. It was calming. The whole atmosphere was hauntingly beautiful. The carved words rang out their meaning.

A few members of the party started to drift away.

Arielle moved back beside Molly and Jean close to the entrance.

"Jean and I are going to head back to the hotel. It's been a long day. Come along when you're ready. We both have our keys. I don't promise to be awake when you come in."

"I won't be much longer, just another look from the other side of the pool," replied Arielle, looking across to where Syd and Grace were standing.

She wove her way silently through the remaining people, glancing at the lion after each couple of steps. The light cast different shadows over his face from each position. A shifting kaleidoscope with each change in angle. Arielle walked behind Grace and then Syd who had moved a good two paces away from her. Arielle continued on another three yards to the edge of the wall. She stopped to watch the light dappled by the tall trees playing on the lion, to listen to the water. She looked back across the pool toward the entrance. Most of the group had worked their way toward the laneway. Grace was still standing in the same place but Syd had shifted to his other foot, moving farther away from Grace and toward Arielle.

Arielle stopped still. She stood still. She was stilled by the harsh beauty of the place. She also knew she was trapped. A sense from Syd was with her. Stay. She was still.

Syd was still. Grace looked at him. He did not look at her.

Grace looked at Arielle. Arielle did not look at her.

Grace took a step toward the last group leaving the park. Syd took a step toward Arielle. They were side by side.

All of Arielle's senses seemed sharper, alert. Her own heart thumped loudly. She could hear Syd's quiet breathing. She heard him swallow.

"Have you made plans for tomorrow?" he asked in a quiet voice.

"Yes. The Richard Wagner Museum on the other shore in the morning, and up the mountain in the cable car for the afternoon." She was matter of fact.

"And your friend Molly?"

"She has plans here in town."

"I thought so. I'm going up the mountain, too. Come with me?"

"Yes." Thoughtful for a moment, then, "I don't like the tourist restaurants at these places, so I take my own food for a picnic. I'll bring enough for you, okay?"

They started toward the last of the group as they were leaving the park, hearing someone say, "Let's all walk down to the lake. The lights will be pretty along the shore and across the covered bridge."

"Twelve noon at the cable car ticket office," Syd suggested.

"Twelve noon, at the ticket office." Arielle agreed.

And they quickened their pace to catch up with the group.

DAY 10: FREE DAY IN LUCERNE

Arielle saw the no-name baseball hat first, waiting in front of the ticket office, leaning on the 'cello' case. She knew he would want to paint and was glad he planned to take the time in spite of asking her to come with him. He expects to maintain his own space and time. Couldn't agree with that more. I hope he expects me to do the same. God knows I can't sit with someone and lose my freedom in dancing attendance on him.

She had this moment of flight. I am going to be with someone all day. I have this wish to withdraw, get out of this, indulge in my own world.

But I realize I must stay with people. It is really unhealthy to be so withdrawn.

Yet I'm apprehensive of any commitment; even short term; a day.

But you had such a wonderful day with this man in Paris.

But that's what bothers me. I'd said to myself that I was finished with men, that I like my own space and time.

I'm feeling rather shy about the attention I'm getting from this man, Syd, because I really want the attention from one man. I like it and I like him.

He makes me feel vulnerable and fussed, but that's what a relationship with a man encompasses. Risk. Emotions on the move, bouncing off someone else's emotions. As close as boxers. Acting and reacting moment by moment. I've been there before, and I love it.

But where's the staying power? Destroy friendship with the recognition of the closeness of maleness and femaleness?

Arielle, she said to herself, this is a trip. You may find out there's not even enough interest between the two of you for even a modicum of friendship, let alone anything else, so don't be silly.

She laughed to herself, I don't believe that for a minute, and was still smiling when she said, "Hello, Syd."

"Good morning, or is it good afternoon?" he said returning her warm smile.

"Both, I think," Arielle added. "Should be a nice afternoon."

Good god, she chided herself, don't talk about the weather the whole afternoon, safe subject as it is. Now settle down. You're the original cool cat.

"Have a good morning?" Syd asked.

"Yes. Richard Wagner Museum. Not surprising, full of memorabilia ... only of interest to a music buff."

"On your own?"

"Yes, why?"

"Nothing, really."

"You have a good morning?" Arielle parried.

"Yes. The Picasso Collection, over in the old part of town. His work, and photos of him at work ... interesting to an art buff," Syd parried back good-naturedly.

"On your own?" Arielle kept it up, in the same tone.

"Actually, no. Jack Track tagged along, which is the only way I can put it."

"I never fancied him to be an art buff. Anything but," said Arielle with a mildly incredulous look on her face.

"He isn't," said Syd.

"Then why did he go?"

"He has his reasons."

Arielle was still looking blank.

"We've got some choices to make," said Syd waving a map and what appeared to be a train schedule.

"It says here on this brochure, for Mount Pilatus ... which is our mountain, we can take the cog-wheel train straight to the top, no stops, or we could take cablecars, which do short runs, and a funicular somewhere along the route."

"Do it in stages? Can we walk around part way up the mountain?" Arielle asked. She was peering over Syd's arm to see the map.

"Yes," said Syd, "here and here."

"So we could stop off somewhere for our picnic ..."

"And I'd like to paint ..."

"And I could wander around and explore ..."

"Sounds good to me," said Syd with a note of finality to the negotiations. "We have to take the bus, the No.1 bus, to Kriens, and then take the cablecars from there. Take a look at the map," he said as he moved closer to Arielle, "... cable station at Frakmuntegg appears to be a good place to stop ..."

"Okay," agreed Arielle. "Shall we activate the treasury?"

Syd patted the pocket on his shirt, and undid it's button.

"How much?" asked Arielle. She pulled some Swiss francs from her purse and fanned them out toward Syd.

"I figured this out before," Syd said, "and I'll take this and this ... but you bought the lunch ... so that's enough." He was calculating as he took the cash.

"I'll hold your cello case while you get the tickets," Arielle said in a light tone.

"My ... cello ...? Oh, you mean my easel! Right. Hey! You're not going to make me, uh, ... Sprechen Sie Deutch?"

Arielle felt relaxed and comfortable at the recognition of their past shared experience. She didn't want to be too familiar, but on the other hand they had spent a rather special day together in Paris.

"You're in luck," she laughed, "my German is limited to some arias from opera, and I'm not about to burst forth!"

"Good," replied Syd as lightly. "Mine's limited to wartime comic-book German, or a few made up words like untergrunden and wisenheimer. Here! I better get these tickets or we'll never leave Lucerne."

I'm having a nice time already, too. Arielle felt at ease and happy.

They rode silently and comfortably on the bus, leaving the city build-up behind; onto the cablecar to Frakmuntegg, enjoying the calm and majesty of the trees and fields below them as they swung over the great mountain.

"Aaron Copland. Appalachians," said Arielle.

"Pardon?"

"I'll tell you sometime," said Arielle, surprising herself.

At the Frakmuntegg station, they made their way along the footpath suggested by kindly climbers, who seemed familiar with the area.

"Edelweiss." Syd pointed at patches of white-flowering plants. He stooped down to look closely at some small pink flowers. "Have to be alpines," he commented.

They found a clearing just off the path, level enough for Syd's easel and big enough to spread their small picnic. Surrounded by mountains.

Arielle pulled the packages of food from her totebag, and then flattened it on the ground to make a tablecloth. She proceeded to unwrap the packages and set out lunch.

"Catered by the deli behind the hotel, Hertensteinstrasse. Bagette ... French bread, Swiss cheese ..."

"That's hardly a surprise!" Syd laughed.

"... salami .... I managed to be understood enough to get it sliced! Tomatoes, celery, grapes and some nice, dark Swiss chocolate. And here's my Swiss Army knife to serve this splendid repast! Also a stack of paper towels for a plate, napkin or whatever."

"I'm impressed," said Syd.

"I just bought bottled water," said Arielle apologetically. "I can't handle beer or wine at lunch, when I'm mountain-climbing! Besides I thought the top of the mountain might be a good place to indulge ..."

"I've become a carrier of the big bottle of water since my experience in Paris. I can paint just as well with it as tap water. Multipurpose water. Can even bathe in it on the street!" Syd looked at Arielle, teasingly.

"What can I say?" was the best retort she could think of.

They sat on the ground at each end of the totebag and served themselves lunch.

"I've seen you eat outside a number of times on this trip," said Syd.

"Yes. I don't like restaurants, and I like real food. I've discovered real food."

"What do you mean?" Syd asked.

He's genuinely curious, thought Arielle. He's curious about me, I believe. I think he would like to know whatever I said. That's nice, she thought.

She told him about her long walks in Toronto, through the ethnic areas and seeing the beautiful displays of produce, and seeing foods she had never known before, and of her concern with nutrition of her dance pupils, and cooking for herself for health; even reading cookbooks about origins of food.

"Did you see the book Monet's Table at the shop at Giverny? A work of art. Also Catherine di Medici. You know, I talked about it in Paris at the Jardin de Tuilieres. I've rabbited on," Arielle said apologetically, "But the older I get, the more I understand that you are what you eat!"

"So that's why the comments in England about the vegetables at Kew," said Syd.

"And I did see those plots ...."

"Allotments..."

"Right, that you told me to watch for ... along the side of the roads in England."

They sat in comfortable silence.

"Then I discovered Still Life paintings. I knew about them before, but I used to think 'so what' ... but now I know. That was nice at the Musee d'Orsay."

They both drifted into silent memory of the shared experience.

"But you're the painter. I saw you absolutely engrossed at Monet's garden." Arielle said, and felt a blush spread over her cheeks. I've given it away. Surely he couldn't intuit just how much I watched him, she thought with alarm. He wouldn't know I took pictures of him!

Syd appeared to take no notice, or did she see a hint of something on his face.

Recovering, she asked "Have you always been a painter?"

"No, and to be truthful, I'm not much of a painter now. Except for my own pleasure in it, and the constant pleasure in the joy of discovery. I overuse the word pleasure!"

Arielle thought she must have looked as interested in what he had to say as he did when she was talking, for he carried on with some highlights of discovering gardening after he had retired from his work, and the wonder of the structure of nature.

"Don't ever ask me about the buds of the lavatera plant as they open up into full flower, because I'll tell you and go on and on and bore you out of your mind." Syd laughed. "Don't say you weren't warned."

"I could never fault anyone for getting absorbed in something," Arielle commented absent-mindedly, as she tidied up the remains of the lunch.

She sat and watched Syd assemble his easel, settle his camp stool on the level, and open his knapsack.

He pulled out a heavy plaid shirt and set it on the ground. "I'm not sure how much it'll cool off at the top of the mountain," he said, and he continued to remove his painting materials.

"Ca va?" he asked.

"Okay." Arielle answered, as she sat on her empty totebag.

She reached over for Syd's big shirt, and asked: "May I?"

Syd nodded, and went on with his paints.

As she folded it up for a pillow, a passing breeze stirred the smell of his maleness caught in his shirt to her nose. A reaction of her own sexuality flared in the depth of her body. Him. Syd. I like him.

Controlled, carefully, deliberately, she pillowed the shirt under her head and stretched out on the ground, eyes closed.

She was wide awake. She was listening to the sounds of the mountain. The air was a whisper of breeze one moment, a swoosh of wind the next. It repeated. It echoed. Songbirds sang over this base. Trees rustled. A melody line from memory played through her mind to this accompaniment. Another part of her brain recognized the Vivaldi. La Primavera. Spring on this mountain-side. She let the music flow through her mind, ever-aware of the sounds of the mountain.

"You asleep?" Syd asked quietly.

"No," Arielle answered.

"Didn't think so," he said. "I want you to look at the light."

"When I finish playing this bit," said Arielle.

"When you finish playing this bit," Syd repeated quietly. Then, "I see, said the blind-man." And he fell silent.

Syd stole some cursory looks at Arielle as she was stretched out on the ground. He knew she was not asleep, in spite of having her eyes closed, as there was an alertness to her face, and her eyelids moved as if blinking.

He had been painting for half an hour and in that time was amazed to see the quality of light change.

He dropped his baseball cap on the ground as he surveyed the heavens for a weather change, but none was evident. It's just the time of day, and this particular place. This light is so clear. Pristine.

He watched Arielle open her eyes and look about.

"The light has changed," she said.

"You can see it?" Syd marvelled.

"Yes. Likely because I've had my eyes closed and it makes a sudden change. If I'd been looking all the time it would have happened so gradually I wouldn't have noticed. I don't suppose you noticed the sounds?"

"There were no sounds in particular," said Syd.

"I suppose it's a cliche now that the hills are alive with the sound of music." Arielle let the spoken words roll into tune.

"What did you mean when you said you had to finish playing that bit. I'm really curious."

"I'm a musician. As well as teaching I play the violin in a symphony orchestra, and for studio work."

"You play professionally?"

"Yes. And I tend to hear the world more than see it. Auditory learner rather than a visual one, like you." She went on to tell him that when learning, it's important to be able to play a piece in your mind within the correct time, and sometimes when at leisure, she actively played a piece in her mind while appearing to be in repose.

"So going to the Wagner Museum today, was more than a touristy music buff." Syd challenged.

"Yes," admitted Arielle.

Syd continued to paint. He remembered from school choir, and he struck a note in a clear baritone, then sang: down up up down down up down up same up; to the words: "Dear land of hope ..."

Arielle brightened in delight. "Not bad. But that's Sibelius'

Finlandia! Wagner is The Pilgrim's Chorus."

"I always got those two mixed up," Syd said, and then struck a lower note, then sang: up down down same up up same up down same down up; to the words: "Once more dear home I with rapture behold you, and ..." He stopped, watching her face light up with complete surprise.

Arielle grabbed Syd's baseball hat and threw it in the air, exclaiming, "I don't believe it! You know some music!"

Syd was looking very pleased with himself. "And why not? Engineers managed to get some culture along the way." He was making fun of himself, and revelling in the joy she exuded.

She looks the way my daughters-in-law look after they've worked out, the way so many of the young women of today do. I like the look of it on them, and she, this Arielle, has the same look. So alive, so healthy, so beautiful, so attractive. He felt full of joy and happiness himself.

Syd turned his attention back to his painting.

He could still see her out of the corner of his eye, and saw her spring to her feet, pick up his baseball hat, whack it on her thigh to remove the dust, and clap it in her head.

"I see why you wear one of these," she said pulling her long curly hair into a pony tail through the back gap. "I'm going to walk a bit. Need to move."

"Okay," Syd said more calmly than he felt. "I'm going to finish up in another fifteen minutes."

"And then we'll go to the top."

I'm at the top, Syd thought to himself as he watched her half run, half walk down the path, her tangly hair bouncing out of his cap.

I'm absolutely hooked on her, he thought to himself. Just a trip be damned. I'm going to enjoy every minute I get to be with her, and I'm going to try to be with her a lot. I'll likely watch her all the rest of the time.

They made one more stop at a cablecar station on the way up, drinking in the majestic sights in the rarefied air.

They seldom spoke, but communicated by eye contact, the odd touch as they pointed out the sights.

The cablecar deposited them at the top of the mountain.

"I'm not about to sing 'I'm sitting on top of the world'," Syd commented to Arielle, "although I do feel like it."

He was turning about for the panoramic view.

"I won't try to paint here, I couldn't capture any of this with my brush. One never knows what to expect," Syd said.

I hope she takes that for literal comment about the geography. I think I really mean my emotions.

"Let's get a drink at the outside bar and sit as close to the edge of this mountain as the proprietors have deemed safe."

Arielle had pulled her cowled sweater on, and Syd his heavy shirt, in the wonderfully cool air.

Not quite stations of the cross, they walked about the walls stopping and leaning over.

First stop, shoulders touched and held together as if glued.

They rarely broke physical contact as they moved on. A slight turn of their head put them in eye contact which neither backed away from, nor wanted to break.

It was only a nudge with an elbow, or a tug on a sleeve, always physical, which caused them to change.

It was when they had come full circle to look over the cross-shaped Lake Lucerne, sparkling lights from the city dancing on the water, to see the first star in the sky that they paused in intimacy and trust.

They moved closer to each other, leaning their elbows on the wall.

"Beautiful," whispered Arielle, as she turned her head toward Syd.

"Yes," he said to her as their eyes locked.

Time stood still.

Eyes. Deep pools. Touching in the depths.

Unafraid, beyond risk, their steady eyes came close, and their moist lips brush each others. Just for a moment.

Their eyes still held as they moved apart, and smiled at the other eyes.

And their lips came together again and held, momentarily out of sight, and slowly caressed each other across once, twice, and drew apart.

Their eyes looked at the sparkles of nature, their beings remained close and still.

They took the non-stop cog-wheel train down, and made their way back to town. Syd had draped his arm across Arielle's shoulder to keep them in physical contact, but in communicative silence.

They decided to walk to the old part of town for late supper at an outdoor cafe.

Cafes were tucked into little side lanes, and they wanted to go far enough that they could back track across the river to the far entrance to the covered bridge and walk it on the way back to the hotel.

As they stepped over the cobblestones, warm and balmy at the bottom of the mountain, Syd switched his easel bag to his other shoulder, as Arielle moved to his other side. He draped his free arm across her shoulders again. They had mastered the manoeuvre as they walked along.

They slowed to peek down a side lane and saw some occupied tables at a cafe that seemed to be doing an evening business.

"Extra fart!" Jack Track's voice rang out.

"Jack!" Ev barked at him as at an unruly child.

"We've found our friends," said Syd gently as he let his arm slide down from Arielle's shoulders.

"Right, Gracie?" Jack's voice was really too loud for the table conversation. "Y' saw it. I showed it to y', on one of the boats at the dock, across from the Mountain ticket office. Around noon, today."

Arielle looked up at Syd. "Jack Track was with you this morning, and then was with Grace around noon across from the ticket ..." Her voice trailed off.

"You've put the two and two together," said Syd, "but have you come up with the correct answer?"

"I've been having a tough time trying to figure out the friendship ..."

"It's not friendship ..."

"Between Jack and ..., ... she, Grace could have come with us today ..."

"Un-huh," said Syd.

"We would've just thrown her off the mountain ..." Arielle said simply, as they approached the tables.

"You horrible little man." Grace spat the words at Jack. "Don't talk to me. Don't ... don't," she was too angry to speak coherently, "... ever, never ever come near me again. If you do," she was shaking her finger at Jack, "I'll tell. I'll ...I'll tell Martin!"

As Jack made space for Syd and Arielle at the table he and Ev were sharing with Barbara and Ross, Grace turned all smiles.

"You," she said dismissing Arielle with a frosty glare and focusing only on Syd, "look as if you've had a nice day."

Jack looked from Syd to Arielle and back to Syd. Nodding his head, Jack quietly said: "Mission accomplished."

Arielle had greeted Molly, who was sitting at the next table with Grace.

Arielle couldn't not hear Grace say to Molly, "He doesn't want her."

"Who knows?" Molly said absently.

"I do," said Grace with brusk authority. "I know men. They don't know what they want. She'll do nothing for him in Toronto. She's not socially connected to get him in if he isn't in already or keep him in if he is. He's just too good-looking to let him go to waste on her. If he'd only cut his hair. He's what I want."

"He may have other ideas," suggested Molly.

"He doesn't," snapped Grace with determination, "not if he knows what's good for him. We'll see it happen tomorrow."

DAY 11: DRIVE TO TUSCANY

Grace followed Syd out of the hotel after breakfast, bringing with her the heavy, lingering scent of one of the modern-day perfumes.

She stood beside him until the coach arrived for the day's drive to Tuscany; followed on his heels into the coach and sat in the seat beside him.

"I said we were going to have a chance to get to know each other," she said sweetly.

Syd had hoped to share his seat with Arielle today. He still felt a closeness to her, and he wanted to connect with her at the start of a new day.

He had watched for Arielle, but when Grace arrived on the scene and he knew he wasn't going to be able to shake her.

Actually Molly and Arielle were among the last to arrive very close to departure time when he was already stuck in the seat by a tenacious Grace. He could feel her grip through the space he worked to maintain between them.

Syd was barely able to mouth a good morning to Arielle as she made her way along the aisle. He thought he detected a slight raise of her eyebrows when she saw Grace sitting beside him. He didn't know how to read her look, but he was concerned that she should have any doubts about him, and what was happening between them.

"Shirley said," Grace started to explain.

"I'm not interested in what Mrs. Wallace said," said Syd firmly. "I've no more than a passing acquaintance with Mrs. Wallace at our church."

Damn this woman anyway.

"Excuse me," Syd said pulling himself up from his seat. "Please may I get out."

He stood with his head crowded under the overhead bin waiting for Grace to move out of the way.

"We're nearly ready to leave," she protested.

Syd watched a pout distort the overly made-up face. It never registered with me how ugly women's cosmetics could be, Syd thought.

"Excuse me," he said as firmly as he dared without creating a scene.

Grace heaved herself awkwardly out of the seat.

I can't stand the sight of this woman. Her made-up face, and then the heavy cloying perfume she was wearing hung in the air so heavily he could hardly breathe.

Be damned if I am going to drive through mountain country with this triumph of consumerism marring my time.

Syd made to the door of the coach as Martin and the driver were battening down the luggage hatch at the bottom of the coach.

Between deep gulps of air, Syd said to the waiting Martin and driver: "I'll step in last. I'm going to sit on that courier's seat beside the door here. Great way to see the mountains."

"Okay, buddy," said Martin. "You're not sick?"

"No, no. I'm fine." Syd reassured him.

It was as good as driving the coach. Syd felt the freedom of the road, the isolation of a long trip on one's own, as the other passengers were out of sight behind him.

He knew he had to do something about Grace. He had no interest in her. He had to be rid of her, notwithstanding she was no connection of his to put aside.

Trouble with a trip like this, there's nowhere to hide. He didn't want to hide. This was his trip. He had met Arielle. He wanted to spend more time with her. Get to be friends with her.

Funny, he thought, only a few days ago he was cautioning himself about the unreality of a trip in getting to know someone. Who's to say this isn't reality, and living and working in Toronto is a fantasy!

Boy, fella, you've come a long way, even considering a thought like that. Face it, now you're a gardener and a painter. Not just botanical watercolours, but aspirations for impressionism. Symbolically a long, long way from the conventional life of your past. It's where I am now, he thought.

Grace is all that I am not any more. I don't even want to consider it. Beyond choice.

I'll be rid of Grace. I'll have to tell her without causing a scene.

Syd mindlessly let the miles roll past, appreciating the scenery, like a wash in a painting.

The coach stopped at eleven.

Syd stood outside while everyone filed off. Grace joined him and waited beside him.

As the last passenger stepped down, Syd said, "Excuse me," and boarded the coach for his knapsack.

Grace was waiting for him when he alighted.

He purposefully strode toward the Rest and Service Centre, watching for Arielle. He couldn't care less that Grace was trying to keep up to his stride.

Was he going to use Arielle to save himself from Grace?

I can't do that, he thought. That's putting too much strain on the beautiful, yet-fragile relationship he and Arielle were experiencing.

I'm not sure she's mine in that old sense, to flaunt at Grace.

That's not the way. I don't want to do that.

It's Grace or not Grace. Arielle doesn't figure into that equation.

It's having Arielle or not having her.

The very thought of having her in all it's sense gave him a lift of excitement and a flood of comfort. Not to own her. Marjorie and I never owned each other in those unlightened days, and it would never ever be a consideration with the free spirited Arielle.

But, of course, does Arielle want me. This is just a trip. We've had some nice times together. Maybe that's all. All she wants. All I want. No, I think I want more. I know I want more.

Grace'll have to go to the ladies' room and I'll be free of her for a while.

He noticed a line-up for the Ladies'. Thank heaven for small mercies, he thought.

Syd got some coffee to go, and went outside, knowing Arielle would be there. She was. Pacing slowly away. One hand with coffee. The other jammed into her pocket.

"Ca va?" Syd asked softly.

Arielle turned at the sound of his voice and acknowledged him hesitantly.

He felt that closeness was gone. Felt a distance between them. Constraint.

His eyes smiled at her. He couldn't find words.

She nodded her head in some small tacit agreement.

They heard Martin call from the coach: "All aboard."

"Trust me," Syd said.

He ambled toward the coach and waited beside the door. Grace waited with him.

"If you're going to sit up at the front, I might as well sit in my regular seat with Jean. You can tell me all about the scenery."

"You sit where you want to sit," Syd said coolly.

Syd waited outside with Martin.

"Tell me, Martin," Syd began, "what're the planned stops for the rest of today's drive?"

"It's eleven fifteen now. We'll stop for lunch from one until two, then straight through. Should arrive at the hotel in Tuscany four-thirty."

With the passenger list in hand, Martin boarded, darting a nervous look at Syd.

Syd noted Grace was not beside Jean, so he chose the courier seat again. He formulated his plan, then sat back to enjoy the drive.

With lunch tray in hand, Syd went back to the cafeteria line to Grace.

"When you have your tray, join me for a meeting."

"Surely, you can't be so serious," Grace replied, all smiles. "Aren't you going to treat me to a nice lunch?"

"No," said Syd. "I'm going to get a table."

When Grace arrived at the table, Syd did not stand.

She said, "A gentlemen usually stands when a lady joins him at the table."

"At this moment," said Syd, "I am not a practising gentleman, I am a pragmatist." He was speaking evenly and deliberately.

"Whatever that is," said Grace sarcastically. Then, "How are we going to carry on a nice conversation ..."

"That's exactly what we're not going to do," said Syd setting aside his soup bowl. "I am going to speak.

"I don't know why you came on this trip," he said, "but if it had something to do with getting to know me, you have made a dreadful mistake."

"But, Shirley said ..."

"I am not responsible for what Mrs. Wallace said," Syd countered, "I'm on this trip to enjoy gardens and scenery and painting, and to chose who I wish to be friends with. If I'm lucky the ones I want to be friends with ..."

"That Arielle," said Grace in derogatory tone.

Syd paused, "I repeat, if I'm lucky the ones I want to be friends with want to be friends with me."

"I want to be friends with you." Grace's voice was rising. "I've been trying the whole trip, but you ..."

"Alas, Grace, I do not want to be friends with you. Nothing more than a polite passing acquaintance."

Syd was eying the remainder of his lunch, trying to time what he had to say with what he had to eat.

Undaunted, Grace carried on. "Why not? We have so much in common."

"I'm not going to be pulled into some kind of an analysis of who you are and who I am."

"I know who you are," Grace said confidently.

Syd put his fork into an apple something. He didn't answer.

"You're a retired professional businessman," Grace explained. "A widower and you'd like your life to carry on just like it used to, like I'd like my life to carry on. When you shave off that beard and cut your hair, I'll bet you look just like you did going to business."

"And we would have enlightened conversations like this?" said Syd, struggling to keep a civil voice.

"Who cares about an enlightened conversation. I'm talking about being a couple. We can forget about that nonsense, like you suggested to Shirley over the phone. I like my own room and want to keep it."

Syd was silent. "I've finished my lunch," he said matter-of-factly, "and I've finished my association with you. Good afternoon."

Syd put his tray on the stand, and headed outdoors.

With nary a glance one way or the other, Syd boarded the bus and unfolded the seat inside the door. He crossed his arms on his chest and watched the traffic and the road as carefully as the driver.

A good hour later Syd realized he was paying attention to the structure of the roads, the sweeping curves, the bridges, the tunnels as raptly as he had when he was a teenager, excited about building, and preparing to enter the university in Civil Engineering.

Taken back to his boyhood, to himself, by these magnificent examples of engineering that built a smooth, efficient, safe transportation system through one of the most mountainous terrains in the world, he felt himself relax. Tension draining away. He felt himself.

Must be close to Italy now, he thought, waiting for the road signs to change to announce the border crossing.

Through the border, and it still looked the same. You know you're in England by looking out the window. Not so here.

Eventually they made the Lombardy plain, passing some languid lakes to by-pass Milan.

On the outskirts, Milan looked like any modern city, with its suburban development and new commercial buildings. He'd have to take the truth of the guidebooks on faith.

They were heading for a small hotel in the hills of Tuscany, northeast of Florence, to stay four nights, then fly out of Milan for Toronto.

Most would be ready to stay put, or to enjoy the day trips on the itinerary. Florence the next day, small Tuscan hill towns the following day, with a farewell end-of-the-trip dinner at their hotel that night. Martin had explained they had to do it one day early because of the optional plan for the last day. Siena, Pisa or Venice.

The coach strained it's way up a steep grade, around a long curve, and pulled into the parking area at the entrance of the hotel. It had been a fifteenth century residence, and was now converted into an intimate country guesthouse.

The view of the surrounding countryside showed rows of cypress, and olive groves; within, a series of sparsely planted courtyards worked their way to a beautiful central garden.

Rooms either looked out unto the hills, or in on the garden.

Syd hung back with the driver and the bellboys who were moving luggage. He let the others get ahead of him and be assigned rooms.

He didn't want to risk any further association with Grace, and he didn't want to appear too eager to be with Arielle. He was sure everyone on the trip was aware of the dynamics he was involved in with both women.

It's just not my style, he thought. I'm never involved in the sensational, except in a private way. Well, he chided himself, you did want to change, to move on. You've got it. Even if it isn't what you expected. You can't control everything, especially when you're stepping off the known path.

As he made his way to the portico at the hotel reception, Grace emerged from behind a pillar.

"Now," Grace said, in a tough voice, "I have something to say to you."

I'm trapped, Syd thought. I don't want to hear what she has to say!

"You made me come on this awful trip," Grace started.

I can't listen to this tirade, thought Syd. All of a sudden, he had a recollection of Arielle saying she used to practice violin in her head.

"All these boring gardens ..."

Sing! In your head! What? Christmas carols! Anything!

As Syd turned sideways to Grace and lent her a deaf ear, inside his head he burst forth with the bass of Joy to the World, the Lord is come, let earth receive her king!

Keep the women's voices going for Let every heart ..., it's working! He drowned out most of Grace's voice.

"... spending all this money, on something I knew I wouldn't like ..."

...counterpoint? ... and heaven and nature sing, and heaven and nature sing .... on into four parts, full organ ...

"... disgusting greasy Italian food, swimming in olive oil and reeking of garlic ..."

Next verse, thought Syd, Joy to the earth, the Saviour reigns, let men their songs employ! He laughed.

"Are you listening to me?" Grace demanded.

...repeat the sounding joy, repeat the sounding...

"I've had enough of you," Grace barked at Syd, turned on her heel and flounced her way into the hotel.

"No more let sins and sorrows grow," he sang softly aloud. He sang, whistled, or hummed the melody, as he made his way to the desk finishing with the words "..and wonders of his love, wonders, and wonders, wonders, of his love."

Syd's room, one flight up, had large glass French doors that opened onto a narrow balcony. Neither the low railing nor the leafy arbour directly below obliterated the view of the garden.

All traditional Tuscan gardens, he knew, of whatever size contain an arbour, a shady sitting-out area furnished with simple chairs and a table where meals could be enjoyed on hot summer evenings.

It was a relief. He needed a garden. More and more he appreciated the calm they induced.

Syd sat on the edge of his bed, took off his mountain shoes and socks, slid out of his beige Gap pants making sure his shirt tails covered his grey cotton-knit boxer shorts.

He spent a few minutes unpacking, hanging up what was fresh, finding a laundry bag for hotel service, putting toiletries in his bathroom.

It was a nice room. Big enough for a double bed centred on the wall at right angles to the balcony. Nice to settle in here for a few days. Help to collect my thoughts.

He stepped into his Birkenstocks, rolled up his shirt sleeves and pulled the armchair in front of the balcony. He could see out, but likely no one could see far enough into the room to invade his privacy.

He didn't want to be seen. He needed to be detached. He had been through more emotional action in the last few days than he had for a long time. A very different kind.

He reached for a sketch book and pencils, and idly drew the garden. It was rather large, with a parterre at his far left coming off the dining room. A few tables and chairs outdoors.

The arbour, directly below him was basically a terraced patio covered by an arch with vines growing over it but looked out onto the garden by the far open side. A loggia. Same view that he had. Long tables and chairs in it. It was for bigger groups to dine al fresco. He knew this was where the last group supper was to be.

It was beautiful. His mind came to peace.

He worked quietly, with minimum movements.

When you come to peace within yourself you think a lot about love, he mused.

Then when you get some loving feelings about a woman, about Arielle, you feel anything but peace. The heightened precipice of risk, and fear of losing the freedom of time and space which brought you to the feeling of peace in the first place. But it's Arielle.

He let his mind drift over the images he had of her, not being able to place her the first few days: well maybe by the water garden, then watching her select clothes in the market. He smiled to himself at that memory. Her calmness at Kew. Then at Sissinghurst ... and Paris ... and he knew she had taken some pictures of him at Giverny. He had sensed where she was all that day.

He set his drawing aside, and dwelt on that perfect day with her on the mountain.

Was that only yesterday?

That closeness, intimacy they felt. He had. He was sure she had. He could almost feel her touch. Even if it was only a shoulder, or a hand on an arm, they had been close. The kind of closeness he had only dreamed of. The deep pools of her eyes. Who had kissed who? It wasn't a kiss. It was a caress.

That closeness was lost. The kind of closeness he and Marjorie had, ultimately got lost. They had moved in and out of each others aura for a while, new shyness to be overcome if they let the distance get too far.

And now, with Arielle. A constraint as a result of the misfortunes of today. A day when he had hoped they could have negotiated tomorrow in Florence. Together. How could he do it now? He did so hope she had trusted him. It was the only thread.

The sun was going down. Dinner was here. Group. Fixed menu. Shower.

Face the world.

DAY 12: FREE DAY IN FLORENCE

The buzz at breakfast was that Grace, who had taken to her bed the evening before, was ill. Arrangements were being made for her to return to Toronto that day.

"Arielle," said Molly, "I'd like to talk to Jean and see how this affects her plans. She's a bit of a timid soul, but intelligent and pleasant company."

Arielle watched as Molly took her coffee cup over to the table where Jean was eating her breakfast with Lorraine, Isobel and Martin.

Syd had been finishing his breakfast when she and Molly had come in. They made eye contact briefly acknowledging a "Good Morning".

Arielle had to admit she was clinging ever so slightly to Molly at this moment. She had that terrible familiar feeling of betrayal that she had experienced during her last few years with B-Man. It had been quite overwhelming at the end, but it had come on so gradually, she had not realized how strong and distasteful it was. Was the familiar feeling upon her now anything to do with Syd? Or was it just afterburn of her own experience?

But yesterday, ... was it only yesterday? ... He had said, "Trust me."

Could she? Was he trustworthy? Deep in her heart of hearts she wanted to believe him. Trust him. Perhaps it was her problem of not believing someone was trustworthy. I may be faced with the most trustworthy man in all Christendom, and I, me, Arielle cannot convince, allow myself, to trust him!

Certainly their day together on the mountain was not some fluke. Was she that bad at judging character? She didn't think so. She'd ultimately judged B-Man correctly. She believed she'd judged Syd correctly.

That closeness, trust they felt. She had. She was sure he had. She could almost feel his touch. Even if it was only a shoulder, or a hand on an arm, they had been close. The kind of closeness and trust she had only dreamed of. The deep pools of his eyes. Who had kissed who? It wasn't a kiss. It was a caress.

Now that closeness was lost. She believed it could stay within range.

She and B-Man could never sustain closeness, try as she may. They had come together on expected occasions: after a party, at night in bed, just because it was the expected thing to do and they were in the same geographical place. Habit, which became meaningless.

And now, with Syd. A constraint as a result of the misfortunes of yesterday. A day when she had hoped they could have made plans to be together in Florence. How could they do it now? She did so hope she could trust him. It was the only thread.

She knew if she went outside, she would find him waiting.

She couldn't.

Molly returned to their table.

"It's all working out rather well," Molly said. "Lorraine is going to move in with Jean, as Jean said she really couldn't stay alone. They are going to adjust Lorraine's single supplement ... well, I don't need to go on about that. I said that I'd pal around with Jean just as Lorraine and I have been doing all along. No change in what we've been doing. Everybody's happy."

Molly was silent for a moment. "Jean says Grace is desperately lonely for the life she had with her husband, and heard through a friend that Syd was looking for a replacement for his wife. Grace assumed Syd wanted what she wanted. Grace is nearly sick trying to make a home for herself."

I can sympathize with Grace on one count, Arielle thought, of making a home for yourself. But that's what you do. Your own self-worth is at stake. Making a home for yourself. Cooking for yourself. Arranging your time yourself. Tough stuff.

On the second count, does he want what I want. What do I want? Simply the trust and love of a man. Syd? Yes. What does he want, though?

Arielle heard Molly say: "Go outside, dear. He'll be waiting for you."

Forget about this being a trip, Arielle thought. You want to be with him.

Without a word, Arielle got up from the table. She walked out the sliding glass doors onto the terrace section of the restaurant, and followed the path toward the garden. Syd was sitting on the steps, expressionlessly watching her approach.

"Ca va?" Arielle said to Syd.

Relief flooded his face. He managed a tentative smile.

"Will you be with me in Florence, today?" he asked her directly.

"Yes," she answered quickly, "but on one condition." She saw a reserved look come over him. "A good condition. Let's keep it private, like, sit in our same seats. I'll ride with Molly and then when we get there ... have you got a guidebook?"

"Get your skates on," Syd said, mockingly bossy, "the coach leaves in twenty minutes. Talk to you in Florence."

"Before we de-bus," Martin said from the microphone, "I'd like to remind you of the plans for the next three days.

"We're settled into the hotel..., and yes, there's lots of shopping in the vicinity,... here in Tuscany until we depart by plane from Milan on Day 15. Tonight, Day 12, we leave Florence at 10 to 10:30pm from the Station," he attempted to say, Stazione, "Centrale, so have your supper in town. Anybody who wishes to stick with Isobel and me, please do. We'll see lots of sights.

"Tomorrow we go to Renaissance gardens at Fiesole and Settignana, hillside villages, then back to our hotel by 6pm, then our final dinner, kind of a banquet there in the arbour in the garden. Gather by 8pm. Isobel and I are having a Happy Hour then, and the food will come along in true Italian style, sometime. It's going to be a leisurely affair.

"We were sorry it couldn't be the very last night, but they couldn't do it here for some reason. Maybe it's worked out just as well. Day 14 is choices. They're partially paid for by your tour cost, but you have to pay a supplement according to where you go. Make your own arrangements at the hotel desk. Vans'll be coming to take you to your destination: Venice, Pisa, or Siena.

"We're letting you off at the Boboli Gardens, see here on your map, Pitti Palace, which is magnifico." Martin held up his map. "You've got all day to get across town to the Station. Have a nice day!"

There was the routine shuffle of getting off the bus and general milling about on the pavement.

Syd stood just aside from Ross and Barbara, not particularly taking any part in their organization, yet not ignoring it.

Arielle stayed with Molly while she waited for Lorraine and Jean.

Molly and Lorraine consulted with Barbara.

All seven started to drift toward the entrance.

Jack Track, with Ev in tow, casually walked past Syd. "Yous okay?" he asked.

"Fine. Fine," answered Syd.

By the time they were through the gate, Syd and Arielle were walking side by side. No one took any notice that they were not keeping up.

How do we get past this strangeness, thought Arielle. I could almost make a comment about the weather, but I'm not going to.

Maybe it's a mistake. That those few days we had were the fun of getting there and then there's nothing.

"Let's stop on these steps and negotiate this garden with each other," Syd suggested.

"Come to think of it we ... we've not done a garden in each other's company," said Arielle shyly. She had fumbled when she said "we". She was grateful that Syd had made the move to put them together.

"Yes we have," said Syd softly. He was taking a sketch book from his knapsack.

Arielle met his eyes.

"Sissinghurst," said Syd.

"It was you who watched me! All day I could sense it. I knew it was you."

"You discovered that garden. I watched you ..."

"Feel it," she said. "It was a work of art."

They just smiled at each other. A shared moment. A shared memory.

"Then, at Giverny, ..." Syd started.

"What about Giverny?" Arielle asked with some alarm.

"How many pictures did you take of me?"

Colour started to creep up Arielle's neck and cheeks.

"What? What are you talking about? You were in a deep concentration over your paints. All day."

"So you were watching me," Syd teased.

"Well, no," denied Arielle sounding quite embarrassed. "Well, maybe."

"So how many pictures did you take?"

"Four, maybe five. You always seemed to be in the right light at the right time. Besides I did want a picture of you, if you must know the truth."

"I also knew exactly where you were all day," said Syd.

"You what?"

"I could feel your presence. It was like a magnet. I could feel the lines of force. I knew when you were behind me, or to the left. It was very strange. I liked it."

"That's the same reason I took the pictures," Arielle confessed. She reached out to touch his forearm.

He caught her hand and held it.

"We'll have to decide on a place in this garden for me to draw you."

"Pardon?"

"To go with the rest of them. Here." Syd handed Arielle his sketch book a bit sheepishly.

Syd leaned back on his elbows to watch her. "If it's confession time, take a look."

Arielle darted a look at him, then opened the book.

"At Greenwich!"

"I do some quick sketches. You were on the path. Gave me perspective. There were other people, I picked you."

"At Beth Chatto's!" Arielle was surprised. "I was hiding in the grass, on the other side, playing Prelude a l'apres-midi d'un faune, Afternoon of the faun. Debussy. It was the grassland and trickle of the water that did it."

"You were so still, for so long. Now I know."

"At Kew! Sissinghurst! At the lunch stop. My wedge dress! And

Giverny."

Syd was looking very sheepish. "Full confession. Allowed myself to be caught out."

He's opened himself to me. Arielle knew he was allowing himself to be vulnerable to her. Extending his trust to her. And what do I give him in response, she thought? My openness. My vulnerability. Not to be exploited. Never. To go with it to closeness. Oneness. Done.

"Let's get down to business," said Arielle slapping the sketch book on his knee. "What do you know about Italian gardens?"

"Before we do, I'd like to say something about yesterday."

"You don't have to."

"I would like to."

"Okay."

"I'm a widower, maybe you know that," Syd looked at Arielle.

"Yes, I think I knew that, I think Molly mentioned it a long while back, but I hadn't thought about marital status at all. You were just you."

"Grace had chosen me! She wants a partner. Had nothing to do with me, except I fill the bill of her expectations!"

"All of that was very obvious to most of us. You don't need to say more."

"Still want to know about Italian gardens? They're very formal. Renaissance gardens ..."

"Which means?"

"Would you believe, masonry, branching staircases, balustrades, cascades, pavilions and pavements. Even the cypress avenues are imitations of colonnades. Take a look up here. Let's find the statue of Neptune."

"In a pool or fountain, I hope," added Arielle.

"You bet. Always water in one of these if they can manage it."

Syd stood up and stretched his hand to Arielle's to pull her to her feet.

Hand in hand they headed for the first set of steps.

"You may not get your picture drawn here," said Syd. "It's a garden, but it is not int...intimate like the others."

Arielle heard him stumble slightly over the word intimate, just as she had stumble over we. She recalled a moment in Paris:

'Tu ...' Syd was stumbling for a word.

'Non.' said Arielle, wagging her finger like a schoolmarm. 'Non, tu. Vous.'

'Mathematique?'

'Oui, mais, vous, pour ordinaire. Tu est pour la intimite.'

'Intimite?'

'Intimacy, en anglais.'

Syd was quiet.

He would never have had intimacy with Grace, thought Arielle. Who am I to say? I wonder if he had it in his marriage. There's a certain something in him when it surfaces. I want intimacy. I wonder if he does? It's high risk. I wonder if he can cope with it. Can I cope with what I believe is his offer of trust? Just as high a risk. The only thing I can do is extend the openness of intimacy to him. Very carefully. In a trusting way.

"Ca va?" Syd asked. "Are you here? You're very quiet."

"Just thinking. This isn't intimate." She smiled at him. "It's a public garden."

"Tomorrow in the Tuscan hills will be better."

"Let's work our way through this. I appreciate the grandeur of it, but it certainly is formal."

"Few flowers."

They appreciated being together more than thoughts of the garden.

"I don't want to organize us," Arielle began.

"I can't speak Italian," said Syd with mock alarm.

"You're in luck," she said with a snort, "I can't either except for adagio, rubato, spiccato. Italian is the language of music."

"I tell a lie. I know a few phrases of construction-site Italian, which I would hesitate to try out in polite company."

"About not organizing us," Arielle continued, "I had jotted down a few things I'd like to see. One of them is Michelangelo's David. It's at The Academy Gallery."

"Let's work from my map."

They sat side by side pouring over it.

"The Academy should be here," Arielle leaned on Syd's arm to point across town.

"It's going to be hot this afternoon," Syd predicted, "Let's see the David this afternoon. Inside. Out of the sun."

"And if we go across one of these bridges, either Ponte Santa Trinita or Ponte Vecchio. Santa Trinita is a work of art. Could we see it better from the other bridge?" Arielle turned her head to look at Syd.

Their faces were bare inches apart. Their gaze softened to knowing, and paused before breaking into smiling, trusting eyes.

"Head for Piazza Della Signoria ...," said Syd.

"Therefore the Ponte Vecchio ...,"

"Right. Meaning correct. The copy of the David is in the Piazza."

"Then along the Via De'Calzaiuoli to the Duomo ..."

"Lunch outside." Syd stated.

"I'll bet we can buy a picnic from a deli or market ... Ah! The treasury," Arielle said as she patted the buttoned breast pocket on Syd's shirt.

There was a comfortable pause as they both knew she was touching him.

"How much?" Syd broke the silence.

"Thousands," Arielle laughed. She spoke lightly and happily. "I think the Italians should apply the decimal point more vigorously!"

Syd laughed. "Haul out your cash and we'll match each other for the kitty."

They were well back to comfort with each other.

Syd buttoned the money into his pocket and once again pulled Arielle to her feet.

They made their way, hand in hand, toward Ponte Vecchio, past obvious groups of tourists, past women fastidiously dressed.

"Beautiful Italian silks," commented Arielle.

"Let's look at some of these shops on the bridge," said Syd. "It's mostly jewellery here. I've always admired Italian craftsmanship even on big construction jobs. Actually I'd like to buy some paper. Notebooks. Watercolour pads. Bound in that marbled paper. Some even bound by hand. To decorate my house."

"To decorate your house! How?"

"The marbled paper is pale yellow to natural." He went on to explain his renovating and experimenting with shades of yellow. "I have very little furniture. A bed. A sofa. Two lamps. A dining table and a few chairs. Steamer style. Wood slatted. Interesting wood. Mabau. Relative of teak, but rosier. Not so tired. Any of these Florentine paper products would look nice around as accents ...."

At the Ponte Vecchio they ambled along from shop to shop using the elbow nudge, or tug on the sleeve. Comfortable, established method of communication.

"Somehow here in Florence, it's right," said Arielle indicating the woman behind the counter of one shop with beautifully coifed hair coloured aubergine.

"I remember when we thought Italian men with hair anything longer than a U.S. Marines' buzz cut was really quite unmanly. Look at me now!" Syd indicated his hair pulled into a queue at the nape of his neck.

Syd stopped at the end of the bridge.

"Since we're on a garden tour, lets see if we can get a peek into either of these two private gardens. Right here." He looked at the map and then up at his surroundings. "Shouldn't be hard to see greenery in downtown Florence, so many red roofs and sandy exteriors."

"This is the Uffizi complex. Correction. I need a word of grand antiquity for it," said Arielle.

"Let's circle it. Turn right. Then we'll perhaps get a glimpse of Palazzo Malenchini and Palazzo Gondi. Should be able to see the high trees above the red-tiled roofs, anyway," Syd said.

"Look," said Arielle, "a wall fountain. Water streaming out of a satyr's mouth."

"How do you know it's a satyr?"

"I know a satyr when I see one ...." She gasped and stopped. Eying Syd, she asked, "How good is your Greek or Roman mythology."

"Non-existent."

"Good."

"I guess I better look up satyr. You know one to see one, do you? ... It doesn't take long walking along these streets to feel you're in an outdoor museum."

"I'll bet most of Italy is," added Arielle.

"In Toronto, we used to laugh at all the statues around Italian homes. Couldn't make a mistake about who lived there. But I've come to realize that if they didn't have all that statuary, they'd think half of their family was missing!"

They were in the Piazza Della Signoria and Palazzo Vecchio.

"Not what you would call a magnificent square," commented Syd.

"Somehow I expected the setting to be more ... planned, after the formality of that garden," said Arielle.

"Read in the guide book, that it was their early meeting place for government. That's the copy of the David. Imagine how long the original stood out here, subject to the elements as well as the human tendency to knock things down." Syd was sounding awestruck.

"Like the action and mood of those people captured in marble under that veranda over there."

"You can tell the locals here are descendants. There's a lot of noise and bustle around us ... have you noticed?"

They made their way through the square, paying more attention to the surroundings than to the crowds and the paving.

Arielle was guiding the way, with Syd walking offset behind her, one hand on her shoulder. She was wearing her scooped-necked black jeans dress. His little finger was on her skin, sometimes caressing it. Neither took any notice. Both knew.

They made their way onto Via De'Calzaiuoli. Fiats and Vespas zipping everywhere.

"This must be a main shopping street. Clothes and shoes. Leathergoods," said Arielle.

The street was narrow and crowded, so Syd was still slightly behind her. Hand still on her shoulder.

"Where will you wear that velvet jacket you bought in the London market?" he asked unselfconsciously.

"For a performance. Symphony or an ensemble concert. Often there's a reception after, and it kind of dresses up my," she laughed, "work dress... you know something absolutely black and plain... that keeps my arms free."

"It must take an incredible amount of time to prepare for a concert," Syd said appreciatively.

"You can imagine that?" asked Arielle incredulously.

"Of course. I know the time it takes our church choir to put our Christmas program together. Longer practices, and pretty intense. And you teach beside. That's full time work."

"But I'm my own boss. Here's an interesting food shop."

They stopped in front of the window of the narrow shop, where the word 'salumerie' hung. It was a take-out shop.

Arielle was caught in a small space between Syd and the glass.

It was a beautiful display of prepared food in crocks, on platters, in baskets.

Arielle pivoted to face Syd. "I'm glad you took the bull by the horns and asked me directly to be with you today," and she reached up to kiss him.

Syd responded by lowering his head, and Arielle touched her lips to his, then gently ran the tip of her tongue along the inside of his upper lip to make his lips part.

Then she pulled away, looking boldly at him.

"I'm very glad you did that," he told her, very softly.

"We better buy our lunch, before they close the shop," she said giving him a shove in the ribs so she could walk to the door.

A lovely smell of rosemary and sage. Sweet not pungent.

They guessed at the ingredients.

White beans cooked in tomato, garlic and sage; broad green noodles with ragu: veal sauteed with red, yellow and green peppers; thick pork chops roasted with herbs; ravioli filled with spinach covered with a creamy tomato sauce; asparagus with chunks of Parmesan cheese; grilled trout with oil and lemon; radicchio salad; rice with chopped bright green spinach and mushrooms; salami; thick coarse peasant bread; gorganzola cheese; salmon mousse; tomatoes stuffed with saffron rice and pine nuts; squash flowers dipped in flour and fried, an anchovy in each gold-green centre; vitello tonnato; cold veal with a puree of tuna; chicken in aspic adorned with prosciutto and tomato; thick salmon steak in pastry crust stuffed with egg yolk and parsley.

"I find these displays of food, awesome, if I may quote my pupils.

Beautiful colours and textures. Does it sound too grand if I say food should nourish the soul as well as the body. And all of this is real food. Surprisingly healthy."

"I'm just beginning to get onto pasta myself."

"You surprise me. Reading up on food?"

"No, just ravenously hungry?"

"I didn't think anyone on the North American continent, ever experienced ravenous hunger."

"One night when I was working on my house. Late. In grubby work clothes. Time got past me. I didn't know what I wanted. In the kitchen cupboard was some spaghetti. I figured I could boil water and follow some simple directions. Found some Parmesan cheese in the refrig. Along with some butter. My daughters-in-law have since educated me on olive oil. A lot of parsley from my garden. Specialty of the house now!"

"Well, what'll we have from here?"

"You chose," said Syd. Then smart-alecky, "I'll pay!"

"How generous," Arielle threw at him mockingly.

"Don't forget two very large bottles of water. For drinking and bathing."

"You're never going to let me forget that."

"No, I'm not."

They left the shop in high spirits.

"Where will we eat?" Syd was looking at the traffic.

"I have in my mind that the Medici palace is somewhere over this way. Maybe we could sit on the steps outside it."

Syd had the map out. "Yes, past the Piazza Duomo, on the way to the Academy."

He juggled his knapsack with the two large bottles of water sticking out, onto the outside shoulder, and took Arielle's elbow to guide them through the crowded street.

Taking in the cathedral with its almost garish green, white and red marbles, they saw a private spot along a street: locked grill gate looking into some private garden greenery, with two marble steps up to it. In the shade.

A typical Florentine courtyard garden incorporating original box-edged beds around the central fountain. The garden was circled by a pergola over which was trained an ancient wisteria. Roses climb the walls.

They took their time over lunch, watching the world go by.

"I think we have to make a choice," Syd said finally. "It's what we do first, the Medici palace or the David. There may be a line-up at for the David."

"I would really like to see it."

"There may be a line-up."

"I can rest on my feet."

"Me, too."

There was a hush in the approaching halls of the Academy where David stood. The building was classical, airy, lit by low arched windows.

They moved with the crowd. David came in full sight.

Arielle gasped. A quick intake of air. Syd looked at her. She had tears in her eyes.

"So beautiful," she whispered almost reverently.

There is a presence, Syd thought to himself.

They were both in a grip of something else. Neither spoke another word, but kept their eyes on that magnificent figure.

The crowd moved them on.

Arielle kept turning back for another last glimpse.

They were out of the hall.

"He has been standing there for four hundred years, and yet is full of motion!" She could hardly speak for emotion.

Syd understood. He recognized the kind of reaction he had had at Sissinghurst. He had not been quite so overwhelmed by this one.

"We've been in the presence of greatness. Made from marble, but looks alive."

Arielle walked toward a window, through a huge space left in a display of other sculpture.

Syd watched her and waited in his own concentration.

She finally turned.

"Ca va?" Syd asked.

Her face brightened, and she walked back to him. "Yes, fine. I was just overwhelmed. I'm almost shaking."

She was breathing evenly.

"Do you want to look at more here?" he asked.

"Would you mind if we didn't? David is so special I don't want anything to deplete him." She put a sardonic look on her face. "That sounds silly, but it was too powerful to have anything else here try to touch it."

"Let's go outside, I want to check something in the guidebook. First, though I want to make an inquiry at the desk."

Arielle stuck close to Syd as they made their way back to the street. She had been deeply touched and wanted some close comfort. She knew it was there for her from him.

As they paused on the street, Syd turned his guidebook open to the page of the church Santa Croce.

"It's a bit of a hike," he said half apologetically, "but it'll be good for you."

They walked, with purpose, noting some of the sights, until they turned the corner into the Piazza di Croce.

"In the church is Michelangelo's tomb. All kinds of great men are buried in this church, or a memorial to them. Let's go in and see."

In spite of the high summer sun, it was dark inside the church.

They wandered around, looking at the ornate structures. Names, besides Michelangelo, were Galileo, Dante, Machiavelli, Bruni, Rossini.

Syd watched Arielle light a candle; then he followed her to the main door, down the steps that led to the market.

"I don't know when anything has hit me so emotionally in a long, long time, if ever," she smiled reassuringly at Syd. "I'm okay. Thanks for being here for me."

Syd put his arm lightly across her shoulders. "Let's amble this way and see if we can find the market, just to have a look at what's around."

Along the way was a collection of stalls covered with awnings.

They looked at some leather purses and brief cases.

"Leathers that feel like butter," Syd commented.

"Silk scarves here. Italian silk is very soft as well," said Arielle moving toward a display of jewellery.

Syd was studying some copies of the David, giving them a critical eye for proportion and energy. One was particularly good. He turned to find Arielle, to bring it to her attention.

The moment he saw her with an earring in her fingers slipping it deftly into the pierced hole in her ear, he felt a very sharp stab of pleasure in his groin. He heard himself expel some air. The merchant at the statues, did a double take: first at Syd, then followed Syd's gaze to Arielle, then back to Syd.

He nodded his head muttering agreeably "Ah-ha, ah-ah, ah-ha," and throwing up his hands, "Da love!"

Arielle was looking at Syd. She raised her eyebrows, as she had in the Portobello market in London, pointing questioningly at the earring, asking for his opinion. It was made of brightly coloured glass beads held together with golden wire. Gypsy earrings.

He walked to her.

"Just asking for your opinion on the earrings, but I can't interpret what your expression is telling me."

"That's the second time I've seen you do that."

"Do what?"

"Put your earring in perfectly by touch alone."

"So?" she asked matter-of-factly.

"It's the sexiest thing I've ever seen a woman do," Syd said boldly.

"Any woman?" Arielle was flirting, "or me?"

Syd knew what he felt was written all over his face. He didn't want to try to conceal it.

"You." He faced her straight on. "You're the sexiest thing I've ever seen."

Still looking flirtatiously at him, she turned to the vendor. "I'll take the earrings."

Syd pulled out his money clip. "A present from me to the lady," he said to the vendor as he extended an Italian banknote.

Looking straight at Syd, Arielle replaced the hoop earring she had been wearing.

No question at all what was going on between us, she thought.

When she took her parcel, Arielle asked, "Now what?"

Their eyes were locked. The happiest of smiles spread across their faces.

Syd said, "I wanted you to see the copies of the David, over here." They burst out laughing.

The statue merchant, threw up his hands. "Mama mamio," and walked away shaking his head.

They just laughed together again.

"We are going to find a nice outdoor cafe and I'm going to drink some beer," Syd announced and deliberately took Arielle's arm and steered a steady course to a cafe.

They settled down without a word, but both aware of the attracting lines of force between them.

Syd ordered beer for himself, and when Arielle could finally focus on the list, an Aperol, the honey and orange-coloured Florentine aperitif.

They just looked at each other, smiling and shaking their heads. Pure joy.

Syd pulled out his sketch book, positioned himself for a good view of Arielle, and settled down to draw her.

Arielle took out the package containing the new earrings. With intent she looked directly at Syd as she removed them from the paper. He watched every move as he continued to draw.

She picked one up and fiddled with it. Then touched her ear.

"You are flirting," Syd accused.

"Just flirting? Or flirting with someone?" she asked confidently.

"With me," Syd said enjoying every minute.

"How am I making out?" she asked with affected coyness.

"H-m-m-m, making out. H-m-m-m. Very well."

"Then I'll keep it up."

"Since you've got it up, you might as well," Syd said matter-of-factly.

They both laughed knowingly.

Very cool, thought Arielle. He's not overplaying anything I'm handing him. Keeping his own counsel. Handing it back very carefully. Very cool.

They sat glowing in each others presence.

An hour or more and another drink for Arielle and two for Syd, with the sun setting, inquiries from the waiter gave them directions for an outdoor restaurant, with a nice view of Florence.

"The walk to the restaurant takes us past that paper shop we saw earlier," Syd was trying to sound businesslike.

He paid the bill, and with map in hand, they stood at the edge of the piazza not focusing on the map in any way.

Syd folded it, and tucked it in a pocket.

He put his hands lightly on Arielle's shoulders and turned her toward him.

They looked honestly and confidently into each others eyes.

Arielle had that feeling of woman deep in her body. The feeling of want.

With eyes locked she took one step toward Syd and balancing on one foot, she arched her back and placed her two hip bones squarely on his.

He, his maleness, his aliveness and want was there held between their two bodies. Both could feel.

Both understood her quiet firm "Yes" as she slid her hips across his and him, then deftly stepped back from him onto the other foot.

He echoed her "Yes".

Mutual consent.

DAY 13: TOUR TUSCANY GARDENS

Martin had the group gathered around him, notes in hand. "This Villa Medici's one of two good Renaissance gardens here in Fiesole. The other one which we're not getting to see today had a connection with that great English gardener, Lawrence Johnston at Hidcote. Speaking of English gardeners, Sir Harold Acton ..."

Syd eased his way to Arielle's side. They'd agreed at dinner last night in Florence to treat their association today the same way as yesterday, and he had the wonderful feeling and knowledge that he could make natural comfortable approaches to her. That basis of what he'd had with Marjorie, but more. The hope of comfortable intimacy. What he wanted. Had always hoped was possible.

I hope she feels the same way, he thought. I'm sure she does. I can only put my trust in it. He had wondered at the bit of sex talk yesterday afternoon. High risk. The fine line to express, but not slide into vulgarity, nor over-the-hill gabble.

He always thought his parents had had an active sex life well on into their seventies, but in those days no one would ever breathe a word about it.

Arielle had just let those words and feelings sit there between them to be enjoyed.

She's wonderful.

"... the typical early Tuscan garden tends towards the domestic in scale ... a cypress avenue, a bowling alley,"

A bowling alley? questioned Syd. Can't be. I'm not paying attention. Who cares!

"... a few 'garden rooms' with simple parterres ..."

"The treasury has enough lira left from yesterday, for today's lunch," said Syd bending to Arielle's ear to whisper.

"What are parterres?" Arielle whispered back.

"Tell you later." Syd liked being close to her ear.

"... Leone Battista Alberti in 1452 set the specific guidelines on what a Renaissance garden was to be ... ordered, geometric, and most importantly, outward looking, incorporating the vistas of Tuscany ... to be simple, mostly green shrubs and trees, often in topiary, reflecting classical architectural designs with few flowering plants ... very important ... views looking out ... this was an innovation since medieval and monastic gardens of earlier centuries. They looked inward to create places of solitude and safety. The Hortus Conclusus...?

"Didn't we see a hortus conclusus yesterday ... eating lunch?"

"Smarty," said Syd poking her in the ribs.

"... classical garden design done with limited palette of plants, emphasizing shades of green with few flowers. Fragrance is provided by ancient citrus trees in terra cotta pots as well as jasmine and magnolia: colour introduced sparingly with oleanders, roses: vertically positioned gardens have water features, non-stop views, symmetrical designs, statuary and bright sunny areas contrasted by densely shaded woods .... I apologize for rushing through my notes, but it's going to be a hot day and ... well I'm here for questions."

The group broke to wander at will.

"We've almost done this trip backward," Ross commented to Syd.

"Particularly when you think of the formal plan of Sissinghurst," Syd replied.

Those urns, thought Syd in a flash. They had satyr-headed handles. Sphinx heads as well. I wonder what exactly a sphinx is. Didn't think to ask at the desk yesterday at the Academia.

"This formal structure," Syd said to Arielle, "these geometric flowerbeds, hedged to hold everything in order. These are parterres." Then with glee in his voice, he said "I know what a satyr is. You know one to see one do you?"

"Where did you find out?" Arielle's voice was high in surprise. "Barbara tell you? Lorraine? I didn't see you talking to anyone."

"The desk at the Academia. What's a sphinx? Vita and Harold had urns with satyr heads and sphinx, and they were such equals, make me wonder."

"I'm not telling," Arielle was teasing.

"All the ones we have seen are old ... " Syd commented.

"Not supposed to have all this colour," Barbara said, pointing to the vivid display in red, pink and white. "However we're well past the Renaissance, so I guess you can do what you want."

"Interesting flower, to get this effect. Godetias, I think," said Lorraine.

"But still symmetrical, and geometric, and in order."

"I think these gardens are closer to theatre, than nature," commented Arielle. "These terraces are almost stages."

"But if you lived in hills like here in Tuscany, you'd have to do something to make them an asset," chuckled Ross.

"Very dramatic," said Arielle.

"But then they lead your eye and you straight into the countryside," said Barbara.

They loaded back into the coach for the short run to Fiesole where the coach stopped in the Piazza Mino.

"We've an hour here," said Martin into the microphone, "for the folks sticking with the bus. For the walkers, just be sure to meet us at Settignano by 3 pm. It's marked on the map of the area that I gave you at breakfast. We've arranged to visit Villa Gamberaia at that time. We're lucky the owner, Princess Ghyka, isn't in residence. She permits visitors when she's away. For those staying with the coach, we have a place to stop for lunch. Everyone else, you may want to buy a picnic here, as there're no eating places on the route. Have a nice day."

Arielle waited for Syd to arrange with Martin where he could pick up his easel bag in Settignano at noon, as the other regulars started across the piazza toward the bronze equestrian statue, on the way to the outdoor Roman Theatre.

"Let's get lunch now," Arielle said, pointing to the stalls in the piazza.

"Yes, so we won't have to backtrack." Syd was looking at his Thomas Cook guide book and Martin's map, both showing the route to Settignano.

Barbara and Ross, Lorraine and Jean followed them to shaded stalls, to the special ambience of the market and square.

And they set off together to the Roman theatre.

Syd and Arielle sat on one of the semi-circular rows of seats facing the stage set so serenely among the trees.

"These are olive groves all around us," commented Syd. "This soft silvery-green colour. I didn't know the trees grew outward, the centres collapsing. Gives a soft look to the structure." Syd had his sketch book in hand.

"Olive oil is lovely. Wonderfully fragrant." Arielle said. "What's more very healthy."

"I said about my daughters-in-law ...," said Syd.

"Daughters-in-law," repeated Arielle. "Therefore you have two or more sons."

"Logic is correct!" laughed Syd, "Just two sons."

"They ..., your sons were with you at the airport."

"You noticed?"

"I saw you. My first reaction was that you looked like Aaron Copland music."

"Huh?"

"But not your sons."

"How could I look like Aaron Copland music?"

"Just look at yourself now. Khaki trousers, denim coloured shirt today. Or jeans, which you had on at the airport. Beige, or khaki shirts. Or a plaid shirt. Would you say you looked like Appalachian Spring or Rodeo?"

Syd looked at his clothes.

"Mountain boots or cowboy boots?" Arielle went on.

"You were humming Tennessee Waltz in Paris," said Syd.

"My train of thought, after Appalachian Mountains. And you said you'd never learned to waltz and I figured you could dance by the way you recovered from that stumble, tucking a little fancy footwork into it to try to make it look smooth and natural. You picked up the step and rhythm so easily, I figured Agnes de Mille could have put you into her ballet Rodeo, maybe even Billy the Kid, if you were wearing cowboy boots."

"If you know so much about classical music, how come you know the Tennessee Waltz?" Syd challenged.

The sweet scented air stirred around them.

"I'm beginning to play some fiddle music. With a quartet. Simple tunes. I'm moving toward simplicity as I age: less is more."

"That's my line," said Syd considering her approvingly.

"We're heading down the road," Ross was calling to them, "Etruscan Tombs."

"Let's have a look," said Arielle.

Syd and Arielle let the others get just beyond hearing distance, giving themselves some privacy.

They maintained a steady pace.

"So you teach music ... piano, violin, and theory?" summarized Syd.

Arielle nodded, then added, "Some dance. Very basic movement and music now. Four to six year olds."

"Like my little grand-daughter. She'd like that. Very important to dance. My sisters taught me .... But you also perform."

"M-m-m-m," said Arielle.

"Symphony ... in a black velvet antique jacket ... and?"

"I'll tell you if you tell me," Arielle offered.

"Huh?"

"Well, here we are, two relative strangers, in the hills of Tuscany ..."

"And I'd like to know you better ..." ventured Syd.

"And all we have in common is this garden tour ..." Arielle snorted a laugh, "and I'm not a gardener!"

"Well I'm having a good time," Syd said looking at her out of the corner of his eye.

Arielle caught his glance. "Me, too," she admitted.

"So I ask, then you ask?" Syd picked up the suggestion..

"Yes," said Arielle, "and you were curious about my performances."

"M-m-m-m," said Syd.

"A quartet, an ensemble, is easier practice arrangement than a full symphony, even sectionals. Four of us got together to do some work for small venues ... concerts, parties, ... that kind of thing."

"Simple tunes like Tennessee Waltz." said Syd.

"And Moon River, plus the familiar classical ones .... Now we're working on another theme, a grouping."

"Like?" Syd was interested.

"Love songs. The whole world loves love songs," Arielle darted Syd a glance.

"I believe that," Syd said looking directly at her.

"Well the funny part about it," Arielle started to laugh, then looked shyly at Syd, "is that most of them are written in the key of A ... you know enough about music ..."

Syd nodded his head.

Arielle laughed again. "If these songs aren't in A, then they're pretty close to it: G, F#, minor key right here, but all close keys. One of the quartet said we should call the program," she hesitated, and looked at Syd cheekily, "not Love in the Key of A, but Music in the Erogenous Zone!"

Syd laughed. She's okay. She's not backing off from sex. Maleness and femaleness. And within the dignity of it as well as the fun. Some of my friends have become old farts as they've aged, or simply asexual. Is it real or a defence mechanism? I had always hoped, Syd shook his head. How lucky can a guy be.

"... my turn," Arielle said.

"Before you do, take a look back. There's the Roman amphitheatre we were at, over the olive groves in the valley," said Syd, standing quietly beside her, looking back.

They walked on toward cultivated land, through a purple haze from sage and rosemary growing wild.

"Okay," said Arielle, "what do you think you'll be doing ... let's see ... a week from today?"

"You want the 8 am eat breakfast kind of thing?"

"Sure," she answered.

"If it's hot, I'll work in the garden, have my breakfast out there, then on toward 11, I'd phone you to see what you're up to ... having talked to you or seen you the day before ..." Syd stopped with a look of concern on his face. "Where do you live? ... There was a sheet with everybody's name, address, phone number ... I've no idea where it is ... oh, yes, I remember, I stuffed it between the paint samples on my clip board ... not important ... then! Where do you live? ... Toronto, I hope ..."

"Yes," said Arielle relieving the tension. "I put that sheet somewhere too ... on my piano ... I think." Then she looked alarmed. "Where do you live?"

Syd was smiling. "Toronto. Where in Toronto do you live?"

"Avenue Road, west side, just south of Eglinton," Arielle answered.

Syd was smiling very broadly. "I live about eight blocks away from you, off Chaplin Crescent."

Syd watched the concerned look melt from her face, and heard her breathe a little sigh of relief, as she reached out to touch his arm.

" ... so you've called me ..." Arielle picked up the scenario.

"Would you be at home?"

"Well, yes, since we had already negotiated my schedule when we were talking yesterday ...."

"Next week's yesterday!" Syd said precisely.

"Right." agreed Arielle.

"Hey, what about tomorrow?"

"Today's tomorrow, or next week's tomorrow," Arielle was having fun with this nothing conversation.

"Today's tomorrow, you know the choice Pisa, Venice or Siena. Where do you want to go?"

"Hm-m-m-m," Arielle was thinking. "If I say, you might agree with me, even if you didn't want to go there."

"And if I said," said Syd, "then you might agree with me."

"I've got an idea," Arielle stated.

"Not another duel!"

"Not quite," Arielle was laughing. "Each makes a fist, and on 'Go' each puts out ... one finger for Pisa, two for Venice and three for Siena. That way we can each say what we want to do."

"What if we don't agree?"

"We'll worry about that after!"

"Okay," said Syd, standing square in front of Arielle. "Fists."

"Ready. Go!"

Fingers shot out on hands held high. They both flipped their heads back and forth observing.

"Venice wins," announced Syd, "two to nil."

"Piece o' cake," said Arielle.

"I'll do the booking when we get back to the hotel," said Syd.

"We'd better get a move on if we're going to get to Settignano, let alone Venice." Arielle gave his shirt sleeve a tug.

Syd touched Arielle's shoulder to indicate a castle clinging to an escarpment.

They followed the group in front of them taking the road to Vincigliata, now entering an open country of vineyards and olive groves.

About half way down the hill they stopped at the castle. On the wall facing the road was a series of plaques giving the names of the notables who visited there, including Princess Beatrice, the daughter of Queen Victoria.

Past the bend, to the left was the Villa I Tatti, once the home of world-famous art historian, Bernard Berenson. It said so on the plaque.

"Never heard of him," said Syd.

"Nice that it's now, what, oh yes, a Centre for Italian Renaissance Studies," said Arielle.

The road continued to descend gently to Ponte a Mensola, an idyllic hamlet with a little river running through it.

"Let's have lunch here," said Syd. "Hills are nice."

They undid packages.

"So much happened here in Italy, you could let your mind drift in and out of your own reality," said Arielle dreamily.

"Like?" Syd was bent over his sketch book.

"Somewhere north of here, Cremona, 'the city of music' where Stradivari made more than a thousand violins. Other stringed instruments. To this day, the most coveted and most expensive in the world."

"I'd like to paint for a bit, here," said Syd. "Do you want to play something? I tried that the other day. Highly effective! It was my saving grace!" He hooted out loud.

They were both quiet as Syd took out materials.

"You were only married once?"

"Oh, yes. I'm a very tradition man." Syd commented.

"Sure you are," said Arielle. "I knew right off from your haircut!"

"Well, I was, but then Marjorie's health deteriorated." Syd decided to tell Arielle how long ago his marriage really had been over. "About twelve years, plus, I guess, that diabetes changed our lives."

Arielle was silent.

"Can I ask you something?" Syd looked at Arielle. Encouraged, he went on: "If my mathematics is correct, you were with a man for eighteen years, and subtracting that from what I estimate to be your age, there seem to be a number of years when you were pretty young but alone. I can't believe someone wasn't with it enough to seek you out."

"Very diplomatically put," Arielle conceded. "I had two strange things happen to me, that now, in the last quarter of the twentieth century no one would even take notice of; but at the time, threw me for a loop. The first man in my life turned out to be gay. Liked my boyish body. Turned out he liked the real thing, and dumped me as I filled out and became womanly."

Syd practically whistled through his teeth.

"Women around the age of thirty don't have a big field of men to chose from. I'm going to tell you. I think you can handle it. Once again in the early sixties. Well, ... I had this relationship with a twenty year old University student. He was painting houses for the summer ... on our street ... and we said hello ... and kind of hung out ... came and went easily ... we could communicate ... talk to each other. He'd not be around for a week or whatever and we'd pick up where we left off.

"He figured out my schedule with summer students, and would show up, or wait, or just check in ... leave a note in the door ... ask for note back, ... for me to leave in my door."

"Kid had the right idea," Syd commented. "Did you go out places?"

"Yes," said Arielle. "I listened to Beatles with him, learned to dance the new way, you know,, no-touch. The Twist. Jungle rhythms. It was considered so primitive ... after the rigid fifties."

"I know the music ... the scene. My son Steve was right into it."

"... I bought a mini-skirt! Loved them. Have had one ever since."

"Sort of like the wedge dress."

"You're observant!" she said.

"So you weren't married, and going out with a twenty year old!"

"And enjoying his company. He was an English Literature major. Really bright. And fun. When university started that fall I finally insisted that he had to get involved at the university, and that we shouldn't see each other any more."

I'll bet they were good together in bed, but I'm not going to ask her, Syd thought with a shock. He liked the idea. "Then you eventually met ...?"

"And expected to marry, but things don't always work out as expected."

"As tradition worked for me." said Syd.

"Maybe deep down, I chose not to settle. Always possibility and adventure. I don't really know."

"Don't take me wrong on this," said Syd hesitantly, "but I think I can say this to you, to open up discussion. I think people's expectations of relationships are too high. We have to be our own person first, and then relate to someone else."

"Like I did with that kid," said Arielle.

"Which I did with Marjorie, to a great extent, within the confines of traditional marriage."

"What's a person like when they're alone?" Arielle asked.

"I think the person who calls himself a loner is using it as a defence mechanism," suggested Syd.

"I need to be alone sometimes. I'm not lonely, but then I want to talk, share ... be with ..." Arielle let the thought dangle.

"M-m-m-m," commented Syd.

Arielle leaned back against the wall, closed her eyes, and started to hum, softly, melodiously.

Syd concentrated on his painting.

When he was finished and putting his things away, he saw Arielle twitch; knew what was happening.

Her eyes still stayed closed.

Syd stretched his foot out and nudged her foot.

She nodded her head; eyes still closed.

Syd leaned over her, and gave her a smacking kiss on the mouth. "Time to push off," he said abruptly. "You can finish playing that as we walk!"

Beside the road were two plaques recording the extraordinary number of famous English and American authors who were attracted to this region. Maybe because Boccaccio spent his childhood here and used one of its buildings, the Villa di Poggio Gherardo, as the setting for some of the early scenes in the Decameron.

Turn left and continue into Settignanao.

Settignano was little town with its own character, despite being so close to Florence. There appeared to be fewer tourist than in Fiesole.

Main square.

Old stone streets contributed to the attractiveness as a place for people to live and work.

The shops displayed their 'signage' with consideration for where they were, within the architectural framework, not plastered all over it.

Syd saw the coach parked just off the square.

"I'm going to get my easel from the coach," he said to Arielle, "and then position myself up the way past the shops, to paint."

"Okay," she said. "I thought I'd have a boo through the shops. Looks like the locals shop here. Not too touristy."

"We've got nearly two hours, according to that clock on the shop."

"I'll work my way toward you ... where you're painting."

Syd set about his task, enjoying the activity in the square. Big outdoor cafe on one side, shops in a row on the rise toward him.

Some kind of bar more than half way along. He had a pretty clear picture. Looks like a local dive, he thought. A bit rough. Some men sitting outside drinking.

He'd been watching Arielle make her way along the shops.

I could almost be accused of stalking her, he thought. Except she's done the same thing to me. Really nice.

He saw her come out of a shop with a parcel under her arm. She's wearing new shoes. Those rope soled ones. Tied around the ankle. Cool, as the kids would say. She's got nice ankles too, swinging under that crinkly brown skirt. Not a lot wrong with her, far as I can see.

She was pawing through some racks of blouses and dresses. Too far for me to discern, Syd thought. She's on her own for this purchase, although he watched her as she held up possibilities against herself, and sought a mirror.

She was inside the shop for quite a while and when she emerged she was looking like a peasant. It was the blouse. Tawny coloured. One of the shades of her skirt. Gathered wide neck, with full puffed sleeves, laced in front with bright ribbon.

Looked like a local.

She was striding toward the men's bar, when Syd heard a loud Italian male voice, "Come va?"

Syd watched Arielle pull up realizing the greeting was directed at her. She looked mildly inquisitive toward the men.

"Mi piace quella gonna. Che bel vestito!"

Syd's construction-site Italian kicked in. I like that something, too, he translated in his head. Beautiful dress.

"Giorgio, sta zitto," called a voice from the table.

Ya, Giorgio, translated Syd, be quiet.

"Lei e molto bella," Giorgio called back to his friend.

Arielle hesitated as she saw the whole group of men focus on her.

Syd watched the very handsome Giorgio, mid-thirties, as best he could tell, walk toward Arielle, smiling, stretching his hand out toward her.

Arielle stepped back.

"Turisti?"

Arielle didn't move.

"Gli italiani sono simpatici."

Italians are nice! Syd translated. He's flirting with her!

Syd felt a pang of jealousy. He watched.

Arielle was shaking her head. "No, no." She was protesting nicely.

She tried to walk on, but the man stayed with her, tried to take her hand.

Take your hands off her: possession nearly made Syd speak out.

She knows, he thought, that she's caught in a harmless mild flirtation, and is graciously trying to diffuse it and move on. He felt better about it.

She caught Syd's eye, and gave him a desperate look to bail her out.

A feeling of deviltry struck him. I'll ignore her and watch the fun. With a broad grin on his face, he turned back to his painting.

"Syd," she called rather insistently.

"L'italiano e una bella lingua ... "

Syd never looked up.

"Syd," she called firmly.

Syd picked out a few words from Giorgio's rapid Italian, "... la donna alta ... simpatico ...elegante ... bella ...." He felt a pride he had long forgotten. He felt she was his. He felt pride of association, even, yes, possession.

"Syd!" There was irritation in Arielle's voice.

"Ah, your man," Giorgio said to Arielle as he pointed at Syd. Continuing in passable English, he said "Maybe he no wanna you," and he reached to touch her shoulder.

He was play flirting with her as much as Syd was play ignoring her!

Well, Arielle, thought Syd, let's see how good you are!

"Come va?" Syd said to Giorgio. He managed to piece together a few word to convey the idea that Giorgio had picked the prettiest woman around, hoping the Toronto construction-site man-talk was not too off-colour.

Arielle looked askance at Syd, then at her Italian friend, who walked toward Syd.

"She's ayours?" Giorgio was speaking with great admiration. "You ... youa, ... un uomo, ...a man, sympatica, bello, she bella, you bed?"

Broken English does get right to the point, Syd thought, all the time hoping his face was not turning completely red. Better get this stopped.

Freed from the attentions of the Italian, Arielle hurried the few steps up the hill and scooted around behind Syd.

As the other men at the bar continued to look on, Giorgio gestured toward Arielle admiringly, and displayed his hands. "Le dita."

Syd said, "La violinista."

"Ah," said Giorgio. "Da ...face, ...le labbra ..."

"Bacio," one of the men shouted.

"You said you couldn't speak Italian," Arielle hissed at Syd, as she stood protectedly behind him.

"I did say construction-site phraseology," Syd was laughing. Very pleased with himself.

"Bacio, bacio," came good-natured chanting from the men at the table. Giorgio took up the cheer.

"What?" asked Arielle.

Syd looked at her daringly. "They want you to give me a kiss!"

"You got me, ... got yourself into this," she said with exasperation. "You could have saved me!"

"You didn't save me from Grace."

"That was different."

The men were still hooting and jeering.

Syd was sitting at the alert on his camp stool.

"You asked for this," Arielle said threateningly.

As she leaned around Syd's shoulder, the men cheered and clapped.

Her hair curtained their faces, and she took Syd's lower lip between teeth.

Jesus! he thought, she is going to bite!

Then in an instant shift in mood, she smoothed her mouth over his, and her tongue sought and found his, in the full intimate expression of the promise that had been building between them.

Suddenly aware of the surroundings, Syd pulled away.

With a final round of applause, the men good-naturedly faded back to their table.

Arielle sat on the pavement a few feet away from Syd.

Syd tried to concentrate on the completion of his painting.

"Bit of commotion up here," said Ross. "Missed it all."

"Just finishing," said Syd. "Is it time to go?"

"If you wanted a gelato before we go to the Villa Gamberaia," said Ross.

"Sounds good to me," said Syd. He raised his eyebrows questionly at Arielle.

She nodded her head.

Syd barely took in any of the details of the Villa Gamberia garden. He and Arielle wandered through it with an aura surrounding them.

They scarcely said a word. They scarcely touched, but stayed within a hand distance of each other.

They felt alone, private, connected, in the classical Sunken Garden.

They hesitated in the lemon garden. Lemon, the symbol of fidelity.

The beauty of the panorama of Settignano above the water parterres held them.

Arielle joined Molly for the ride back to the hotel.

It was still hot when Jack Track and Ev joined Syd in the far corner of the arbour for Martin and Isobel's Happy Hour.

"Still wearin' the same uniform," said Jack, indicating Syd's light denim coloured chambray shirt and light beige cotton twills.

Syd good-naturedly pointed to Jack and Ev, "Bought new T-shirts here in Florence."

"Souvenirs. Don't wanna cart around a lota useless stuff." Looking down at Syd's feet, Jack said, "Y' like them Jesus shoes? Always thought they was a bit fruity myself."

Not much of a reply for that, thought Syd, yet from Jack it seems okay. I quite like him.

"Actually, they're cool in hot weather, and you can slide your feet out of them if it's really hot." Pleasant conversation.

"She looks as if she just got outta the shower. Her hair's still wet," said Jack to Syd as they watched the arbour fill with their fellow travellers.

Syd had no doubt who Jack was talking about. Jack knew he knew.

"Certain cooling effect as it dries," Syd said absent-mindedly. He had seen Arielle immediately and thought she looked fresh as an Appalachian Spring herself.

She was wearing her new peasant blouse and her same crinkly brown skirt. Big gold bracelets. No earrings! Syd had fully expected she would wear the ones he had bought for her in the market.

Martin and Isobel were circulating, chatting to their guests.

Opened bottles of white and rose wine stood in ice buckets on the tables, with red beside them. Trays of antipasta were generously set around.

The usual groups were together. The shoppers. The sight-seers. The gardeners.

Molly stopped by the bench with Jean and Lorraine. Some had taken their places at the long supper tables in the centre.

"Arielle, come on over here," Jack Track called from the far corner of the arbour, "I've saved a seat for y' beside me."

He indicated a spare chair to his right, between him and Syd.

Syd gave her a sly smile.

She walked over to the place saved for her.

"Jack Track doesn't miss much," Syd said.

"He likes you," said Arielle.

"I think he likes you, too."

"Knew yous two should get together," said Jack, He turned back. "That there with Grace, was a ... a..."

"An imbroglio," Arielle put in.

"Yea," said Jack, "and it was a mixed up state of affairs. Personal like."

Arielle would have laughed right out had not Syd, holding his sides, kicked her under the table with his bare foot.

Fortunately, Jack turned his attention to Ev and the others.

Arielle pulled the Florentine market earrings out of her skirt pocket, and held them out to see the light dance through the glass.

"You wouldn't dare," Syd eyed her suspiciously. "Not here! Start something ..."

"Nobody else knows. I thought you ...," she was teasing, as she dramatically threaded one earring in one ear and then the other.

"Tu. No mistake."

Voices soft as the Tuscan air.

"Yes. Tu."

"English can only handle you and yous," Syd said, indicating Jack Track. "The French have it made with vous and tu," Syd said seriously to Arielle. "This evening I am speaking to tu. Make no mistake about it."

He felt very comfortable talking intimately with her. That which he had wondered about and wanted to experience was close, within range.

"Let's pull up these ice cream parlour chairs," someone called out, indicating the sturdy ubiquitous green European cafe chair, with slats for the seat and two slats at the back on a strong metal frame.

Fueled by copious amounts of wine, the party took off.

Between courses, which arrived spasmodically over the next couple of hours, Martin made a pleasant appreciative speech, and invited others to tell of their favourite part of the trip.

Syd and Arielle just sat on the fringe of the party, Jack Track almost obscuring them from others' view.

Waiters wove in and out, serving and tidying up.

It was getting late. Comfortably cooler sage and rosemary scented air was coming off the hills. The party started to break.

When he saw others start leave, Syd put one finger on Arielle's arm, to detain her.

They were leaning their elbows on the table. Their knees touching.

Jack Track was ushering the last few stragglers out of the arbour and the garden.

They were alone.

"Tu," Syd said softly.

Arielle turned, slid her hand on to Syd's back and nuzzled her nose against his bare cheek, above his beard, then nuzzled a kiss under the clean-shaven corner of his jaw and nibbled up to his earlobe.

Syd put his hand under her chin and gently drew her mouth to his, the tip of his tongue inviting hers.

His hand slid down her neck to caress along the base of her throat with his thumb, as they let the kiss linger.

The kiss broke as Arielle lost her balance on the edge of her chair.

With her right hand still on Syd's back, she reached her left across his body for his right shoulder, and she swivelled to sit side-saddle on his left thigh.

With the lightest of touch, she reached up and stroked her fingers across his brow, around his ear to the tie at the nape of his neck and gently loosened his hair.

"I like your hair loose, too," he breathed, as his fingers caught in the tangles of curls. "Light sparkling from your halo."

Their faces were close and they let the space diminish until they felt their lips exploring again.

"Hands ... to explore ..., too," said Syd intermittently.

"M-m-m-m," responded Arielle, as both of hers caressed his back.

Her fingers came around to the buttons on his shirt as his left hand touched her breast beneath the fabric of her blouse. "No bra," he said with pleasant surprise, as he cupped her tentatively.

She undid all the buttons of his shirt.

Slowly, he started a circular pressure on her nipple and felt it come alive under his hand.

Arielle pushed his shirt aside and bent her head down to brush his nipple with her lips. Same effect.

She lifted her head to smile into his eyes as she played with his nipples with each thumb.

Syd was fumbling with the ribbon on her blouse. "Does this undo ... oh ... simple bow."

He took his time, touching and kissing the cool skin of her body, and she in turn caressed and kissed his face and licked his ear, and let her hand move to his maleness.

She pressed him for a moment, as he brought his eyes to hers.

Both sparkled for themselves and for each other.

Syd gathered the crinkly material of her skirt at her knee and caressed her bare thigh to her hip. His hand stopped at a silky, highcut, underthing.

Arielle put her right hand over Syd's on the band of the highcut, folded his thumb and finger around the band and together they slid the underthing down.

Deftly in one move Arielle stepped out of the thing and slipped it in her pocket.

Just as deftly, she lifted her skirt free, and with a high wide step, sat straddled across Syd's thighs.

Syd put his hands on her waist; he touched her bared breast; he reached under her knees and pulled her toward him.

Arielle nibbled more kisses, alternately pulling his lip with her teeth, darting her tongue to his, or caressing his lip.

Syd slid his hands up the inside of her bare thighs. He stopped.

"Don't stop," Arielle voice was a caress.

"My room 's up there," Syd breathed.

"The mood's here," murmured Arielle.

"Yes."

Syd drew Arielle's right arm up around his neck, as he slid his fingers into her moist, ready, femaleness.

His lips sought hers with hunger.

Arielle drew back to give herself space to stroke him while she undid the buckle, undid the button and undid the zipper.

She momentarily took her weight off Syd's thighs, on her tiptoes, and leaned on her hands on the chair seat beside his hips.

"Wiggle down a bit and wiggle those clothes down a bit," she whispered as she caressed his ear with her tongue. "No one can see, my skirt's covering."

She settled back onto his thighs, and touched him as he was touching her.

Very gently she raised herself up and toward him. Both using hands to guide, he came up inside her.

His hands held her firmly at the waist.

Arielle's arms were on his shoulders. Their faces and mouths searched each other.

Arielle tightened the muscles in the floor of her pelvis.

Syd made a little gasping sound.

She relaxed the muscles. Then tightened.

"You can caress that way?" He groaned with pleasure.

He moved up into her, a small thrust, and pulled back.

"Not much space," he breathed, and moved upward again.

She timed her tightening with his upward, and relaxed with his pull back.

Their mouths echoed what their other body parts were doing. Intense. Close. Intimate. Oneness.

Arielle's body tensed and arched holding Syd's hardness in a tight grip. A moan escaped her lips as she pressed her face into Syd's shoulder.

Syd muffled a sound in his throat, and he wrapped his arms around her and pressed her body close to his upward spasming groin.

They stayed wrapped in each other as the energy of love drained from them.

Still joined, Syd raised Arielle's head with soft hands to kiss her with tenderness and wonderment.

"Stay with me tonight." Syd stated to Arielle.

"Yes."

Time drifted as they remained contentedly wrapped in each other's arms.

Finally, Syd's leg twitched.

"I've never made love on an ice cream parlour chair before," Syd said with a laugh. "I feel kind of trapped."

"One move and I'll be flat on my backside on the ground," Arielle responded with a little laugh of her own,

Syd held her by the waist as she climbed off his thighs.

"Let's go in, Jack Track needs to get some sleep."

"Pardon?" asked Arielle.

"Wouldn't you bet Jack stood sentinel, to make sure our privacy wasn't invaded?" asked Syd as he drew Arielle close.

DAY 14: FULL DAY IN PISA, VENICE, OR SIENA

She woke to a sensation of her hair being stroked from her temple onto the pillow close to him. Cool enough to have the sheet draped over her shoulders.

She could feel his breath slow and steady near her ear.

A peep from a slit in her eyelids saw early light.

"Really early," he whispered. "Five thirty-five. We don't leave for Venice until eight."

She nestled under the sheet and turned her face toward him.

Propped on one elbow, he reached across her forehead to stroke her hair back and brushed some kisses across her hairline.

She turned her body toward him and put her right hand on his ribs. Breathing was deeper.

He ran his thumb around her ear, as he explored her face with more brush kisses.

She let her hand trail across his hip, then belly, down until it met with his hard uprightness.

"Satyr," he said, "You did say you knew one when ... you ... saw! ... one ...."

She caressed him, then hesitated with her thumb on his sensitivity.

He drew in a deep breath.

"Bed's a suitable place to meet one ..."

Slowly, mouths nibbled at each other; hands caressed nipples and breasts, hips and thighs.

Lips and tongues played.

Fingers sought moistness.

He rolled her onto her back, as she steadied him on top of her.

His knee touched both of hers, pressing one away.

She made room for him.

He hovered above her, on his elbows, to stroke her face and see her eyes sparkle in the beginning of morning light.

She opened the pools of her eyes as his maleness touched the entry to her femaleness.

Her hands stroked his back down to his buttocks as she pushed her knees farther apart, and he slipped in.

Small noises of pleasure accompanied the rhythm of togetherness.

He thrust and shuddered, as she wrapped her legs around his hips.

"Stay. Stay," she gasped, pulling him deeper, as her body spasmed.

He relaxed his body against hers.

"Stay! stay!" she whispered, tightening her muscles on his reduced swolleness.

Her body arched and spasmed again as she pressed her mound and sensitivity against his root and pelvis.

Released, she caressed his neck and jawline with wet kisses.

Time passed.

Syd slid off her to his side.

"Ca va?" he asked.

"M-m-m-m," Arielle answered in a most satisfied way.

"Did you ... twice?" he asked most quietly.

"Yes," she answered. "Sometimes ... when ... you ... tu ... special ..."

"Would you mind if I just enjoyed you?" Syd asked contentedly. "You have such a nice warm, alive mind and body."

They were quiet.

Arielle took a deep soft breath, then let the air out of her lungs slowly and deliberately.

"This intimacy ...," she looked cautiously at Syd, "...it's here ...." Their eyes held. She saw him nod in agreement. "Does it ever survive the light of day...?" Neither broke eye contact. "I've been here a number of times ... experienced ... but it's always denied the next day and is lost. This oneness I feel ... is it too raw? ... too high? ... too much emotion? ... too alive? ... that no one can go with it, let it slide down and know it was there and may be or will be there again?"

"Faith ..., belief ..., trust ...," said Syd.

"You say that. I always thought that. So I have to have faith ... belief ... trust ... that you mean it."

"That's all any of us can do," Syd said. "That it'll lead to the intimacy we all hope for, wish for ... "

"A heady, high risk place to be," Arielle whispered.

"To open up and hope and trust someone can and will match that risk ...," Syd said softly.

"We're both feeling secure enough to even say these things," Arielle murmured.

"Yes," Syd agreed.

"I like you."

"I like tu."

They turned to look at each other again with confidence.

Syd wrapped his arms around her and gave her a big bear hug. She tightened her arms around him, then started to struggle for release.

"A wrestling match should wake us up for the day," she laughed.

Syd released his hold. "I'll phone room service for some breakfast ... I'd like that. Couldn't go to the dining room this morning."

"Me neither. Lots of tea."

"And real food. I know."

As he was waiting on the bedside phone, Arielle slid out of bed and stepped toward the chair where their clothes were piled.

"What's that?" Syd said to her bare back.

"What? Oh, that," Arielle said dismissing by touching the coloured coin-sized patch on the ridge of her left hip. "A tattoo."

"A tattoo?"

"Just an apple."

"Jesus, lady," said Syd full of surprise, "excuse my language, but you are something else."

As Syd ordered breakfast from room service, Arielle picked up the denim-coloured chambray shirt Syd had been wearing last night and slid it on as a shorty dressing gown.

"I never thought that shirt looked so good," Syd said.

"I thought it looked pretty good yesterday."

They let that exchange hang in the air.

"Those grey boxer shorts, toss them to me, would you?"

"Cotton knit, with a Calvin label. Very trendy," Arielle looked at the broad elastic waist. "I saw those in a GQ magazine ad. B-Man thought I was gross looking at a man's magazine."

She tossed the boxers to him.

"I have to believe," Arielle said, "that five years ago you didn't dress the way you do now."

"No, I didn't," said Syd. "It's a demonstration of my life changing drastically. Having to go on. No going back. Besides, if I'm spending my days renovating a house, digging in a garden or painting at an easel, I'm not going to wear business suits. And if I don't wear them, what would I wear. Not Jack Track's choice!"

Arielle laughed appreciatively.

Breakfast came.

They finished.

"Half hour 'til the van leaves," said Syd.

"I'll meet you at the front desk," said Arielle, as she pulled on her crinkle skirt, tied Syd's shirt around her waist and stepped into her sandals.

With a shy look at Syd, she checked her skirt pocket briefly showing him the satiny item stuffed in it. She carefully rolled up her peasant blouse, and headed for the door.

"My shirt," said Syd.

"You're not going to wear it today." Arielle stated.

"No, but ...,"

"Pick it up in Toronto, unless I decide to keep it. I've never worn blue!"

As she closed to door behind her, she heard Syd say, "Jesus, lady, you're something else."

Arielle swung the door open again. "So are you."

The van took them across the Ponte della Liberta to the Piazzale Roma.

With too many Venetians they piled into the waterbus, the vaporetto, that would deposit them at the Piazzetta, which fronts on the Grand Canal and leads into St. Mark's Square.

Arielle, gave Syd one hand, as she gathered the long skirt of her black cotton dress with the other. The full easy shape from the shirred empire waist made it easy for her to climb out of the boat onto the landing dock.

They stopped to look at the two huge columns: the Lion of St. Mark and St. Theodore spearing a crocodile, and walked into the square.

Arielle drew in her breath, as she looked around.

"Somebody said that this is the world's greatest drawing room."

"It invites you to stay, doesn't it," Syd commented.

"Let's," said Arielle. "Let's sit at one of the cafes and soak it up. I could look at the details ..."

"Or the over-all ... more of the great outdoor museum ..."

Neither needed to finish sentences.

They settled at their table and agreed on a "petit dejeuner" as Arielle said to the waiter, who understood. "I'm not about to risk your brand of Italian," she said cheekily to Syd.

"Mosaics?" asked Syd.

"Byzantine," said Arielle. "Horses, gold?"

"Not likely. Bronze. Or amalgam of copper, silver, some gold."

Pigeons fluttered, and fought over crumbs.

"Tourists," said Arielle.

"We're not tourists," said Syd off-handedly.

"No-o-o-o," Arielle drew the word out, "there's another word for us," and she leaned over to kiss him. "They say Venice is for lovers."

"North American males back off that word like the plague," Syd commented.

"Pity," said Arielle. "Want to try saying it? Part of truth, faith and what have you?"

Syd gave an embarrassed laugh.

"Go ahead, try it." She was almost gazing adoringly at him.

"Okay. Lovers." He looked shyly at her. "Venice is for lovers. For us. And I demand a rewarding kiss."

Business finished, and settling back with his coffee cup, Syd said, "A person certainly would never feel alone here."

Arielle said, "It changed my life, living alone."

"Changed mine, too. Living alone. What was the biggest thing about it for you?" Syd asked without side.

"Having my own time and space. Independence of thought. Knowing I wasn't going to be put on the defensive, nor have to try to figure out where somebody else is, so I can respond being myself. I have that working with pupils. The advanced ones. What about you?"

"Being retired takes away a big chunk of intelligent company. And my wife had been among other things, my friend. She was her own person, and I liked it. Her illness, ... I think, interfered with us developing a deeper relationship. She died. I had to discover more depth in myself. To find challenges. Independent ones. Real work. Like real food." Syd made a joke about Arielle's attitude toward food.

He put his hand on her bare arm below the rolled up sleeves. "I can only think about this stuff for so long ... let's see more of Venice."

They headed out a narrow exit into back alleys, small canals, small bridges.

Syd had his hand on Arielle's shoulder as they walked.

They stopped at shops, at statues, at fountains, at waters-edge.

Arielle slid her arm around his waist.

"'How now, Bassanio, what news on the Rialto?'" quoted Arielle.

"Come again?" said Syd.

"Shakespeare," said Arielle. "Merchant of ..."

"Venice, of course!" said Syd. "How do you know?"

"My mother was a fan! Think of my name!" Arielle waited a moment. "Ariel. The Tempest."

"Oh, yes," recalled Syd. "Rings a bell. Many years ago, in high school. Complete change of subject," he took a deep breath and plowed on, "we were both adult enough, to overcome that ... constraint ...over that episode with Grace."

"You said, 'Trust me'," said Arielle. She was quiet and pensive. "I hadn't had trust for so long, I nearly couldn't. But you said it. So I had to go to you with my trust."

"And have to get to know someone again. Even the little we knew each other, to get it back. Take it back. to get to know you better. I had quite a bit of that in my marriage to Marjorie."

"I've never had it except with that kid. Who knows if it would have happened in the long run."

"Both have to work at it, and not back off."

"There's this internal conflict," said Arielle. "The natural reluctance to let go, to expose too much, to become vulnerable."

"That's where trust comes in," said Syd.

"You're so lucky to have had all that," said Arielle.

"I didn't quite have all. After a point," said Syd cautiously, "and I'll say for health reasons, we ceased to be together. Led parallel lives."

"Speaking of parallel," said Arielle, "there's not a straight route, except for an alley of shops, anywhere in Venice, is there?"

"Makes it interesting. Where do you want to go?" asked Syd.

"Get lost and see what we find," said Arielle.

Syd gave her an appreciative hug.

"Find Vivaldi's church, see the Bridge of Sighs, go to the market ..., ride in a gondola .... The Treasury!"

"Not to-day!" Syd sounded adamant.

Arielle looked at him.

"A date. I'm taking you out on a date."

"But the sense of equality. My independence."

"Maybe I want to see if you can be slightly dependent."

"On someone who wants the responsibility, who I believe wants to do it this way." Arielle considered for a moment. She nodded her head. She continued, "This trip especially in Italy, may not be real when we get home. Home is real."

"Then we'll have to come back here." Syd solved the problem.

"You can paint, and I can play violin," said Arielle sardonically.

"I grant you the competition may be pretty tough! However since we eat outdoors, and do other things outdoors ...," Syd observed her knowingly, "expenses wouldn't be too high!"

"Let's find the market, then."

The sandwiches were works of art. Decided on two. They bought olives folded in a paper. They passed up gold marrow-flowers for peaches, cherries and apricots which they bought because of their colours. Freshly cooked Venetian scampi. Asiago cheese.

They seemed to criss-cross St. Mark's square on every mission, until it became as familiar as home.

They sat on the steps of a bridge over a canal.

"I'm not going to invite myself to stay with you tonight," Arielle said to Syd, "I'd like to finish the trip with Molly."

"That's nice," said Syd. "What about at the airport in Toronto?"

"The local taxi driver who looks after Molly and my mother is booked to meet us."

"If you need any help at the Milan airport or in Toronto, just let me know."

"Thanks," said Arielle.

"I'll be watching you all the time, anyway!"

"Nice."

In the fading light of early evening, they took a gondola.

They commented on the odour of Venice! They commented on the noise of Italian cities. They commented on the flowers all over: high up on small balconies, in doorways, spotting colour in the buildings and the water. They commented on the twice as much concept of Venice: everything reflected in the water.

They settled back on the upholstered seat. Syd had his arm around Arielle's shoulder. She leaned comfortably on him.

The gondola slid silently through the water.

"I don't want to live with someone," said Arielle, "but, I don't want to live without someone." She made a wry laugh. "How does a person live their life with someone?" she asked. "I haven't been able to do it, and I feel secure enough with you to ask about it."

"I think," said Syd, "that it's easy when you're both following the traditional roles as Marjorie and I did. You just do what you do. I worked and earned the bread and Marjorie ran the household and our social life. Although, to some extent that was along traditional lines. Family. Us as the children first. Then when we had children, we carried the family load with church and business ties. Patterned. We were busy and happy. It worked for us."

"And since I've always earned my own way, in spite of living in B-Man's apartment I've really supported myself and never had that family extension that our world in Toronto works on. I've got wonderful friends and many of my music and dance pupils are my friends and I have extensions through them. But how would two people like you and me live or be together?"

"Just that. We be together. Bad grammar," he said with a little laugh. "But I think we both have to live our own lives. Coming and going as we want to do and negotiate what we do together."

"Will that work? To satisfy my want to be with you and my need to have independence?"

"It has to. It's the only way. To count on someone without controlling them. To be independent but available. You have to believe."

"Believe in what?"

"Just believe," said Syd. "Have faith. I think it's the basis of the trust that people have between them, if they care. Care for each other. Care about themselves. Believe. Have faith. Care. Trust."

His words plucked her heart strings, gave her being a lurch. There it was. He knows trust. It's part of him. That which she had always wanted. Hoped for. Believed could happen. Believed was possible. Had faith she could find it. "Such simple concepts," said Arielle. "Belief. Faith. Care. Trust. But the biggies."

Arielle shifted so she could look at Syd.

Syd was thoughtful, "I have to believe it'll work because the traditional way I had doesn't exist for me any more. I've moved beyond it. I couldn't conceive of finding or wanting someone to fit into Marjorie's shoes and perhaps me fit into some deceased husbands shoes and we carry on without missing a beat, living some kind of thoughtless unconnected life, making traditional patterned moves. That was Grace."

Their eyes moved away from each other to look out over the lagoon. They sat quietly, listening to the dipping of the oar, feeling the rocking of the boat. Still. Both afraid to break the magic of the water softly lapping against the canal walls, and the lights of the city dancing in the water.

The shriek of a police siren on the street behind them broke the spell.

Syd smiled at Arielle and she returned his smile, both with eyes sparkling as the light on the lagoon.

They pulled into the dock.

Syd squeezed her shoulder, and let his hand slide down her arm to take her hand.

"Let's go.

They spent the rest of the evening in St. Mark's square, walking with arms around each other; dining al fresco on roast kid and risotto; and watching Venice and the water mirrors of Venice.

They waited for the vaporetto to take them back to the van.

"I'm afraid to say that it's au revoir ..." said Arielle.

"Until Toronto ..." said Syd.

"Yes."

"Tu?"

"Tu."

"Tu."

DAY 15: DEPART MILAN FOR TORONTO

Syd came through the Arrival doors to a sea of faces beyond the barrier.

"Dad," shouted Steve.

Syd spotted Hughie and Steve just outside the gate.

"Great to see you." Syd was genuinely happy.

"You look terrific," said Hugh. "Look at him, Steve."

Both sons had grabbed an arm of their Dad's and were thumping or pumping.

"Like, you do look terrific, not that you didn't before, but .... " Steve was giving Syd the once over.

Syd just stood there as they enthusiastically grabbed his gear.

"You look like a new man," commented Hughie, swinging the easel bag over his shoulder.

"I am," said Syd, matter-of-factly.

"Must be the middle of the night for you, with the time change from Milan," said Steve, picking up Syd's suitcase.

"We'll have to hear all about this. Driving you directly home," announced Hugh.

"We'll just pull off Avenue Road, below Eglinton," said Syd. He patted the envelope of marbled Florentine paper sticking out of the unbuttoned pocket on his shirt. "I have to drop off a message in the mail box, first door around the corner."

About the Author

Georgia Brock lives in Port Perry, Ontario. She graduated from the University of Toronto and taught school in Ontario and England. She is an avid gardener.

She visits gardens when on holiday with her daughter in England or on other trips to places in United States, Europe, China, & Israel.